THE REBEL WITCH

THE COVEN: ELEMENTAL MAGIC BOOK THREE

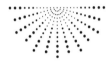

CHANDELLE LAVAUN

WANDERLOST PUBLISHING

For Jerry and Daltrey,
One of you stuck a hose in my diaper, the other ate all my
food, but you're still the best brothers I could ask for.
Thanks for all the great material, my characters wouldn't
be the same without your inspirational shenanigans...

CHAPTER ONE

EMERSYN

"Remind me what we're looking for." I craned my neck back to look up at the fountain in front of me.

Somehow in the two days since Tegan had blown it up, the cement-fairy monstrosity had been magically reconstructed already. The polished surface shimmered under the falling water.

When my sister didn't respond to me, I glanced over my shoulder and spotted her glaring into the distance. "Tegan? I said, remind me what we're looking for."

Her dark hair blended in with the black sky above. "What are we doing here?"

"No, I know what we're *doing* here. I said what are we looking for."

I knew exactly what we were doing there, and I

knew whose fault it was. *Mine.* The prophecy on Bentley's arm had warned us to be ready for a lie, for a trick, and yet two days ago, I'd fallen for it. Sure, it wasn't my fault Henley had been possessed...but it *was* my fault that the Gap was opened for a greater demon to come in. My fault that my friend was now trapped in her own body in another realm. No one wanted to admit that realm was probably Hell. So yeah, I knew what my twin and I were doing. We were looking for answers. For clues. For *anything.*

Except, now that we'd arrived at Hidden Kingdom, I wasn't sure what that might be.

Tegan's pale green eyes met mine, and the fire in them almost made me take a step back. Almost. She was my twin, my best friend. I knew she was on *my* side. Still, with every passing day, her power grew stronger and more intimidating. Every day she stood a little taller, her eyes shined a little brighter, and her aura grew a little more terrifying.

"A clue that might tell us what kind of demon this was." She narrowed her eyes and glared into the distance again. Her long black hair was braided to one side, and it made my heart hurt. She'd been wearing it like that to honor Libby. "I think she was possessed here at the park."

2

I followed her stare, but I saw nothing. Just the cobblestone path that led to the castle and the forest surrounding the courtyard. I pushed my magic out, the way Uncle Kessler had trained me, to see if there were things my eyes missed. Except I still saw nothing. "What makes you so sure?"

She wiggled her fingers, and her magic spilled into the air in a shimmering rainbow mist. "Do you remember the night the shadow monster arrived and attacked them here at the park? Royce told us how Henley had been fighting it until it just vanished."

I shivered and turned back to the fountain. My gaze traveled down to the pool at its base...to the last place I'd seen Henley. "They thought they killed it."

"Not dead," a soft female voice said from above me.

"Saffie!" Tegan ran up beside me with a big grin on her face. "I was hoping we'd run into you tonight."

Saffie's fiery red hair blew across her face, so she tucked it back behind her pointed ears. Her lavender eyes looked kind of gray in the orange glow from the lanterns around the courtyard. She cocked her head to the side. "You wanted to see me?"

"Of course. We're friends."

"Friends." Saffie smiled and her eyes twinkled like the stars above her. She flew down until her eyes were level with ours then hovered in the air, her translucent pink wings fluttering behind her back. "I was worried about you, after you blew up the fountain. But no one has come by since."

I frowned. There was something *off* about my twin's fairy friend. Sometimes she spoke almost like a toddler, and in third person, yet other times, she spoke the same as we did. And why didn't she ever leave the theme park?

Don't ask what you're thinking, twin. Not yet.

I smirked and rolled my eyes. Tegan's telepathic gift was just not fair. *Wait. How did she know what I was thinking?* Was I that obvious? What did my face look like? I rubbed my face with my hand, and when I pulled it away, I made sure to smile.

"I'm sorry no one told you I was okay, Saffie. I assumed Tennessee came by since." Tegan sat down on the ledge of the pool. She spun sideways and let one foot drop into the water.

Saffie sighed and plopped down beside my twin. She shook her head. "No one has come. Not even my friend Tennessee. You're not hurt though?"

Tegan shook her head and smiled. "I'm not hurt."

"Good." She glanced up to me with wide eyes. "Are you my friend?"

4

I frowned. "Of course I'm your friend." I hated that she even had to ask.

She clapped her hands and squealed. "Now I have *three* friends."

My stomach dropped. Who was this little fairy and why was she so alone?

Seriously, Em. Control your face. We're not digging into that yet.

I groaned and sat down on the other side of Saffie. Apparently I had problems with my face and how easily my emotions showed. How was one to fix that, anyway?

Saffie gasped and grabbed Tegan's hand. She pulled it up to her face and stared at the gold wave ring with wide eyes. She glanced back and forth between Tegan and Tegan's ring. "*Keltie?*"

Tegan's lips curled into a mischievous smirk. She nodded. With the hand Saffie wasn't holding, she pushed her black hair behind her ears, revealing the gold earrings the siren had given her. They wrapped all the way up her ear in little gold cuff hoops, and some had etchings and crystals. One was the same wave shape as on her hand.

"Keltie and I had a conversation," Tegan said.

Saffie leaned forward and ran her thin fingers over the golden cuffs on Tegan's ears. She glanced over her shoulder at me, like she wanted to be sure I saw them too. Her lavender eyes filled with tears. She looked back to Tegan. The two of them seemed to be communicating silently. Well actually, with Tegan's telepathy, they could've been doing exactly that.

I cleared my throat to remind them I was still there. "Those rings have fairy magic, right?"

Saffie shook her head, and her red hair flew around. "No, no. This is *much* older magic. This is ocean magic."

"Ocean magic? I don't know what that is." Which wasn't precisely a new thing. Most of the time, I didn't know what was going on. I hated that. I told myself I'd do better.

Tegan frowned and cocked her head to the side. She pursed her lips and narrowed her pale green eyes. Finally, she shook her head. "I don't either."

"You will, Tegan. The ocean's jewels can only be worn by someone who has the soul of the sea inside them." Saffie pointed to Tegan's chest. "Keltie felt the ocean in you."

"Keltie said—"

Saffie gasped and dove forward, covering Tegan's mouth with her thin hands. "You must not tell me anything! Keltie will tell us when."

Tegan blinked a few times then nodded.

That's it? I didn't understand how she could be so calm about all of this. Like it was *no big deal.* I was taking mental notes, trying to put it all together. Leyka knew the Crones, and somehow they connected to Saffie. Apparently, Keltie knew Saffie. Whatever was said in the aquarium tank to Tegan, Saffie was part of it. I wanted desperately to know what it was.

She held Tegan's finger with the wave ring up to her ear and sighed. It was the first time I saw her relax a little. After a long minute, she dropped Tegan's hand. "Don't lose these. They will protect you."

I narrowed my eyes. *She knows stuff.* "Saffie, do you know anything about Henley getting possessed?"

She closed her eyes and nodded. "When it vanished, it took her."

My heart sank. It happened right in front of Royce, and he didn't even know it. For days our friend was possessed and living among us without us knowing.

"Do you know anything else?" I asked.

Saffie grabbed both our hands then flew into the air, pulling us along with her. She guided us closer to the edge of the courtyard, near the forest. "This is where it happened. The Cards will tell you more here."

"We are the Cards, Saffie. We don't know."

"She means I need to read the Tarot deck right here." Tegan spun in a slow circle, eyeing the ground. "Don't you, Saffie?"

"Yup. Yup. Yup."

A wild sparkle twinkled in Tegan's eyes, and my stomach dropped. In the few weeks I'd known her, I'd already learned to be nervous of that look. I didn't know what she was thinking, but I suddenly regretted not bringing backup.

"Um, Tegan?" I tucked my hair behind my ears and looked around. "Maybe we should call the others before you start? Like maybe Tennessee at least?"

She cringed and shook her head. "I can't...with him... can't... We can't... No." She sighed.

The only thing more unsettling than Tegan's wild side was her stuttering side. She was confident and sure of herself in a way I'd probably never be. So when she got nervous or panicked, I wanted nothing to do with the cause. Not that Tennessee would hurt her, or me. But she told me about the ridiculous law forbidding the three of us from dating anyone until we were middle-aged—or else be stripped of our magic. Not a consequence worth testing. I couldn't imagine what it felt like for my sister...to fall in love with a guy, then have that door be closed, locked, and vacuum-sealed shut.

"I'm just going to read the Tarot. Henley did it without being attacked, so we should be fine. Besides, there are three of us."

Saffie nodded and waved her skinny pointer finger in

the air. A large white crystal sparkled like glass on her finger. "Tennessee moves fast, too."

Good point. If something went wrong, I'd call Tennessee, and he'd be here within minutes. The three of us could hold anything off until then. "Okay, just be careful. And fast."

Tegan reached into the back pocket of her black jeans and pulled the stack of cards out. The Tarot, given to The Coven by the Goddess herself. A tool to be used by the High Priestess.

"You carry them on you?"

Tegan shrugged and sat down on the cobblestone ground. "Henley said in times like these, I needed to always be ready. So yes, I carry them. I need you to be ready, too. Watch our backs."

"This doesn't make me feel better."

She placed the deck of cards facedown on the ground. With her hands hovering in the air above them, she whispered a few words in our ancient language. "Uncle Kessler said for the High Priestess, reading the Tarot can sometimes blind me of my surroundings until the ritual is over."

"Fantastic."

She rolled her pretty, pale green eyes. "You're the Empress. You got this."

I opened my mouth to say...*nothing.* I had absolutely nothing to say back to that. She was right. Of course she was. I didn't know what my problem was. I knew I had powerful magic. I knew my gifts were strong. I just never knew what to do with it. In the heat of the moment, I tended to panic. That was the difference between me and my sister. When I froze, she acted.

The truth was...it scared me.

A warm breeze slammed into my face. My hair flew over my shoulders like a kite in a hurricane. I squinted and refocused on my sister sitting on the ground. Rainbow mist and white lightning circled around her in a tornado of magic. The lights in the courtyard flickered.

"Oops," Saffie whispered.

"Oops? Oops what?" I peeled my eyes off Tegan's magic swirl and spun toward Saffie. *Why did she say—* I gasped and stumbled back a few steps. "Why?!"

"Oops. Oops." Saffie flew behind me and gripped my shoulder. "Uh-oh. Too fast. Too fast."

My pulse quickened and my palms grew sweaty. Those ghost-fairies were back. About a dozen were perched on the newly-rebuilt fountain...just *watching* us.

"Why did they come?" I whispered. "She just started!"

Saffie mumbled a string of words in a language I

didn't recognize. "Too much magic, too fast. They come. They come."

I swallowed through a lump of fear. "Will they attack us?"

"Yes," Saffie whispered back without hesitation. "Now, Empress. *Now*."

I shook my head and took a few steps back. My heart pounded in my ears, drowning out whatever Saffie was saying to me. Tegan was there, but she wasn't *there*. This meant Saffie and I were on our own, and I wasn't entirely sure what my living fairy friend could do. The ghost-fairies jumped off their perches and flew in circles over my head like vultures.

"Ready now. Ready. Now. We fight them." Saffie fidgeted with her dress. "They come."

I need a weapon. Why didn't I keep Mom's dagger?

Think, Emersyn. Think.

I tried to summon some fire or smoke, but my magic just crackled around my fingers. My hands trembled. Why couldn't I *do* this? I'd done it before. I glanced around me, searching for something I could use as a weapon. All I needed to do was stall. I pulled my phone out of my pocket and hit the home button to unlock it.

It vibrated in my hand. Try Again. I readjusted my finger placement. Try Again.

"Oh, c'mon!" I groaned. "Hey, Siri, call Tennessee."

"I'm sorry, I didn't get that."

The ghost-fairies froze. Their eyes aimed lasers at me. Their wings fluttered.

"Hey, Siri, call Tennessee."

"The capital of Tennessee is Nashville," Siri answered.

"Are you kidding me right now?" I shouted at my phone.

The ghost-fairies screeched and flew toward me. I gasped and threw my hands up. I pushed all of my energy out. Red-hot energy prickled against my fingertips. I had no idea what it was, but I grabbed ahold of the lifeline and channeled all of my magic into it. The ghost-fairies slammed into me. Their hands were ice against my bare skin. But that magic was still waiting for me. I curled my fingers around it and pulled. The ghost-fairies shrieked in a high pitch that pierced my ears.

"YES!" Saffie shouted, startling me. "More, Empress! MORE!"

What did I do? When I spotted Saffie, she hovered nearby with a long crystal wand, pointing and gesturing. I followed her hands and saw little round discs of bronze and silver soaring through the air. My eyes widened. *Oh my, what have I done?* The pennies and nickels from the fountain's pool flew around the fountain like an asteroid field. My jaw dropped. *How...?*

The fairies ducked and tried to dodge the metal discs. I glanced behind me to Tegan to ask how she'd done that, except I found her still locked inside her own magic, completely unaware.

"EMPRESS! More!"

My heart skipped a beat. Adrenaline rushed through my veins. Somehow I'd done that. I had no idea *how*. But it didn't even matter. I raised my hands and pushed my magic. The coins swerved under my command. Dozens of tiny purple eyes narrowed on me. I clenched my teeth and sent the change charging after the ghost-fairies like a swarm of killer bees. They hissed and shrieked in pain. *Yes!* I narrowed my eyes and focused my energy on one ghost-fairy at a time. One by one, I plucked them out of the sky like I was at a shooting range until all of them were gone.

"Holy shit," Tegan whispered.

I jumped at the sound of her voice. When I glanced over my shoulder, she was on her feet with the Tarot clutched in one hand and her jaw hanging wide open. I stood there panting.

"That was so dark and twisted!" She bent over and laughed. "With pennies!"

"Well..." I threw my hands in the air. "You weren't here!"

She clapped her hands together. "You see?! I *told* you. Amazing."

Saffie flew over to us, waving her hands frantically. "Not done. Not done. More."

I frowned and turned back to the fountain in time to see ghost-fairies pouring out of the fountain like a fireman's hose. Within thirty seconds, we were surrounding by dozens and dozens of them. My stomach dropped. Sweat dripped down my spine.

"Okay...maybe my decision-making skills were slightly altered recently," Tegan mumbled under her breath. She took a few steps forward then bent down and pulled our mother's white-hilted dagger from her boot. The Tarot deck poked out the top of her pants pocket. She glanced over her shoulder at me with that wild grin. "I want you to repeat that like it's your favorite song, girl. You got it?"

I nodded and flexed my fingers. The coins responded immediately, hovering a few feet in the air. My magic sizzled with the need to use it. "In theory."

"Tegan, remember?" Saffie asked from behind me.

A dark, black cloud rose from the ground. The earth trembled under my feet. Warm, salty wind whipped up my back then wrapped around the courtyard. Thunder rumbled above our heads, and lightning cracked across the black sky. The water in the fountain turned to solid ice.

Tegan held her left hand up, and her *II* Mark stood out against her fair skin. The golden wave ring glistened. Her magic coiled around her fingers. It was a rainbow mist of menace and fury, just waiting to be released. She twirled the dagger in her other hand. She looked back over her shoulder, and her eyes sparkled like diamonds. "Oh, I remember."

CHAPTER TWO

TEGAN

"Em, are you okay?" I narrowed my eyes at my twin and waited for her to respond. Then I waited some more. "Emersyn?"

My sister seemed to be functioning on a different wavelength this morning. Wherever her thoughts were, I certainly wasn't getting through. Normally, my twin talked my ear off our entire drive to school. Yet she'd parked our car in the student parking lot a solid two minutes ago and still hadn't spoken. Not that I was in a rush to get to class, but something was off with her.

"Earth to Emersyn." I took my seat belt off and spun to face her. Except all I got was her profile. The morning sunshine made her hair and eyes look like liquid gold. I frowned. Maybe I had to try a different approach. I focused my energy on my twin, then spoke to her with my mind. *All right, what's going on in that head over there?*

Emersyn jumped. She pressed her hand to her chest. Her wide eyes found mine. "What?"

"Finally. Damn." I shook my head and laughed. "What is happening in the driver's seat right now? We parked like an hour ago. Talk to me."

She cursed and dropped her forehead to the steering wheel.

"I love it when you curse. Did you know that? So feisty. But seriously. Start talking."

"I was trying to get our story straight," she mumbled against the steering wheel.

I frowned. "Our story?"

"Yes." She turned her head to look at me without picking it up. "Our story, for why we went to the park last night. You know Mom told Uncle Kessler, which means everyone else knows. Which means they're going to ask us why, and we need to be ready."

I reached over and pulled the keys out of the ignition. "We didn't do anything wrong, Em. We don't need an alibi." I threw the keys in my backpack then climbed out.

"But what are we gonna say?"

I leaned down into the open doorway. "The truth,

17

obviously." I winked and closed the door before she could panic any further.

Once out of my twin's sight, I sighed and eyed the surrounding parking lot. The beach was *just* close enough for me to smell the hint of salt in the air. The sky was vivid blue without a single cloud. The sun beat down on me in all its awful glory, burning against my chest. I squinted and slid my sunglasses into place. The air was wet and sticky. I'd only been standing in the heat for mere seconds, and sweat dripped down my spine. Every time the wind blew, it felt like someone was breathing down my neck.

I turned around—and froze in place. My heart climbed up my throat. Tennessee stood behind our car with his tan arms crossed over his muscled chest. His glare was hot and filled my stomach with butterflies. *Damn it, he looks good.* I didn't think I'd ever get used to the sight of him or the effect he had on my body. His black hair grazed the bottom of his jaw. The waves were wild and tangled, like he'd run his hands through the strands all night. His mismatched eyes narrowed and looked up and down my body. I shivered and licked my lips, then took a tentative step closer. That was when I noticed belatedly the rest of our Coven standing right behind him...with the exact same expression.

Cooper's nostrils flared, and I knew if he had fire

magic, he'd be breathing smoke like a dragon. His shoulders rose and fell as he breathed heavily. The muscles in his arms flexed. Beside him, Royce's sapphire eyes were bloodshot and glaring at me like I was his enemy. As a matter of fact, they *all* glared at me.

Emersyn's door opened behind me. "For my own sanity can we—" She gasped.

Don't say it, I whispered to my sister's mind.

"Your sanity? *Your* sanity?" Cooper said through clenched teeth. "I'd love to know where the hell your sanity is right now. Or should I say where it was last night?"

I cleared my throat and pushed my sunglasses on top of my head. "We had perfectly sane intentions last night."

"How the hell do you figure that?" Cooper yelled, his face flushed bright red.

"Don't yell at us like we're children," I snapped back.

"Then don't act like children!" he shouted.

"What's the matter, Cooper, don't like when people keep secrets from you?" I said through clenched teeth. My voice came out low and rougher than I'd ever heard it. I pushed my shoulders back and took a step closer to him. My magic pulsed under the surface, begging to be used. "The audacity in your hypocrisy is laughable, *big brother.* You lost the right to scold us when you lied to our faces. Don't make the mistake of thinking I forgot."

Emersyn stepped up beside me and wrapped her hand around my elbow. It was both a sign of support and a warning to back off. Had anyone else pulled that, I might've flipped out, but my twin had my back. I knew we messed up by going by ourselves to the park, but how dare he speak to us like that.

"You don't get to choose when to be our brother, Cooper," Emersyn snapped. "Perhaps if you lived with your own family, we could've had this conversation last night."

"Unless of course you'd like to see sibling rivalry take a magical turn." I arched my eyebrow.

The air around us shimmered like glitter. In my peripheral vision, I saw Willow in the back of the group, holding her hands in the air.

Easton jumped in between us, forcing us to take a few steps back. He shook his head and cursed. His silver, magical armor covered both of his arms and shoulders, like he was afraid one of us would strike him. His sky-blue eyes were missing their usual playful sparkle. "Same team, guys. Same. Damn. Team. You have family drama, then you handle it at home, like the rest of us."

Lily walked up behind him, her black hair a stark

contrast to the two blonds in front of me. "Back off. All of you."

I glanced to Tennessee, but he stood frozen like a statue, still glaring at me. He hadn't spoken a single word. I wasn't even sure he was breathing. I had to look away. My emotions and my magic were too on edge to be near him without giving us both away.

"We came here to talk," Larissa said from my other side.

"What were you thinking?" Cooper said in a calmer voice, though his face was still red.

I sighed and threw my hands in the air. "That Henley needs our help and may not have time to wait for Kenneth to figure it out! We just went looking for clues."

"Why would you go by yourselves?" Braison asked. He scratched the back of his red head. "You know exactly what lurks in the park, so why not ask us to go with you?"

Because I'm trying to stay away from him. I bit my lip to stop myself from saying that out loud. I hated that it was the reason. I hated that he affected me so much. I hated that my brain turned to slush because of him. I hated the stupid law that said we couldn't be together. Now that I knew he was my soulmate, I wasn't sure how to act around him. Or more specifically, how to act around him in front of other people.

"We didn't do it intentionally, y'all," Emersyn said with a soft voice.

I did. My gaze flicked up to Tennessee without my permission. He loomed over me like a thunderstorm waiting to strike me down.

Emersyn groaned. "It's just... It's *my* fault Henley was taken. I couldn't sleep, so we went."

Paulina flinched like we'd slapped her. "No. No, no, no. That was not your fault. We *all* played a part in that, even if only by not telling you how the gaps work."

"Besides, its plan may have always been to leave our realm," Chutney said as she walked up from behind Cooper. She rubbed his back. "We can't start blaming each other."

Royce scoffed. "I'll blame myself enough for the rest of you."

My throat burned. "Royce..."

"Royce, don't say that," Emersyn cried.

"I knew something was off with her, and I did nothing." He shook his head and looked down at the ground. "You both *knew* going there alone was a terrible idea, yet you did it anyway. Looks like we're all idiots."

"Royce..."

"Why didn't you at least ask *me*? It's my sister who was possessed. My sister who's in another realm right now." He slammed his lips shut and blinked his eyes, like he was losing control of his emotions. He waved his hands in the air then stormed off toward the school.

"Royce, wait! Please!" Emersyn shouted and ran after him, her platinum blonde hair flying in the wind behind her like a cape.

"That was foolish. Reckless. Downright stupid." Cooper put his hands on his hips and shook his head. "You're a lot of things, Tegan, but none of those. Try to remember that."

Without another word, he turned and followed after Royce and Emersyn.

I sighed and looked at the rest of my friends. "Guys, I didn't mean anything by it. We just...got an idea to go look for clues, and it was stupid, okay? I'm sorry."

Easton nodded and his magical armor vanished. "You just scared the shit out of us, ya' know? We're a Coven, remember? We care about your well-being. That was hella dangerous."

"Come on, we better get to class." Lily took Easton by the hand and pulled him toward campus. "At lunch we'll discuss what happened last night."

One by one, the rest of my Coven walked off for class, leaving me alone in the parking lot. Well...not *alone*. The heat off Tennessee's stare was hotter than the sun. I wondered if anyone else noticed he hadn't moved a muscle, or perhaps no one else was as attuned to him?

Tennessee wasn't the most talkative guy, but he always had *something* to say in conversations like those. Usually the others looked to him for direction. Yet somehow his stony silence went undetected.

I licked my lips and glanced around us. There were only a few straggling groups of students lingering by their cars, but none of them were paying any attention to us. A Mustang convertible and a fancy Porsche 911 pulled into the parking lot in the back, but I knew no one in my Coven or witch community drove those.

I cleared my throat then finally turned my gaze to meet his. "Tennessee..."

He reached out, grabbed me by the back of the head, and dragged my lips to his. His kiss was hot and rough and everything I needed. I sighed and sank into his chest. All of the stress and fear inside me dissolved against his lips. But then he broke away and pushed back.

"Don't *ever* do that again," he growled, then stormed off.

CHAPTER THREE

DEACON

"Deacon, I just don't understand why you had to move down there."

I rolled my eyes and pulled into the parking lot at Gulf Shores High School. There wasn't a sign for where students parked, but I followed a convertible Mustang full of teenage girls. I assumed I was in the right spot.

"Deacon! Are you even listening to me?"

I scoffed. "I'm honestly trying not to, Mother."

"Not humorous."

"On the contrary." I chuckled. "Do you hear yourself? I was *Marked*, Mother. I'm a Card now. A member of The Coven. Whether you approve or not, I no longer belong in Manhattan."

"You don't belong in *Florida* either. Why didn't you go to Salem or Eden? At least there's some prestige." She made a hissing sound. "Like you'll fit in down there."

I sighed and pulled into an open parking spot near the back of the lot. "I don't know what you're talking about. There's nothing but Porsches in the parking lot." There wasn't. Mine was the only one. I asked for a truck or something casual, but no. When I got off the plane in Tampa, my parents had a brand-new Porsche 911 waiting for me. Not that I was complaining. It was just... Were they trying to set me up to fail?

"Deacon."

"Mother."

"Why didn't you go to Eden?"

"Because most of The Coven lives *here*."

"Says whom?"

"Royce and Henley Redd. You know, my cousins who've been acting members of The Coven for fifteen years."

She sighed. "Well, have they at least been welcoming to you?"

I opened my mouth then shut it again. I'd called Royce and Henley several times since my Mark appeared thirty-six hours ago, but I hadn't gotten ahold of them yet. It wasn't unheard of to not hear back from them for a few days. However, I'd hoped to stay with them. Kessler Bishop, the Card in charge of all the underage ones, was welcoming though. He'd let me drop my stuff at his house then ushered me off to school, promising we'd all get together afterward. He also told me where to find my Coven-mates at lunch.

"*Deacon.*"

"Yes?"

"I'm trying to have a conversation with you. Can you resist ogling the girls down there for a moment?"

I looked out my windshield and around the parking lot. There were a few dozen girls hanging around. I leaned forward and did exactly what my mother just told me not to do. There was a group of bleach blondes standing in a circle, all wearing ripped-up jean shorts far shorter than any dress code would allow. They wore flip-flops and tank tops. They looked like they were headed to the pool, not school. I glanced around, but I found more of the same. I mean, sure, it was hot as hell outside. The thermometer in my car read 105. But surely that didn't mean everyone ignored fashion...did it?

Don't I sound like a pretentious ass. I wasn't expecting Tyra Banks or Kim Kardashian, but I was accustomed to Manhattan girls who dressed with pizazz and style. So far, everyone in Tampa just looked sweaty. I'd never seen so much workout clothing outside the gym. Everywhere I looked, the students were all so... unimpressive. Was this what the rest of the world was like?

I sighed and leaned back in my seat, but then my

gaze landed on something interesting. Standing on the other side of the parking lot beside a little green sedan was a girl with purple-tipped black hair. She looked taller than average, with long legs covered in black leather pants. They were probably leggings. Whatever. She looked fantastic. Instead of rubber flip-flops or sneakers, she had on black combat boots with little studs. *Those are badass.* She turned toward me and I smiled. Her white T-shirt had Tom Petty on the front. Maybe there was hope for this town after all. This girl was hot. I couldn't see the details of her face under her black aviator sunglasses, but she looked pretty, and her style was awesome. *I need to meet this girl.*

"Oh, for Goddess' sake, Deacon."

I chuckled. "Sorry, Mother. You said ogle girls, and I got distracted."

She mumbled something in our ancient language under her breath.

"If you wanted to continue to use our ancient language in conversation, you should've done a better job teaching it to me, Mother." I told my parents I couldn't speak it. I lied. I should've felt guilty about it but I didn't.

"Deacon. The world isn't what you may think. There are serious demon problems and witches who dabble in dark magic. I need you to not be so blasé about this."

I looked down at the black *XV* etched into my left forearm. "I'm the Devil now, Mother. The rest of the world needs to worry about me, not the other way around."

CHAPTER FOUR

TEGAN

"Royce, I thought you were mad at me," I said before I could stop myself. When he didn't respond right away, I gripped his arm. "Please don't be. I couldn't handle it."

He smiled, but it only lasted a fraction of a second. "No, I'm not. I'm sorry I snapped at you this morning. You just scared the hell out of us. We can't lose anyone else."

My stomach twisted into knots. "Henley isn't gone."

"Yet," he whispered.

"Royce..." I needed to tell him what I saw in my Tarot reading, but I didn't want to.

He sighed and shook his head. "Where's Emersyn?"

"Talking to a teacher— Hey, no changing the subject!" We stepped out from under the covered hallway into the grass and I hissed. The midday sunshine was the worst part of Florida. *Why is it always so damn bright?* I raised my hand to shield my face from the attack and groaned.

"Oh no," Royce whispered. He flipped my hair over my shoulder and poked my throat. "We're too late! The vampire process has begun already!"

I smacked his arm away and stormed toward our picnic tables. "Why do we sit outside?"

"Because we're witches, and witches *love* nature."

"Who said that? I can't see you." I looked up and squinted through the bright assault on my eyes. The sunlight dimmed down a few notches, then darkness swept over me. I sighed with relief and blinked. I looked around and found my Coven sprawled out over two picnic tables under an oak tree. Our usual spot. They laughed and it was definitely *at* me.

"That better?" Braison asked with a dimpled smile.

"I could make the sun set if you'd like," Lily said with a laugh. "Only like seven hours early. I doubt anyone would notice."

I shook my head and laughed along with them. Being a witch was still a new and awesome thing to me. I took my tray and plopped down on the bench then dropped my backpack to the grass. My stomach growled, like it somehow knew it was about to get food.

"Better, little sister?"

I snarled in my older brother's direction. "Depends what we're discussing, *big bro.*"

Truthfully, I was torn when it came to Cooper. Him being my full biological brother made so much sense. In hindsight, his behavior was stupid obvious. I *liked* Cooper. Finding out he was my brother was actually kind of cool. I now had a big family. I tried to empathize with him. It couldn't have been easy to keep that secret from me, from *us.* But he did. And it *hurt.* I didn't want to forgive him yet. I didn't want to just say it was okay because it wasn't.

"Tegan..."

I held my hand up to stop him. It didn't matter what he said—the deed was done. I looked over to Tennessee for assistance— *Wait. That's not Tennessee.* It was Easton sitting behind Cooper with a black hat on. I frowned and scanned the group, but he wasn't there. *Where is he?* He'd been in the parking lot before school when everyone yelled at us, so where was he now? My pulse quickened. My mind flashed a dozen horrible scenarios for his disappearance. *Calm down, Tegan. You're overreacting.* Cooper wouldn't be calm if something was wrong with Tennessee. So he had to be fine, wherever he was.

I licked my lips and took a deep breath. "Where's Tennessee?"

Cooper frowned and shook his head, like my question came completely out of left field. "Um, he left school for the day. Why?"

"He left school for the day?" Easton took his hat off and threw it in the grass. His blond head looked white in the sunlight. "Why does he get to leave?"

I took a bite out of my pizza to hide my reaction to talking about him. I seriously needed to learn how to control my face, or more specifically, my blushing. It was going to get both our magic stripped if I didn't figure something out. Tennessee made it look so easy.

"I gave up asking those questions." Cooper sighed and scratched the back of his head. "Why do you ask, Tegan?"

Uh-oh. Um...think. Think. Think. I cleared my throat and shrugged. "I was going to talk about my Tarot reading last night, but he's not here."

"No, but *that guy* is." Larissa pointed toward the cafeteria behind us. Her skin looked like peanut butter fudge in the sunlight. Her hazel-green eyes sparkled. "*Hel*-lo."

Paulina spun around on the bench to look and whistled. "He better be coming over here."

Braison's red eyebrows scrunched together. "We don't invite Sapiens over here."

"No, we don't," Easton grumbled.

"Fine, I'll invite him over to my house later," Paulina said with a wicked grin and a thick accent.

My thoughts went immediately to Libby and Henley. They were our most outspoken girls when it came to boys, especially Libby. I heard her voice saying their words, and it made my heart hurt. I pictured the two of them sitting side by side on top of the table, whispering to each other. They'd use their magic to get the mystery boy's attention, then flirt with him from across the lawn. They'd toy with him, leading him on only to forget he existed soon after they got their fill. We'd never get Libby back, but we still had a chance with Henley. If the visions I saw in the Tarot were legit, it was possible to save her.

"Easton's just mad there are other pretty blond boys," Willow teased and threw a piece of food at him from an opposite table.

"Don't be ridiculous." Easton rolled his beautiful sky-blue eyes. "Cooper is a pretty blond boy, too."

Cooper placed his palm to his chest. "Thank you, Easy E."

Lily groaned. "That nickname *has* to stop, or I'm going to hunt down every single one of his conquests and kill them. Choice is yours."

I threw my hand over my mouth to hide my laugh. She was serious, and I didn't blame her. If all of our friends openly joked about the girls Tennessee hooked up with before me, I... *Oh my God. Other girls?* My stomach turned, and I had the sudden urge to vomit. I'd never even considered Tennessee might've been with other girls before we met. How many were there? Were any of them serious? Did I know any of them? *Oh, God. What if he's still hooking up with other girls?*

"Royce, Earth to Royce!" Chutney waved her hand in the air. "We're objectifying a cute boy. We need you to weigh in."

I frowned and looked over at my friend. Royce was always quick to comment on attractive guys, yet he'd remained silent. He sighed and picked his head up. His eyes were tired, the bags under them growing darker every hour. He was thinking about Henley, too. Had our friends not noticed him suffering, or was this their way of distracting him? I looked around at their expectant eyes and warm smiles. Distracting, definitely.

"Royce, tell them no guy should wear white pants that tight or rolled up above his ankles." Easton leaned forward with his elbows on his knees. "Tell them."

"Damn it, now I have to look," Royce mumbled, though I wasn't sure if anyone else had heard him. He glanced over his shoulder and blanched. "DEACON?"

Wait, he knows him? I spun around to look, and my eyes widened. I totally understood the girls' reactions.

This guy, Deacon as Royce called him, was a walking movie poster. He was tall and lean, but with muscles like maybe he was a runner. His hair was a soft, sandy blond that reminded me of the beach back in South Carolina. It was short on the sides and long on the top, swept back in an effortlessly sexy way. Actually, the hairstyle reminded me of Royce's.

"Deacon, what...what are you doing here?" Royce stepped away from the table toward the incomer.

Deacon smiled and it sent a shiver down my spine. *This one is wild.* I didn't know how I knew—I just *knew.* I couldn't see his eyes behind his blue aviator sunglasses, but I felt his magic from ten feet away. He was a witch. He was definitely hot. And he was the exact opposite of Tennessee. Where Tenn wore black, Deacon wore pristine white. Like head-to-toe. White crew-neck T-shirt. Long white cardigan unbuttoned and pushed almost up to his elbows. White slim-fitting jeans rolled three inches above his ankles. White Adidas sneakers...with the laces tucked inside, like all the cool kids wore.

Deacon chuckled. "Here to make trouble, like always."

"Royce, you know him?" I asked the question I knew everyone was thinking.

Royce sighed and nodded. "This is my cousin, Deacon English." He stepped forward and greeted him in that standard guy way of shaking hands and slapping each other on the back.

"Deacon English? It's been a long time. I didn't recognize you," Cooper said from behind me.

"Yet you look exactly the same, except twice the size," Deacon said with a grin. His voice was smooth like silk. He moved through the group to greet my brother the same way he had Royce. "What's it been, a decade?"

"At least," Cooper said with a chuckle. He leaned back against the picnic table and gestured toward the rest of us. "I don't think you got to meet most of The Coven back then, did you?"

"My parents shipped him back home before he got the chance, if I remember correctly." Royce leaned against the table beside me. His voice was light and teasing, but his eyes were sharp and wary. "How'd you convince your mother to let you return?"

"I'm eighteen. I do what I want now." He slid his sunglasses to the top of his head, revealing a dashing pair of violet eyes. He winked at his cousin then turned to the rest of us. "Hey, everyone, I'm Deacon. I'm a witch. I'm from Manhattan, and I like tacos."

I narrowed my eyes. "Wait, is that a euphemism?"

He grinned and turned toward me. His eyes widened and his smile got a little warmer. "Hey, I saw you in the parking lot this morning."

"You saw me? That's random." I frowned. There were dozens of students in the parking lot that morning, including the whole Coven...yet he saw *me*.

He shrugged. "So are hot chicks with purple hair."

I blushed. "Um...thanks?" My thoughts immediately went to Tennessee. I was both glad he wasn't there to hear that, and mad that he couldn't be there to mark his territory.

"You're definitely welcome, beautiful." Deacon stepped toward me with his palm out. "What's your name?"

I took his hand and shook it. "Tegan."

"Tegan? That's fun. I feel like I've heard it before."

"Dude, no hitting on my sister," Cooper muttered.

"Deacon, stop flirting with our High Priestess," Royce said before Deacon could respond. "Tell us what you're doing here. I know there's a reason."

Deacon's blond eyebrows rose. He looked back and forth between Cooper and me. "I only see it in the eyes. Well, it is an honor to meet you, High Priestess."

"I said no flirting," Royce said.

"Royce, baby cousin, I'm not flirting. It *is* an honor to meet our High Priestess after all this time." He frowned and looked around the group with sharp eyes. "Wait, where's Henley?"

Silence.

Deacon's frown deepened. "Guys...where is Henley? Royce?"

But Royce's face was blank and as white as Deacon's outfit.

The awkward silence wasn't going to help anyone. I cleared my throat. *How do I say this?* I considered a variety of sugarcoated statements, but they felt like an insult to Henley. The truth was always the best option, in my opinion.

"Deacon, Henley was possessed by a demon last week, and a few days ago, she was taken through the Gap into another realm," I said.

Deacon's face fell. His skin paled, and gone were any hints of humor. He walked over to Royce and gripped him in a tight hug. Then he held on a little longer. "Royce, I'm so sorry. I had no idea. I would've come sooner." He pulled back and squeezed Royce's shoulder.

"There was nothing you could've done," Royce mumbled and sank onto the bench.

Deacon's eyes watered, but he blinked the emotions away. He turned to face the rest of us. "Is there...any hope of getting her back?"

"Yes," I answered immediately.

Everyone's eyes widened, and they spun to face me.

I held my hand in the air to stop them from asking

questions. "I read the Tarot last night, in the very spot she was possessed. I was waiting to tell the whole Coven together. I might not be able to tell it twice." I wasn't sure I could tell it once, the images were too scarring.

Cooper cursed. "That's why you asked where Tennessee was."

No, it really wasn't but okay. I nodded. "Yeah."

"The infamous Tennessee Wildes. I had noticed his absence," Deacon said. "Who else is missing?"

"Emersyn is in a meeting with a teacher." I picked up my pizza and took a bite. I didn't want to talk about my visions yet. Not without Tennessee. Not without Bentley.

"Libby," Willow whispered.

Deacon nodded. "I'm sorry for your loss. I always heard great things about her."

"You knew she passed?" Cooper frowned and scratched the back of his head. "The Coven hasn't announced it yet."

Deacon shifted his weight from foot to foot. "I was... notified..." He pushed his left cardigan sleeve up to his elbow.

Everyone gasped and leaned forward, like we needed a closer look despite the fact it was visible from across a football field. *XV* was Marked in black into his left forearm. The Mark of the Devil.

"Oh my Goddess," Royce mumbled and leaned back.

Deacon shrugged. "I was as shocked as you are, trust me. But when it showed, I knew I had to come here, to take my place in The Coven. I imagine this will be hard for you guys, and I really *am* sorry about Libby. I didn't choose to replace her."

The Devil in white.

Interesting. That wildness in his smile made so much more sense now. He was the living, breathing embodiment of temptation and desire.

I looked around at my crew, and I saw their pain in their eyes. They'd had to replace two of their dearest friends within days of each other. At least with Bentley, we had a sense of relief when we found him after the Hierophant's quests. Plus, he was a little boy. He was nothing like Cassandra, and it would be a long, long time before we had a similar relationship with him because he was so young. But Deacon was our age. I understood how they'd feel territorial and hurt by his arrival.

I also understood what it was like to be the new fish in the pond. They'd been warm and welcoming for Emersyn and me. Henley and Royce in particular. Deacon was their cousin. I owed it to them to show him the same comfort they gave me. *Don't I?*

"It's okay, Deacon," I said. "We all know how it

works, and it wasn't your fault. Welcome to The Coven. It's bat shit crazy here."

He chuckled and scrubbed his face. "Thanks, Tegan."

"Want a slice?" I patted the empty bench seat beside me. "Come on, I'll share for the newbie."

"Well, I can't say no to that." He grinned and took the seat I pointed to, then plucked a slice of pizza off my tray and took a bite. "Not bad. Six slices?"

"Half are for my sister."

"Hey, does Kessler know you're here?" Cooper asked as he pulled out his phone.

"Yeah, Kessler knows. He told me I'd find you out here during lunch." He pointed his half-eaten slice at my brother. "Though you would've been easy to find, I felt like I was following the yellow brick road of magic."

Cooper nodded and typed something on his phone. A few seconds later, a round of beeps and vibrations echoed through the group chat. I pulled my phone out of my boot and found a text from Cooper.

Deacon is here with us.

Three little bubbles popped up immediately, then Kessler's response appeared. Great. We have to initiate him tonight at midnight, so everyone meet at the beach at eleven thirty. Ceremonial white.

More bubbles popped up, then a text from a 212

phone number that wasn't saved in my phone appeared. Am I supposed to have ceremonial white?

Kessler responded immediately. No, ceremonial white is not common among civilian witches outside of Eden. Come over tonight and you can borrow.

Royce's name popped up with a text. It's okay, Kess. I've got an extra, we're about the same size.

"Who the hell is Deacon?"

Everyone jumped at the sound of Emersyn's voice. We'd all been so focused on the group chat we'd missed her arrival. We were a special breed of witch, apparently.

"That would be me," Deacon answered while turning to face her. When his eyes found her, they widened and lit up like fireworks. It was a look of recognition, like he already knew her. He blinked a few times, just staring at her. After a second, he shook himself and stood to greet her, sticking his hand out. "Hi. I'm Deacon English."

Her cheeks were a pinkish color, though that could've been from the sun. She stared at his hand for several awkward seconds before shaking it. "I'm Emersyn."

"Our new Devil. He just arrived today." I frowned and glanced back and forth between them. *What is happening here?* "Do y'all know each other?"

Emersyn shook her head and narrowed her eyes. "No."

Deacon smiled but it was a little wobbly. "Nice to meet you, Empress."

Emersyn glared at him. "Likewise." She took her hand back then moved to sit on the other side of me.

I turned toward her to ask what her problem was when my phone vibrated again. This time it was a text from Bentley just to Emersyn and me. Will you guys take me to HK after school, before dark? I left something in lookout tower I need for Deacon's initiation tonight.

I shot back my answer. Of course, B.

Emersyn's response came in right after mine. We'll pick you up right after school, so be ready. Tell Mom and Dad, though.

Awesome. I'll tell them. Can we do rides too, though?

I chuckled. Absolutely.

When I looked up from my phone, I found everyone in their own little bubbles. Lily and Easton were seconds away from a make-out session I didn't want to see. Cooper texted on his phone, probably to Uncle Kessler or Tennessee. The others were just having little side conversations. Except Deacon. He sat beside me, staring at the wooden table and eating the slice I'd given him.

I felt bad for the circumstances of his arrival.

44

Replacing a beloved friend who'd just died was a rough break. But at the same time, his arrival and initiation were easy compared to mine and Em's. I would've loved to meet the crew in the middle of the day and do my initiation ritual in a calm manner...not in a panic on a boat headed for a dangerous quest.

"Hey, Deacon?"

He looked over to me with a smile. "Yes, gorgeous?"

"Em and I are taking our little brother, Bentley, to Hidden Kingdom after school. Would you like to join us?" I opened my bag of Doritos to try and look casual. The last thing I needed was for this guy to think I was flirting with him. "Figure you might want to see it in the daylight first? Em and I didn't get that opportunity."

"Bentley, as in the new Hierophant?" When I nodded, he whistled. "Scary powerful family, man. But yes, I'd love to join you. Thanks for asking."

CHAPTER FIVE

TENNESSEE

I never needed much reason to ditch school. If I thought of an excuse, I used it. My father stopped giving me a hard time once I got my license. We both knew as Emperor, I'd never have a regular Sapien job. He only asked I try to keep good grades and be a good role model for my peers. I did that, and my report cards were worthy of approval...even if my absentee tally wasn't.

When I first learned Tegan went to Hidden Kingdom at night by herself, I about had a panic attack. I figured it was typical reckless, stubborn behavior we saw in new witches when they thought their magic was invincible. I thought she was overconfident in her abilities. Not that I'd blame her. Tegan was the Aether Witch. That meant she could create and control any element she wanted right from her fingertips. Once she learned practical magic, she'd be terrifying.

But this morning, I learned she'd gone to the park looking for clues to save Henley...and, well, it was exactly something I would've done. I'd already planned to do that exact thing after school, but I'd decided to ditch school and get an early start. So, being mad at her was hypocritical to say the least. But she was my soulmate. I had the right to worry, especially after losing Cassandra and Libby.

For the last four or five hours, I'd searched every surface imaginable for any kind of clue to help us save Henley. I came up empty-handed.

"Hello, my friend!"

I recognized her voice in an instant. *Saffie.* I smiled and turned to find her sitting on a low-hanging oak tree branch. Her fiery red hair was tied down behind her head, which was unusual for her. The pink translucent wings on her back fluttered lazily.

"Hi, Saffie."

She pouted. "I missed you, Tennessee."

"I know. I'm sorry. My father wouldn't let me come. I missed you, too." I sighed as I stepped up to her branch and rested my hand on it. "I've been looking for you all day."

She grinned and it made her lavender eyes sparkle.

"Last night scared me, so I didn't sleep. So I nap today. Then I was with Tegan."

"She's here now?" What the hell was she doing back? Did she not get the message this morning?

"Yup. Yup. Yup." Saffie nodded and picked flower petals out of her red hair.

My pulse kicked into overdrive. *Relax, dude. You've been here for hours. There's nothing here.*

I licked my lips and tried to keep my voice calm and casual. "Can you show me where?"

"Yup. Yup. Yup. Let's go, friend."

I smiled. *Friend.* I couldn't believe I'd avoided her for all these years. My Coven-mates were all afraid of her. Knowing her now, I felt awful. I knew in my gut Saffie was a good person. Her soul and heart were pure. Whatever had happened to her... Well, I was going to find out and make it right. Somehow. I owed it to her.

I followed her between the trees and off the paved pathway. Her little pink wings fluttered as she zipped over and under thick branches. Every few seconds, she looked over her shoulder to make sure I was there.

The sun poked through the sprawling oak trees in little patches. Twigs and fallen leaves cracked under my boots, but the dirt was a welcome cushion after all the cement. It was impossible to block the sounds of the theme park around me, but with every step deeper into the forest area, the smell of nature grew stronger. There was also a hint of maple syrup in the air. Demons. They weren't out now during daylight, so I pushed those thoughts away. I had to keep my head on straight if I was about to see Tegan. In public. Where anyone could see us.

Saffie spun around to face me and smiled, holding her thumbs up. "Almost there."

I loved that she took me the back way. It was more proof we were meant to be friends. I hated taking the path the Sapiens did. None of my friends shared this interest. *I wonder if Tegan will?* Heat spread across my chest and into my left shoulder. It burned deep down into my bones, like it came from inside me. Then again, I supposed it did. It meant Tegan was close by. I clenched my teeth and breathed through the pain. *When is this part going to stop?*

Saffie made a sharp left turn and waved me along. "They're right here."

I frowned. "They?"

"Yup. Yup. Yup." She nodded and flew ahead of me. When I caught up, she'd stopped along the edge of the forest. She pointed. "Tegan and new boy."

I stood straight. *New boy? What the hell?* The sun was so bright it took my eyes a moment to readjust back. I spotted her in an instant, like my eyes had a built-in GPS for her location. She stood beside the fairy fountain, the same one she'd blown up a few days ago. Her legs looked a mile long in those leather leggings. Her combat boots were filthy. Even from thirty feet away, I saw the mud and demon blood caked on the soles. She looked entirely out of place in a Florida theme park, surrounded by fanny packs and cargo shorts. And it filled me with the warm-and-fuzzies. I loved that she was different from everyone else.

Her black hair was tied up on top of her head, for the moment at least. It looked like one good gust of wind would knock the bun over. *Should I? Yes, yes, I should.* I held my hand in the air and pushed a strong breeze across the courtyard. It slammed into her from the side and knocked her hair down. Those purple tips I loved fell down to her waist and whipped around in the wind. I chuckled and leaned against the tree next to me.

She reached up and rolled the short sleeves of her white T-shirt almost all the way up to her shoulders. I wondered what she'd wear if she wasn't hiding our soul-mate glyph. I longed for the day we didn't have to hide. She turned to the person beside her, and that was when I saw him.

The new boy.

"He's pretty. Like a sunflower." Saffie giggled.

I frowned. He *was* pretty. And standing way too close to my girl.

His stupid blond hair was the same color as beach sand. I couldn't see under his obnoxious blue sunglasses, but judging by his sharp jawline and perfectly shaped eyebrows, I had a feeling his stupid eyes were pretty too. He said something to her, and she threw her head back and laughed.

A weird growl-like noise came out of my throat, and I didn't try to stop it. My magic swirled inside me, and the ground trembled.

Mister Pretty Boy raised his arm and pointed—

I gasped. My stomach dropped like I was on a roller-coaster.

There on his left arm was the Mark of the Devil.

No. No, no. This can't be happening. Not already. It's too soon. I didn't know why I was shocked. That was how the process worked. When a Card died, a new witch was chosen immediately. I scrambled for my cell phone tucked in my back pocket. I'd put it on Do Not Disturb when I'd left school. When I pulled it out, I had dozens of missed text messages. I cursed. Of course the one day I hid away, I missed something big. I scanned through the texts. Most were from the Coven group chat but my brother and father also. One word stuck out like a thorn.

Deacon.

My heart sank.

No. No, no, no. Not him.

Why him??

Deacon English.

Of all the people. Of all the witches in the world, why had She chosen the hot-headed, party-boy, never-suffered-a-day-in-his-life Deacon. Heat shot down my spine as my power raged to the surface. He was our replacement for Libby? *I call bullshit.* We weren't getting the better end of the bargain. I'd only met Royce's cousin once, back when we were kids. He'd come down for a two-week vacation, and Royce's parents had shipped him back after only a few days. He'd been impossible to handle. Zero discipline. He never listened to *anyone.* He didn't care if he got me, Cooper, Royce, and Henley suspended from school for *his* actions.

But yeah, let's make him the Devil.

I hadn't seen him in almost a decade, so there was a chance he'd grown up into a decent human being. But he also lived a cushioned lifestyle on the Upper East Side, with hired help to brush his teeth if he didn't feel like moving. Besides, I'd heard stories about him from his cousins over the years. Particularly the last few. It didn't sound like he'd changed.

Tegan said something to him then turned and

walked away. I followed after her without hesitation. A group of foreign tourists with matching neon-yellow shirts cut in front of me, blocking my path. I snarled and released some of my magic. Everyone around me jumped out of my way like I'd physically put my hands on them. I dashed across the courtyard and into the women's restroom I'd seen Tegan walk in.

In the back of my mind, I knew I shouldn't have been in there. It was all kinds of inappropriate. Except all of my focus was on my soulmate. A few girls shrieked and sprinted past me, but I didn't pay them any attention. I slammed each stall door open as I walked to make sure they were empty. I knew where *she* was. I could feel her aura pulsing from the back of the bathroom. With every step, my glyph seared my skin. A toilet flushed in the handicap stall all the way at the end. *Tegan.* I paused outside the door, waiting. She may have been my soulmate, but I wasn't going to invade her privacy. When the sink water turned off, I couldn't hold back any longer. I pushed my magic out, and the stall door flew open.

Tegan gasped and spun around. Her face was white...until she saw *me*. Her cheeks flushed pink, and her pale green eyes dilated a tad. She shook her hands, and the water evaporated.

She narrowed her eyes. "Where have you been?"

"Stay away from Deacon English." That was *not*

what I'd intended to say. I meant to answer her question, but the words slipped out before I could stop them.

Tegan arched one black eyebrow. "Feeling jealous, Tenn?"

"You don't know him like I do. You don't know the kind of guy he is," I snapped, ignoring her question yet again. "He's trouble. Reckless. Selfish. He's a rich brat with more notches on his belt than—"

"I'm gonna stop you right there, gorgeous." Her fists balled at her sides. "First of all, I can't even wear a tank top in this God-awful heat because of you, so don't you *dare* finish that sentence like his love life is of any concern of mine."

"That's not—"

"Important?" She stepped closer to me. "Relevant?"

I grabbed her by the jaw and dragged her lips to mine. She gripped the front of my shirt and pulled. We stumbled back with our lips locked until we collided with the cool tiled wall. The metal door rattled against the lock. I pushed against her and angled her chin to deepen our kiss. She was everywhere, invading all of my senses at once. She was everything I needed. The rest of the world slipped away. Her fingers tangled in my hair, drawing a tortured groan out of my mouth. My chest burned from lack of oxygen, and I didn't care. All of my stress and worry melted against her lips.

"Tegan?"

The real world crashed back into my brain at the sound of Emersyn's voice. I pulled back, but Tegan's teeth sank into my bottom lip and pulled me in. A low growl escaped around our lips as I took her face between my palms and kissed her with everything I had. With all of my pain, with all my torture. I let it all pour out of me with every brush of our lips.

"Was that a *growl?*" Emersyn's voice grew closer, too close. "Tegan, are you okay? Is there a monster in here?"

Yeah. Me. I dropped my hands and jumped back from my soulmate. I didn't look at her before I turned away. I knew I wasn't strong enough to say no. My heavy footsteps echoed around the bathroom.

Emersyn's aura filled with anxiety. I threw the stall door open, and it slammed against the wall.

Emersyn stood just on the other side. Her golden eyes widened. "Tennessee."

"Emersyn." I nodded my head in her direction then sprinted for the door.

CHAPTER SIX

B *loody hell.*
I'm not cut out for this kind of torture.

The second Tennessee was out of sight, I dropped. The only thing preventing me from sitting my butt on the nasty theme park bathroom floor was the conveniently located handicap sink. The cold porcelain against my fingers did nothing to simmer the fire raging out of control inside me.

That boy made me a mess.

"What...just happened?"

I groaned and rested my forehead against my arm. "Euthanize me, Em. I can't take it."

Her boots clicked closer on the tile. "Where did Tennessee come from?"

A chuckle escaped my mouth. I shook my head. "Girl, I've been asking myself that for weeks."

"I mean, was he already in the park? Or did he follow us here?"

I used the sink to pull myself back to my feet. My gaze immediately latched onto my reflection in the mirror. Dark eyes, pink cheeks, and puffy lips. My hair was disheveled and wild. My skin tingled everywhere he'd touched me.

"Tegan?"

I met my sister's stare in the mirror and shrugged. "I have no idea, Em. He didn't say." I turned the handle and let the water rush out of the faucet.

She frowned and crossed her arms over her chest. "He didn't say? What were y'all doing in here? Making out?"

I stared at her without speaking.

She gasped and a light flush covered her cheeks. She glanced around us then moved closer. "What happened?"

I hung my head and focused my attention on the cold water running over my fingers. "I came in here to use the restroom, then *boom*. There he was. One second we were arguing, the next...well..."

"Arguing? Why?"

If other people entered the bathroom, I couldn't tell over the pounding of my heart in my ears. Energy ran through my body like raw electricity.

I sighed. "He just started yelling at me to stay away from Deacon because he's awful and a total player, though not in such nice words."

"Playboy?"

I willed the water off, then stared at the droplets on my skin. "He's trouble, evidently. Reckless, selfish, rich brat who sleeps around—according to Tennessee." I turned away from my reflection and headed for the door.

"Oh, lovely," Emersyn whispered behind me.

"Come on. Let's get what Bentley needs and go home."

CHAPTER SEVEN

TENNESSEE

I needed answers. My life was now full of questions and uncertainties. I hated it. I hated not knowing. I couldn't prepare for unknowns. I was flying blind, and it made my skin crawl. I used to think I was like a cat, that no matter how far I fell, I'd always land on my feet. But after losing two of my closest friends within days of each other, I wasn't so sure of those nine lives. What if this was my last life? What if the next battle got the best of me? What if it got the best of Tegan?

My stomach turned. *Don't think like that.* Tegan was the Aether Witch. She had more power than any other witch. Ever. Or at least in many, many centuries, if not longer. Every day her control got stronger, her behavior more confident. *She'll be fine. She will.*

I parked my Jeep in the front of the lot then jumped out. The salty ocean air rushed by my face. Something about being at the beach chipped away at the tension inside me. I took a deep breath and tried to rein in my thoughts. Deacon's initiation had to happen right at midnight. I glanced down at my watch and sighed. I only had twenty minutes until everyone else would arrive. My Coven didn't need to know what I was doing. They didn't need to know my confidence was a flimsy façade.

Okay, here goes nothing. I pushed my shoulders back and stepped onto the beach. My boots sank in the sand with every step, but I trudged forward. The waves crashing onto the shore comforted me like a lullaby, and not for the first time, I wished I could curl up in the sand and sleep. When I got to the shore, I willed the ocean to harden under my feet. If it had been daylight, I would've walked under the surface, but at night it would be pitch-black down there, and I didn't want to draw any attention to myself. The demons were playing a new game with us, except we didn't know the rules yet.

I pulled George out of my pocket. The crystal responded to me immediately. The purple and blue mist spilled into the air like it was stretching. I thought it might've sighed, then I thought I might've been losing my mind.

"Good evening, George," I said to my pendulum without slowing my pace. "Care to help me out?"

Energy shot up the chain and into my fingers, sending tingles up my arm. *YES*.

I chuckled. "Well, okay then. Do you know what I'm doing?" I'd gotten over the weirdness of talking to a crystal like it was a living, breathing person a long time ago. Somehow, George always knew what was going on, and he *felt* real.

Yes.

"Perfect." I nodded and glanced at the horizon in front of me. In the dark, I only knew it was there by the shimmer in the waves under the half moon. "Do you know where the best place will be to send it?"

Yes.

I loved when my pendulum knew what I was thinking. "Am I there yet?"

NO. If a crystal could roll its eyes, it just did.

"Show me?"

It swung to the right, veering my path a few feet over. I kept my eyes on the pendulum until it spun in a tight counterclockwise circle. I frowned and stopped walking. "Here?"

YES.

"All the way to the ocean floor?"

Yes.

I narrowed my eyes and pushed my magic out. "George, are there any demons near me right now?"

No.

George had never led me astray before, so I had no reason not to trust him. Regardless of how many times I'd seen demons at this very beach. Then again, the demons had been quiet ever since Henley was taken through the Gap. I sighed and pushed thoughts of her away. *One step at a time, Tenn. Now, focus.*

The water moved at my command. It split open and formed a staircase. The first few steps glistened in the moonlight like glass, then it was nothing but darkness. It was a staircase into a black hole. I willed my body to glow then began my descent. About twenty steps later, I got impatient and turned the stairs into a slide. Gravity took over. My boots slammed into the ocean floor mere seconds later.

With George still gripped tightly in my hand, I stood and looked around. I saw only more darkness, but my magic sensed life force nearby. The water rippled over me in small, gentle waves. Whatever was there, it meant me no harm. The glow off my body lit up a ten-foot radius of sand and saltwater.

I cleared my throat. "George, is this the right spot?"

Yes.

"Is this going to work?"

Yes.

"Leyka is going to get my note?"

YES.

"Is he going to respond?"

I don't know.

Well, that was expected. I nodded. "Thanks again." I tucked my pendulum back into my front jeans pocket where it would be safe from harm. If it was on my body, then the water wouldn't hurt it.

Now that I'd found the right location, I willed the ocean to cover me. It was like someone just wrapped a warm blanket around my shoulders. Once the water calmed, I reached into my back pocket and pulled out the note I'd written up for Leyka.

Cooper had been dreaming about our angel friend Leyka for days. I knew we needed to reach out to him somehow. With the help of the New Book, The Coven's replacement for the lost Book of Shadows, we'd found this method of communication. We didn't want anyone knowing we were communicating with him. If he'd wanted people to know, he wouldn't have gone through all the measures he had. The pig. The Sirens. Keltie. No, we had to be discreet.

My father, Cooper, and I had spent the last few hours choosing the right words. Leyka may have been cool when we saw him, but there was no guarantee we'd get the same hospitality. I'd written the note on special parchment treated with privacy charms. The note itself was written in blood. *My* blood. It was short and concise.

I knelt down on one knee and pulled my dagger from my boot. With the tip of the blade, I sliced a circle in the sand around me. I placed the folded up parchment right in front of me then buried it. I sliced my left palm open and let my blood pour onto the sand over the note. Blue energy swirled around my hand. I pushed it down and whispered in the ancient language. The sand rippled and pulsed. I willed the grains to wrap around my note and lift into the water. It looked like a snowball, hovering in front of my face.

"I call upon Water's power, carry mine gift to Leyka this midnight hour."

CHAPTER EIGHT

TEGAN

pparently, the initiation for each Card was different. Emersyn and I had to have help from the Crones because of the blocking spells placed on us as babies. For our ritual, the Crones had drawn a massive black pentagram into the dirt and had Royce cover the lines with his flowers. The process was wild and full of raw magic, mixed with the power of the elements. But during Bentley's initiation, the pentagram was made up of candles in varying sizes and colors. It was calm and serene, done right at sunrise.

Deacon was the Devil though. Something told me this wasn't going to be like Bentley's.

"All right, y'all." Dad pulled the truck into the parking lot and grabbed a spot up near the front. He glanced over his shoulder and grinned. "Let's do this."

Mom opened her door and then jumped out. She

leaned her head back into the truck and focused on my little brother. "Bentley, stay close to me, okay?"

"There aren't going to be any demon attacks on us tonight, Mom."

"You don't know that," she snapped back.

"Yes, I do. I'm psychic." Bentley grinned.

"Bentley."

"Okay, Mother. I'll stay close." He sighed and climbed over the console to go out Mom's door.

As soon as we were alone in the truck, Emersyn groaned. "We don't have to stay here after, do we?"

I frowned and looked over at her in the seat across from me. "I know you're not the night owl I am, but what's your problem?"

Her blonde eyebrows were scrunched down low over her eyes, and her lips were pursed. "Nothing. I just don't want to be here." She threw her door open and slid out, then slammed it shut behind her.

"Yeah, that much is clear," I mumbled to myself and got out of the car.

I followed my family toward the beach, but my mind was elsewhere. Something was bothering my twin. I just couldn't fathom what that would be. I watched her out of the corner of my eye. Normally she had a bounce to her step and a clean aura around her. Tonight, she stomped through the sand with her hands in fists at her sides and a cloud of smoke under her feet. Her long platinum blonde hair was uncharacteristically tangled. The hem of her ceremonial white gown was wrinkled, also completely not like her. *What is up with her?*

"Hey, guys!"

I jumped and spun toward the male voice with my hands raised. My magic responded to the rush of adrenaline and slipped out. Water splashed onto Deacon's face like from a fireman's hose.

I gasped and pulled my power back. "Crap, Deacon, I'm sorry!"

He laughed and wiped the droplets off his skin. "Nah, it's okay."

"How is sneaking up on your own Coven-mate *okay*, Deacon?" Emersyn snapped from a foot away from me. Waves of heat rolled out of her as her golden eyes aimed lasers at him. "She could've hurt you, or are you that reckless? Or maybe it's careless?"

Deacon opened his mouth then shut it again. He shook his head. "Emersyn...I..."

But she just rolled her eyes and stormed off toward the shoreline where the rest of our Coven sat around a bonfire.

"Tegan, I didn't mean to scare you," Deacon said in a rush. His violet eyes were wide and his face a little pale. He raised both hands in the air. Water dripped down his face in little rivers. "Honest. I just got here and saw you, so I called out."

"I have absolutely no idea what *that* was about." I pointed toward my twin's back. I smiled and waved my hand, drying the wetness I'd made. "But you don't need to apologize. I need to not space out quite so deep."

He chuckled and ran his hand through his hair. His cheeks flushed a light pink, or at least it seemed so. There weren't any lights on at this part of the beach, or the parking lot. All we had was the moon...and apparently the glow of my skin. I hadn't even realized I'd lit up. I rolled my eyes at my own overreaction and reined my magic in until I was no longer luminescent. When I looked back up to Deacon, I found him watching my sister with a strained look in his eyes.

Deacon seemed to annoy her, despite the fact we'd just met him a few hours ago and that he'd been nothing but friendly. I'd get to the bottom of it eventually. My twin loved people. She was the epitome of an extravert—she *needed* to be around others. Emersyn only disliked a person if they were mean to her. Innocent until proven guilty was her motto.

But with Deacon? She never smiled. She straight up glared at him. Her words were short and clipped. If I hadn't known any better, I'd think they knew each other. Except Deacon told me they didn't while he was asking me a million questions about her. He seemed rather engrossed by her. He had a thing for her—that was painfully obvious. And he was *nice* to her, so it didn't make any sense at all.

In fact, I didn't see the guy Tennessee said he was at all.

Who did I trust? My intuition had never led me astray, not in my entire life. Tennessee was my soulmate, but he'd blatantly lied to my face. But then Emersyn's reaction to Deacon confused everything. When the person who loved everyone hated someone... Well, it gave cause for concern. *Guess I'll have to do some digging of my own.*

A gust of wind blew off the ocean and swept over me. My hair flew back and coiled around my bicep. The salty air broke through my thoughts, bringing me back to the present. We were at the beach to initiate Deacon into The Coven. That was all. And they appeared to be waiting for us.

I glanced over at my new friend again. He sure looked damn good in white. Just like the other guys in The Coven, wearing a dress didn't seem to make him uncomfortable. His arms were bare and cut with lean muscle, not quite like Tennessee's—well, no one looked like *him*.

I cleared my throat. *Don't think about him right now.*

I wrapped my arm around Deacon's elbow and urged him forward. "C'mon, Devil, let's get you initiated."

"I just don't understand what I did to her," he whispered as we walked.

I shrugged, suddenly aware of how much of our skin touched. Would Tennessee be pissed if he saw? He'd certainly seemed the jealous type earlier at the park. I took a deep breath and braced myself for the pain in my chest, but it didn't come. *Is he not here?* The glyph always burned when my soulmate was near. I tried to keep my face neutral while I scanned the group, but it was too dark to see everyone clearly.

"...tell her for me?"

I blinked back to Deacon who apparently had still been talking to me. *Oops.* "Listen, Deacon. Although I have no idea what crawled up her ass and died today, I do know that we've been through hell in the last couple weeks. My sister puts a lot of unnecessary blame on herself for what happened with Henley, and you're Henley's cousin. I suggest you just back off a bit and let her collect herself."

Deacon frowned, but he nodded. "Okay. I can do that."

"Good." I squeezed his arm then pulled mine out of

his as we joined the group. "All right, how we doing this?"

"We're not all here yet." Uncle Kessler glanced down at his watch then glared at the ocean. He turned and walked to where my parents stood a few feet back, talking to Bentley.

"Who's not here?" Emersyn crossed her arms over her chest and looked around.

Cooper rolled his eyes, and he looked *just* like Emersyn when he did. "Who do you think?" He shook his head and smirked, his stare locked on the ocean too.

Tennessee.

"Emperors are never late. That's the saying, right?" Easton stood and brushed sand off his ceremonial white.

"No, it's 'a queen is never late.'" Royce walked up to his cousin and fist bumped him. "And trust me, that boy is no queen."

"Thank the Goddess for that." Larissa threw something into the bonfire. Her white dress was a stark contrast to her mocha skin, especially with only firelight. "Y'all gotta leave some of the pretty ones for us, too."

For us. My stomach turned. That was my soulmate they were talking about. *Not us. Me. For me. Only me.* I wanted so badly to claim my territory. He was mine, and I couldn't tell anyone.

"All right, let's get in position so we're ready as soon

as he gets here." Uncle Kessler rejoined us, with my parents and Bentley hot on his heels. "Willow?"

She jumped up from the sand and skipped away from the bonfire, toward the shoreline. Her strawberry-blonde hair looked carrot orange. About halfway between us and the water, she stopped and spun around to face us. She wiggled her fingers until sparks of pink and orange flickered, then she raised her hands into the air. Shadows shot out from her feet and spread across the sand. I frowned and moved closer...and then I saw it.

A pentagram. "Just like on Crone Island..."

"Great, that went well," Emersyn mumbled behind me.

"Seriously." Royce whistled low. "I got a bad feeling about this."

I opened my mouth to agree with them when my body filled with warmth. It was comfortable and relaxing, like being cuddled under fuzzy blankets. I smiled and sighed.

My father stepped into my line of view. Golden, glittery mist shimmered around his hands. He smiled at us. "This is not going to be like Tegan and Emersyn's initiation, so everyone just breathe. If anything goes haywire, well, there's a whole hell of a lot of us here."

My dad has magic. That was something I may never get used to. In hindsight, his gift was stupid obvious. He could control people's emotions, and it clarified a lot of my youth.

I smiled. "Thanks, Dad. Now, Uncle Kessler, where do you want us?"

"Tegan, stand at the top point. Emersyn and Tennessee—whenever he decides to join us—will take the bottom two points." He walked over and stood on the circle line around the pentagram, directly between the bottom two points. "Bentley, please stand right behind Tegan. Everyone else, spread out around the circle."

Everyone jumped into action, moving to their designated spots. I only had to take a few steps to get to my point. The sand was cool and soft under my bare feet. Straight ahead of me, behind my Coven, the Gulf of Mexico was flat and calm. The moon was a tiny sliver of a crescent moon, hanging low and bright in the black sky. Behind me, to my right, was Bentley. He hummed something and seemed overall happy to be there. To my left, standing just outside the circle, was Deacon. He shifted his weight back and forth between his legs. His energy was nervous and buzzing.

"You okay?"

He nodded. "I'm not wondering what happened in your initiation at all."

I chuckled and opened my mouth to reassure him when red-hot heat seared through my chest. The pain filled my lungs and shot down my right arm. I gasped and held a hand to my chest, unable to stop myself. I clenched my teeth together and breathed through my nose. It would only be unbearable for a few seconds, then it would simmer. I knew this pain well. *Tennessee.* I scanned the parking lot in the distance, looking for a fresh set of headlights, but everything was dark.

"Have demons ever attacked you guys here?" Deacon asked with a clipped tone.

"Yes, but they won't tonight," Bentley answered in a calm voice.

"Then what is *that?*"

I spun back around and followed Deacon's gaze. Despite my brother's confidence, my own flickered. My magic swirled around my fingers, ready to defend us. The ocean rippled off in the distance, then it *cracked.* The water split open at the horizon, parting like the Red Sea in a straight line toward the shore. The pain and heat in my chest intensified with every inch closer the crack got.

"Tennessee," I breathed.

"What?"

Oops. I gotta stop doing that.

Before I recomposed myself enough to answer, Tennessee's tall, dark form emerged from the parted water. His black hair was windblown and wild. His ceremonial white gown was wrinkled like it'd been balled up on his bedroom floor since the last time he wore it. Even still, he looked beautiful. He stepped onto the shore with bare feet and a nasty grimace.

"Oh my Goddess," Deacon whispered. "That's him."

I frowned and stole a glance back at Deacon, only to find him grinning like a madman. "You okay back there?" Had I missed something? Was Deacon playing for the same team Royce was? I thought he was crushing on Emersyn.

Deacon nodded and covered his mouth with his hands. "I'm cool. I'm cool. It's just...he's the *Emperor*. The only time I met him, we were little kids, like it didn't mean anything to me back then. But now?" He whistled, just like his cousin always did.

I raised my eyebrows and watched the way his eyes lit up. "And now?"

"Seriously? Oh right, you're new to our world." He threw his hands in the air. He kept his voice at a whisper, like maybe he didn't want anyone else to hear us. "He's easily the most famous person in our entire society. *Everyone* knows who he is. He's definitely going to be leader one day. Everyone knows it. I mean, did you see the way he walked out of the ocean like that?"

I chuckled. "Are you fangirling over Tennessee right now, or crushing?"

"What? No. No, no. I like girls." His eyes flicked over to Emersyn then jumped back to Tennessee. It was subtle, but I saw it. He shook his head. "He's just... I can't believe I'm actually meeting him again. My friends back home will die when I tell them. You don't understand."

Oh, I do. Though, perhaps for entirely different reasons. I found his reaction comical considering the way Tennessee reacted to seeing him at the park. Whatever happened when they were kids was definitely not still in Deacon's memory. I turned back to face the group and tried not to look at Tennessee.

Uncle Kessler raised his eyebrows. "Well?"

Tennessee nodded, but his expression was unreadable. "Done."

"What's done?" I asked before I could stop myself.

"Nothing to worry about," Cooper answered.

"Not yet anyway, right? You prefer to wait sixteen years."

"Tegan." Cooper sighed.

"Okay, we have to start *now*," Uncle Kessler shouted from the other side of the circle. "Tennessee, take the point beside Emersyn. Deacon, please stand in the middle."

"Cool. Cool. Cool," Deacon mumbled under his breath. When he got to the center, he spun and faced me. "Ready to initiate, boss."

Uncle Kessler nodded. "Devon, fill in the blanks, please?"

"On it." My mother nodded. A wall of shimmery silver mist covered her then shot out around the circle.

The mist swirled and moved until it took the form of my mother, like a clone. In the flash of a second, there had to be a dozen of my mother standing around the circle. They were exact copies. I couldn't even tell which was the real person and which was magic. *Whoa.* Cooper had told us our mother's gift was astral projection, but apparently I hadn't realized what he meant.

"Thanks, Devon. Now..." Uncle Kessler smiled and turned toward me, but his eyes were aimed lower. "Hierophant, would you like to get us started?"

"Yep." He grinned and looked up at me. The golden, ancient locket hung around his neck. "High Priestess, please draw our pentagram with flames. Use Willow's illusion lines as guides."

I smiled. Every time I thought of my little brother as a normal kid, or even as a normal witch, he went and did something to remind me of who he really was. Our Hierophant. He had the gift of psychic ability. So even though I hadn't told anyone I'd learned to manipulate fire...he knew.

"Yes, sir." I took a deep breath and reached out to the bonfire with my magic. I knew I could create it on my own, but I was still practicing that part. I raised my hand and grabbed ahold of the hot energy, then pulled it toward me. Flames danced around my hand without touching my skin. I narrowed my eyes on Willow's black lines then shot the fire into the sand.

A chorus of gasps and shouts of surprise echoed around our circle, but I ignored them. My gaze latched on to Tennessee's across the sand. The flames stood two feet tall, swaying and flickering in the wind. Tennessee's eyes bored into me with more heat than the fire.

Bentley shouted in our ancient language. Somewhere in the back of my mind, I wondered when and how he'd learned it so fast, but it was a fleeting thought. With Tennessee's eyes on me, my brain was sluggish. I licked my lips and tried to concentrate on breathing. His black hair glistened like oil. His skin was deliciously tan. The flames shot up over our heads, and it took everything in me not to take a step backward.

These were *my* flames. I could control them. Stop them, if I had to. I couldn't see anyone on the other side of the circle, or next to me for that matter. I heard Bentley's voice chanting in our ancient language, but I couldn't *see* him. His aura was calm and serene. In front of me, in the dead center, Deacon dropped to the sand on his knees. His hands were balled at his sides. His eyes squeezed shut. His sandy blond hair looked neon orange.

I raised my hands and pulled my magic back just a tad. The sky above us rumbled like a stampede, then lightning the color of blood shot out of the darkness and struck the ground at Deacon's knees. His back arched. The same red lightning erupted from his chest.

A cold chill crawled up my spine and shot into my fingers. I called my magic back to me, and it obeyed without hesitation. The flames vanished in an instant. White smoke billowed from the sand everywhere the fire had touched. It swirled and turned crimson. The smoke slithered across the ground toward Deacon. When it reached him, it wrapped around his body then shot up to the clouds.

Red lightning flashed in Deacon's eyes like something out of *X-Men*. The bolts struck the crimson smoke in rapid fire. The smoke sparked and glowed. It swirled around above Deacon's head.

I narrowed my eyes and watched with my jaw wide open. Within the smoke, fiery red lightning bolts thickened in the shape of letters...until they formed words...

THE DEVIL MARKS THE START.

CHAPTER NINE

TEGAN

The smoke crackled and sparked like a broken power line. The words grew larger and brighter. They looked like a neon bar sign against the blackness. The sky thundered and the ground trembled. Red lightning shot out of Deacon's chest and struck the ground in a line, traveling across the pentagram to where Bentley stood right behind me. I gasped and spun toward my brother. The red smoke coiled around his feet then slithered up his body like a snake. I lit my body up and raised my hands to shine some light on him.

Bentley's amber eyes twinkled like stars. He smiled softly and raised his left arm in the air. He whispered something in the ancient language, and the smoke stretched up and down to his fingers. My eyes widened and my pulse quickened. I knew what was about to happen. Judging by Bentley's calm, expectant expression, he knew, too.

No one spoke. I didn't need to turn around to know everyone's eyes were locked on our Hierophant's arm. The red smoke circled around his forearm like a tornado. It darkened from crimson to purple to blue and then to black. After a second, the smoke turned to dust and vanished. Two lines were written in elegant black script on Bentley's arm, just under his *V* Mark.

"What's it say?" Easton half whispered from somewhere behind me. "Guys...guys, what's it say?"

"The Devil marks the start..." Braison whispered back.

"No, I saw that. What does his arm say?"

I gasped. *Deacon!*

"Deacon?" Tennessee called out before I got my mouth to work. "Deacon, are you all right?"

My heart filled with pride. My soulmate thought horrible things of Deacon, warned me to stay away from him, yet there he was making sure he wasn't hurt.

Except Deacon didn't respond. I glanced over my shoulder and found our Devil on his knees with his shoulders slouched and his head hanging down.

"Deacon?" I called.

Behind him, Emersyn glared at his back. Her face was ashen. "Is he breathing?"

"Deacon? Can I go to him or do I have to stay here?" Royce's voice rose in worry, a tone I wasn't used to hearing from him.

There was a beat of silence while everyone just stared at Deacon's nonmoving body...then we all rushed forward at the same time. Royce got there first. He dropped to his knees and gripped both of his cousin's shoulders.

Deacon gasped and snapped his head back. His eyes widened, then he blinked rapidly. "Cool, cool, cool. That was unexpected."

Royce sighed. "You're okay?"

"Yeah, totally normal." Deacon chuckled nervously and ran a hand over his hair. "What did I miss? Did I see words in the sky, or did I lose my mind?"

"The Devil marks the start." Tennessee crossed his arms over his ceremonial white dress. His mismatched eyes stared off into space, looking at nothing in particular.

"Listen, I'm happy Deacon is okay, but..." Easton turned back to Bentley and pointed his finger. "Can we see what his arm says *now*?"

Oh, right. I spun around and found my baby brother standing silently behind us. If I expected Bentley to be nervous under all of our gazes, I was wrong. He was one tough nine-year-old. He held his left forearm out for us all to see.

I held my glowing hand up and read the lines out loud. "*Call upon the Magic Mirror, all chosen wands will shine clearer.*"

"Wonderful," Larissa mumbled.

"Well, now, what the hell does *that* mean?" Royce grumbled.

Easton groaned. "I hate these riddles. Can't we get a suggestion box and request easy instructions?"

"Magic mirror? Maybe it means like our reflection on the ocean?" Chutney said softly.

"Oh, maybe I'm supposed to conjure a mirror with my magic?" Willow asked.

"No." Tennessee cleared his throat. The low, rough edge to his voice sent warm shivers down my spine that I prayed no one else noticed. "It's capitalized, so it's referring to an actual Magic Mirror."

"That's a real thing?" Chutney asked with a frown.

"Glad I'm not the only one who didn't know," Emersyn mumbled. Her arms were wrapped around her stomach.

"A Magic Mirror is a tool we use to help see things as they really are." Uncle Kessler narrowed his eyes and turned to face my parents.

My father shook his head. "I never used those, wasn't my thing."

"I did," my mother said with a nod. "They're usually full of spells and charms, properly cleansed and magically charged. I haven't seen one in years, not since Rebecca."

"Who's Rebecca?" Emersyn asked.

"The Hierophant when I was a child, two before Cassandra."

I frowned and looked back over to Bentley. Everyone always acted like our Hierophant was supposed to have all the answers, but my brother certainly didn't. Though he definitely was more knowledgeable and connected than before. If this Rebecca had and used a Magic Mirror, maybe it had something to do with the Hierophant. Maybe it was the locket. If I remembered correctly, there was a nice reflection off that thing. Besides, we went through hell to get it, and it had all the secrets.

"Claudette used to talk about her Magic Mirror, but she'd never show it to anyone." Uncle Kessler tugged at his bottom lip with his fingers.

Emersyn sighed and threw her hands in the air. "Who was Claudette?"

"The High Priestess before Tegan," my mother said softly, her light green eyes full of pain.

Wait. Hold up. The High Priestess had one, and so did a former Hierophant, yet no one else in The Coven did or knew about it. So it wasn't a common object, but the Goddess wanted us to use it. In fact, she didn't tell us to go find it—she just told us to use it. Meaning we already had it. *What will we use it for?*

"That was my next question," Deacon said and relaxed his crouch in the sand.

I meant to look at him, but my eyes caught Tennessee's and refused to budge. His stare held mine with an intensity no one should've witnessed. I didn't look away. Someone suggested it meant we had to make a wand... Then a few others argued over how they were to be made.

I shook my head and waved my hand. "No, it said *chosen wands.*"

Tennessee nodded. "Right. Not something we make, but something that will enhance how we see something."

"Maybe it's saying we have to go find this chosen wand? Like a quest?" Deacon asked, still sitting on the sand.

"No, that's way too short to be a quest prophecy." Cooper shook his head.

I peeled my gaze off Tennessee and looked to the horizon. The first quest we'd gone on started right at the same beach, kind of late at night as well. For that, the

Goddess had used the stars to spell out which Card was to go on the quest. Then during the purification ritual of the locket, Henley used the Tarot to figure out which Cards were required for ritual.

Wait. Could it be?

All of our crew were still discussing and debating.

I turned to Bentley and focused my thoughts. *Bentley.*

His golden eyes looked at me. He raised one eyebrow and cocked his head slightly to the side. If anyone else had seen, they would've assumed he was deep in thought.

It means the Tarot, doesn't it? The back of the cards are black, but they reflect everything. Have you seen them before?

Bentley shook his head, but I recognized the sharp look in his eyes. It was the expression he wore whenever he was thinking really hard. I saw it every time I helped him with homework. Then his eyes lit up. He tapped on the locket and nodded. I had no idea what he'd seen in the ancient jewel, but there was a reason we'd tortured ourselves to find it.

Did the last High Priestess call the Tarot her Magic Mirror?

Bentley gripped the locket in his palm and closed his eyes. White light shimmered between his fingers. His eyes moved back and forth under his closed eyelids. After a few seconds, he opened them and looked back at me. He nodded, then pointed to the second line, then made a circular motion with his finger.

I nodded. *Exactly. She wants us to read the cards to tell who is going on the quest.*

"For the Book," he whispered.

"Yes." I grinned. It was a relief knowing someone knew what was coming besides me.

"Where is the Tarot?"

"In my bag, in the car." I shrugged. "No pockets."

He smiled. "Go get them. I'll get everyone ready."

I didn't waste another second. I sprinted across the sand and into the parking lot. The uneven gravel burned against my bare feet, but I didn't slow my pace. My hair whipped around my body, tangling itself into a knot I'd spend forever combing out. When I got to my dad's pickup truck, I ran around to the back door. I placed my palm to the handle and pushed with my magic until I heard the click of the lock popping. I threw the door open and dove for my book bag. My Tarot deck sat just inside the zipper, right on top of everything else. I grabbed it and spun back around. I gasped and stumbled back against the car.

Tennessee stood looming over me, with his arms crossed over his chest.

I exhaled and pushed my hair out of my face. With my heart in my throat, I shook my head. "You scared the hell out of me."

"Good." He narrowed his eyes and leaned close enough for me to get a good whiff of his fresh rain scent but not enough to kiss him. "You need to pay more attention to your surroundings. I could've been a demon or spirit. You could've been possessed."

"Tenn..."

His arm moved in a blur. He pressed his finger to my lips to stop me from talking. "I can't lose you, too, Tegan." His voice cracked, and it broke something inside of me.

I understood. The idea of...of... I couldn't even think it. I wouldn't survive something happening to him.

I nodded. "I'll be more careful," I whispered against his finger.

He sighed and dropped his hand. "Just stop going *anywhere* alone. And Emersyn does not count. Wherever you go, take someone with you. Even if it's not me."

"Even if it's Deacon?"

He snarled and made this low, growl-like noise that totally did weird things to me. "Even. If. It's. Deacon. You understand? I need you alive."

I took a deep breath. It wasn't often I got Tennessee to actually *talk* to me about us, about how he felt for me.

These weren't those three words, but they were damn close.

I licked my lips and nodded. "Okay, but promise it back in return."

He scoffed. "Tegan, I'm—"

"Not human? I know." I grabbed a handful of his white gown and pulled him closer. Those three words were right on the tip of my tongue, but I held them back. This wasn't the time or place. "I know you're amazing and practically invincible. And it's not enough for me. I need you, too."

His heavy gaze traveled over my face then lingered on my lips. "Deal?" He held his pinky up in the air.

I smiled and hooked my pinky around his. A shot of electricity tingled up my arm. "Deal."

He smiled and dropped his hand, though his pinky still held on to mine. "Come on, let's get back. Bentley is getting everyone set up for you."

I let him lead me back to our spot in the sand. We walked in silence, and it was mostly comfortable. The heat radiating off his skin made me want to cozy up and go to sleep. We got back to the group way faster than I wanted. We never got enough alone time.

Tennessee stomped through the sand away from me. "No one goes anywhere alone for the foreseeable future."

"But we haven't seen a single demon since the night Tegan blew up the fountain," Larissa said with narrowed eyes. "Maybe they can't get through yet."

"No," Bentley said with more force than I'd ever heard from him. Him being a prominent figure in The Coven would take some getting used to. "This is the calm before the storm. Tennessee is right. We need to be ready for disaster at every moment."

"They're right." Uncle Kessler looked each and every one of us in the eye. "No one alone, not even to go to the bathroom at school. This goes for you, too, Tennessee."

Mismatched eyes met mine and I smiled.

He nodded. "Of course."

"Okay, let's get started." Bentley waved his arm. "We have cards to read."

It was at that moment I realized the group sat in a circle with their legs crisscrossed and knees touching. They all had their hands resting on their thighs, palms up. It was an impressive sight with everyone in ceremonial white on the beach. Tennessee walked ahead of me and filled in one of the empty spots on the circle, right beside Deacon. Bentley waved me forward.

I nodded and walked to the center of the circle, then dropped to my knees. The Tarot in my hand tingled with magic, its energy pulsing with anticipation. I looked up and found Bentley sitting in the circle with everyone else, but he'd positioned himself right in front of me.

Bentley cleared his throat. "Okay, these two lines mean for Tegan to read the Tarot to see which of us are about to go on a quest. An extremely crucial quest. Everyone just chill where you're at. We'll do the rest."

"Wait." Royce raised his hand. "Why talk about the Magic Mirror instead of just saying read the Tarot?"

"Because it's not a normal reading, not even for us." Bentley returned his focus to me. "I'm going to lead the ritual. You just lay the cards out."

I smiled. "You got it, B-man."

I placed all twenty-two Tarot cards on the sand in a circle shape, face down with the black backs showing. When I finished, I held my palms over the cards. My magic poured out of me in a rainbow mist swirling around my fingers. Bentley chanted a few words in our ancient language, and a jolt prickled my hands. My body glowed brighter than a full moon, yet even still, the backs of the cards looked jet black.

A shimmery silver wave rolled over the cards from left to right. When it passed over the center of all the cards, a giant *II* in sparkling metallic silver glistened up at me. A white light flashed over the cards like a fire-work, then it shot out and slammed into my chest. I flinched and braced myself for pain, but it never came.

When I looked down, I saw a glowing white cord connecting me to the cards. *First chosen is High Priestess.*

I waved my hands over the cards again, and this time a *III* glimmered up at us. That white cord stretched out to Emersyn's chest. Her eyes widened but she nodded. *Second chosen is Empress.* I repeated the process five more times, and each time the cord connected on someone else. *Star. Devil. Wheel of Fortune. Magician. The Fool.* I frowned. Cooper, Deacon, and Royce made sense for a quest—along with myself and Emersyn. However, I couldn't foresee a reason to have Willow and Chutney go. They were young and not at all prepared or willing for combat. *She has a reason. I just gotta remember that.*

I paused with my hands over the cards, trembling slightly. Seven Cards had been chosen. Not only was that a lot, but that was how many we took on our last quest. And Tennessee wasn't selected.

My brain screamed in panic. My heart thundered through my entire body. *Please select him. Please select him.* I took a deep breath, then waved my hands over the cards again. A burst of white light blasted out from the cards then shot over to Tennessee. I sighed. *Thank Goddess.*

I heard a round of relieved sighs throughout the

circle. I smiled. Apparently I wasn't the only one counting on having our Emperor on the quest. I cleared my throat and repeated the process again, except that time the cards remained stoic black and the tingling energy was gone. I nodded and met Bentley's stare.

"Okay, we have our next quest list." Uncle Kessler stood and brushed sand off his legs. "Tegan, Emersyn, Cooper, Deacon, Royce, Willow, Chutney, and Tennessee."

Bentley sat up straight and looked down to his left arm with wide eyes. "GUYS."

The quest prophecy?

Bentley nodded without taking his eyes off his arm. Words etched into his skin. Everyone scurried to the center of the circle. Bentley raised his arm higher for everyone to read.

Where only Eden and the chalice knows, Your fate lies in The Book of Shadows. Between the balefire the runes shall dance, From within the cauldron comes your chance.

I opened my mouth to speak, but Bentley shushed me.

He waved his hand in the air. "No one speak. I need to process this. Cooper, watch my dreams tonight and make sure I don't miss anything."

CHAPTER TEN

"We're gonna do *what?*"

I rolled my eyes. "Open your ears, Deacon. He literally just told us."

"Yeah, but...but...it's crazy."

Please stop talking. Stop smiling. Stop being everywhere I go. A girl couldn't even go to training session without him being all over everything.

Something moved in my peripheral, except when I looked, I only found Tegan watching me. *Great.* My twin was way too observant sometimes. Always. She was going to ask me what my problem was. Again. Except I still didn't have an answer. Deacon just irritated me. I couldn't put my finger on what it was exactly, and until then, I couldn't talk about it. I'd only sound insane.

My chest burned to breathe. The pain spread down into my stomach. I'd had about a dozen Rolaids before training, but all the exercise must've made them wear off sooner.

"Does no one else think this is nuts?" Deacon looked around at the group with his blond eyebrows raised. "Do you do this a lot?"

No, we didn't. Though I wasn't about to go to his aid. Why did he need to ask so many questions? If Uncle Kessler told us to do something, he needed to just listen. I didn't care if he was the Devil. I didn't care if he was new here. I was still new, but I did what I was told. I didn't think I was above the rules. If Uncle Kessler wanted us to do some crazy training technique, then he had a reason. Although in the back of my mind, I questioned it as well. We'd been training for an hour already, and now Uncle Kessler wanted to pull this?

"Kessler, could you just elaborate on this for a hot second?" Easton used his wooden training sword to scratch his back under his training gear.

"Yeah, 'cause"—Royce wiped a towel across his face —"Tennessee ain't human."

Uncle Kessler grinned. "Exactly."

"I got a bad feeling about this," Braison whispered. He raised his hand, and the shadows from surrounding trees spread over the backyard. "We should've stayed in school today."

"I did *not* get enough sleep for this," Cooper

mumbled and walked over to his water bottle. "Could've given me a day to recoup after Bentley's dreams."

Bentley frowned and raised his hand. For a moment, all I saw was the quest prophecy on his skin. "Um, yeah, I don't have to participate, right?"

"No, Bentley."

"Guys, really? All of us against him? I think that sounds like a fair fight." Tegan adjusted her ponytail. Sweat dripped down her neck but vanished before it touched her shirt.

"No magic, Tegan." Uncle Kessler pointed his finger at her.

Tegan cursed.

No magic? Not that I was the queen of magic or anything, but still. I may have been Empress, but I was no match for anyone even *with* my powers. How the hell were we going to fight Tennessee in hand-to-hand combat? I looked over to where I'd last seen Tennessee standing, expecting to find a cocky smile on his face. Instead, I found him scowling as hard as everyone else.

"Do *I* get a say in this?" our Emperor asked. His long jet-black hair was soaking wet and dripping sweat onto his arms, though he didn't appear to notice or mind. Unlike everyone else, he was breathing steadily. The sweat was simply a byproduct of Florida summer humidity.

I didn't even want to see what I looked like.

Uncle Kessler cocked his head to the side. "Are you going to take over as Leader?"

If possible, Tennessee's scowl deepened. "No," he all but growled.

"Then no, you get no say either." Uncle Kessler grinned. He walked to the center of our training circle. "Though I give you full permission to thoroughly kick their asses."

"Wait, what?"

"Hold up."

"Dude, no."

"Why you hate us?"

"Do you want us to die?"

At *that*, a wide grin spread over Tennessee's face. The other girls probably all swooned at the sight. Tenn didn't grin often. The sight of it made my stomach drop and a cold chill slide down my spine. He scared the hell out of me. I knew he wouldn't hurt me for real. I knew he'd protect me in the real world. But he was the single most terrifying person I'd ever met. I glanced over to my twin and found her cheeks freshly flushed. She buried her face in her arm to hide her smile. They'd be the most petrifying couple ever.

Yeah, hence why it's forbidden with the cost of their magic on the line. The rule sucked for them, but it made sense. I wondered if a Hierophant in the past had seen the two of them in a psychic vision and created the no-dating rule as a precautionary measure. Sure, the rule included the Empress as well, but that was of no concern to me. I had *zero* interest in boys. Or girls, for that matter. *Nope, no thanks. I'll be a cat lady. I'm a witch. It's fitting.*

Please tell me you're picturing all your future cats right now.

I jumped at the sound of my sister's voice in my head. "Stop doing that." She always seemed to know exactly what I was thinking. It was irritating to be so transparent.

"What did I do?" Deacon flinched back with his hands up in the air. "I just asked if you were okay."

Heat rushed to my cheeks. "Well, then don't." I snapped my mouth closed before anything else could come out.

Ouch, bruh.

Deacon's blond eyebrows raised in surprise. His mouth twitched then curved into a sideways smirk. "Feisty. Okay." He shook his head and turned away from me to join the others at the other side of the circle.

I heard Tegan's laughter in my mind. Telepathic laughing was worse than talking or yelling. She nodded and pursed her lips. *A deep conversation coming, I see,* she said in her best Yoda impersonation.

I narrowed my eyes and tried to send my response back telepathically, but it just hurt my head.

I wish you could talk like this, too, though I'd miss seeing that constipated look on your face all the time. She winked playfully then walked away. *Come on, Empress. Time for me to embarrass myself watching Tennessee be amazing and hot.*

I laughed and followed after her. By the time we caught up with everyone else, we only heard the tail end of Uncle Kessler's instructions.

"...no magic. I'm serious. The point of this is to learn to fight as a team against something immensely stronger than you."

Easton scoffed. "Don't let him hear you say that."

Royce shook his head. "He ain't human. He already knows, dude."

"Pretend he's a greater demon. Yes, you have magic, but so do they, and kinds you don't have. We need to learn to fight as an extension of each other," Uncle Kessler said, completely ignoring the guys' comments. "I told him not to hold back, so you can't either."

"So, if we die today, do we get excused from the quest..." Deacon turned to Bentley. "Or nah?"

Bentley looked down at the prophecy lines on his arm then back to Deacon. "Nah."

"You boys are so dramatic." Lily rolled her eyes. "We're wearing magical training gear and using wooden swords."

"If you get a splinter, I've got a potion to heal it." Larissa patted Deacon's shoulder and winked.

I rolled my eyes. *Flirting, really?*

Man, that conversation is coming soon. Cool your face, bruh.

I turned to my right and glared at my twin. She shrugged. She had a point. I had no idea what my problem was.

Focus, Em. I looked down at my gear and tightened the straps, readjusting the pads into proper placement. The gear was pretty awesome. The pieces were small and lean, as to mimic our real body and not affect our movement while at the same time protecting us. If we received a fatal hit, bright-colored smoke would explode from the gear. It made practice visually appealing, anyway.

"All right, let's get started. As usual, you smoke up, you're out." Uncle Kessler yanked my chest pad higher and tightened the strap. "Drop where you fall. Have fun."

Uncle Kessler turned and walked over to the low

brick wall surrounding his porch. He sat and crossed his arms over his chest, an eager smile on face. I took a deep breath and waited for someone to tell me where to go. I frowned and stood up straight. Tennessee was the one who told us where to go and what to do. He was the one who led us in battles, both real and in training. I glanced around my group. Without the adult Coven members and Tennessee, there were only twelve of us huddled together on one side of the yard. And no one took lead yet.

I cleared my throat. "So, um...where do I go?"

"Where should I stand? Where are you standing?" Chutney asked behind me, her voice raised a few octaves more than normal. She was the youngest in the group, and she never did combat outside of basic training. "Do we stand in a line? Or a circle?"

"Can I be in the back?" Willow gripped her wooden training sword in both palms. Although she'd seen her fair share of fights, she *always* used her power of illusion. "No one wants me to be in the front, right? Right?"

"Wait, is his speed part of his magic?" Paulina frowned. She slid toward the back of the group, between Willow and Chutney. "Cooper?"

"I've never been sure." My brother sighed. He twirled his wooden sword in his hand. "It doesn't matter anyway. He can't turn it off. And he's not going to warn us before attacking."

"He's not going to attack us straight on," Tegan said in a low voice. She swung her wooden sword around in the air while looking around the yard. "We need to get in a formation."

"Where *is* he?" Deacon asked. He spun in circles. "I don't see him anywhere."

"You won't. That's the whole point." Tegan turned to face our brother. "You know how everyone fights better."

"Easton, Royce, Paulina, and Lily take the back." Cooper pointed without looking. "Deacon take the left. Braison the right. Willow, Chutney, hang in the middle between them. Tegan, Emersyn, and Larissa, we've got the front."

I nodded and jumped into action. I stood just on Tegan's right side with my sword gripped in both palms. *No magic. No magic. No magic.* "How are we supposed to fight while in a circle?"

"If we're not together, he'll pick us off one by one." Tegan's eyes sparkled like gemstones in the sunlight. "Weapons at the ready, guys. He's coming."

I opened my mouth to speak when I spotted Tennessee out of the corner of my eye, but when I turned to face him, he was gone. A dark shadow passed in front of me. I gasped and jumped backward just as Chutney's chest exploded with hot pink smoke.

Chutney shrieked and fell to the ground.

"WHAT?" Deacon pushed his hair back. His purple eyes were wide. He cursed then threw his head back and laughed. "Holy mother of Earth. She was in the middle! How?"

How was right. Chutney was surrounded by eleven people. How did Tennessee get in and out of the group without detection? My pulse skipped a beat. Adrenaline pumped through my veins so loud I couldn't hear myself think. I whipped my head back and forth, searching for the recognizable head of long black hair but he was nowhere to be seen.

Another streak of darkness ripped through the center of the circle in one big blur of black and purple smoke. We spun toward it with our weapons drawn, but we were too late. Willow dropped her sword and stared down at what would've been a hole through her stomach. She blinked and sat down in the same spot.

"Dude, seriously?" Cooper shouted. He walked a few steps forward, away from our formation. He raised his arms out. "Those two?"

Tennessee appeared at the far side of the property, laughing and twirling his sword around like a toy. "Oh, c'mon, I put them out of their misery. Did you *see* the panic on their faces?" He grinned and charged toward us, running at what looked like full speed.

When Cooper leapt forward to meet him in battle, Tennessee slid under his feet in a blur of motion. Larissa gasped and clutched her throat. Purple smoke billowed from her neck strap. She stomped her foot and dropped to the ground. Braison shouted in alarm. Orange smoke erupted from his back. He shouted in pain and plunged to the grass.

"No!" Cooper cursed violently and raced back to our cluster.

Tennessee had capitalized on Cooper stepping outside.

Deacon cursed but that grin was still plastered on his face. "Amazing."

I turned my back toward my twin's and raised my wooden sword in the air. Tennessee jumped out in front of me. I gasped and sliced my sword through the air. Wood smashed into wood, sending little tremors up through my arms. He spun in a tight circle then slammed me right in the chest. Pain flared and oxygen grew tight. Black smoke billowed out from my training gear and into my face.

CRAP. I was so busy watching, I forgot to fight. I dropped down to my knees as we'd been told. *At least I wasn't the first killed.* I sank to my butt and crossed my legs in front of me. Royce shouted in surprise. When I looked over to his spot, I found him flying through the air doing spins. He landed on his stomach, and yellow smoke exploded under him like a popped beanbag chair.

"Don't play with your food!" Paulina spit out a line in Spanish which I assumed was cursing.

"Yeah, come and give us a chance!" Lily shouted.

"As you wish, ladies," Tennessee said with a chuckle as he appeared right behind the two girls.

He swung his wooden sword in the air like it was a whip. Paulina leapt forward in a beautiful arch and aimed her sword for his neck. Tennessee ducked under her caramel arm and sliced through her back pad. Easton dashed to their aid, but it was too late. Tennessee was *faster.* Orange smoke seeped out from Paulina's midback. Lily screamed and charged, jumping through the air like a gazelle. Tennessee moved so fast he was a blur of black sliding under her body. He dragged his sword with him, chopping Lily right above the knees. Purple smoke poured out from the backs of Lily's legs like actual blood.

Tennessee appeared on the opposite end of the yard. "Then there were four."

"We can't just stand here with our thumbs up our asses!" Tegan crouched into fighting stance with her sword ready to swing. She rolled onto her toes. "We have to attack."

"On it!" Deacon yelled. He charged forward with a grin still plastered on his stupid face.

"Deacon, no!" Cooper shouted. He took a step then stopped.

Tennessee chuckled and shook his head. "Deacon, yes." He rested his wooden sword on his shoulder and watched Deacon run toward him. His mismatched eyes twinkled. He was the picture of ease, not even slightly concerned.

What does that feel like?

Deacon raced ahead. Tennessee watched without moving while Deacon charged for him. I thought he was going to engage, swing his weapon at him or something. Except he only narrowed his eyes and cocked his head to the side, like he was waiting to see what Deacon would do. When Deacon ducked down, Tennessee's shoulders dropped. He shook his head, like he was unimpressed with the attack. He rolled to the balls of his feet then jumped over Deacon's head. Just straight up leapt *over* him.

I'd never seen anything like the way Tennessee moved. It was graceful and elegant and entirely unhuman. His toes hadn't even touched the grass again before he swung his sword against the backs of Deacon's legs.

The red smoke from our Devil's gear was eerily similar to the prophecy the night before. Deacon face-planted in the grass with a thud and a string of curse words I'd never heard in such a combination.

"Now!" Tegan screamed and sprinted forward.

Tennessee's eyebrows rose. He smiled. "Oh...devious." He slammed the tip of his sword into Deacon's back without looking then moved toward his oncoming attackers.

Cooper reached him first. Their wooden swords clashed together, and the thud echoed through the yard. They seemed to anticipate each other's moves as they slashed and swiped in a duel they clearly had had before. Easton was seconds behind. He didn't hesitate to jump into the fight. The two blond guys danced around Tennessee, but he blocked each and every one of their advances.

Wait, where's Tegan? I peeled my eyes off the three boys and spotted my twin stealing Deacon's dropped sword. She spun around with a weapon gripped in each hand and a wicked smirk on her face.

What's with the smiling in a fight? What is wrong with them?

Tegan bounced on her toes, watching the tango in front of her. After a few seconds, she leapt forward. Tennessee's back faced her. His long black hair flew in the air around his head, possibly even blocking his peripheral view.

This was planned. I leaned forward, my heart pounding with adrenaline. They were going to do it. Tennessee hadn't noticed Tegan creeping up behind him with *two* swords. All of his attention was on Cooper and Easton, who were doing a great job holding their own against him.

Tegan slid in closer, silent as a mouse. She bit her bottom lip and raised her sword. I glanced back and forth. All she needed was the beat of a second with the right angle and she'd win.

Easton and Cooper ignored her. Their faces were tight and strained, with flushed cheeks and sweat dripping. The muscles in their arms twitched with fatigue. If I saw it, then Tennessee probably did too. Tenn leapt to his left, landed on one foot then sailed into the air. I wasn't even sure what I saw after that besides a black blur flying around Easton then under Cooper.

Easton and Cooper slammed into the grass like meteors. Tennessee landed on his feet right in front of Tegan. She gasped and glanced down at the guys. They were moving and groaning, but their gear hadn't received a fatal blow so they were still in the game. Which meant Tennessee had been *playing* with them. He'd totally seen Tegan creeping up on him.

I released a breath. *Amazing.*

Tennessee chuckled. "Show me what you've got, High Priestess," he whispered.

A brilliant pink flush filled my sister's cheeks, but she didn't hold back or hesitate. She growled like a tiger and attacked. For a moment, I was lost in Tegan's skills with a weapon. She ducked and spun as they fought, constantly moving. She swung and jabbed her swords in perfect form.

My jaw dropped. I had no idea when she'd learned to fight like that or where I was when she did.

Except it didn't matter.

Tennessee was incredible. He blocked and countered every one of her moves without strain. Even the ones I didn't think he saw coming, he dodged.

Tegan was panting. Purple dye dripped off the tips of her hair and onto her arms from sweat. Tennessee lunged forward, swinging his sword in an upward arc right across Tegan's arms. Both of her swords went flying across the yard. He brought his arm around in a full circle then swept her feet out from under her.

Her body crashed into the grass. He flipped his sword upside down and slammed the hilt against her chest gear. Rainbow smoke exploded right in his face, but he paid it no mind. He spun around then leapt over to where the guys were climbing back to their knees. He jumped over Cooper and somehow *threw* my brother through the air like a baseball. Cooper was a solid six-foot-three, two-hundred-thirty-pound heap slamming into Easton's chest.

WHAT?

The impact exploded Cooper's training gear in a wave of green smoke. Tennessee strolled over and yanked Cooper's limp body off of Easton's chest, then poked the neck pad strapped across Easton's throat. Blue smoke poured from the fake wound. Easton coughed and dropped his head to the grass. Cooper rolled to his side, groaning. Tennessee spun around in a circle like he actually thought there was anyone left to fight him.

"Dude, what was that?" Cooper said between breaths as he slowly pushed himself off the ground. "Really?"

Tennessee grinned and shrugged one shoulder. "I did what I was told."

"If that was a real greater demon, we'd be screwed." Tegan sighed and wiped her forehead with the back of her wrist.

Royce scoffed. "He's *not* human. I told you," he yelled from where he'd fallen.

Easton jumped to his feet then stumbled backwards. "Rematch. We can do this."

"Yeah, maybe after thirty rounds and he gets—"

Tegan gasped. Her pale green eyes went wide and her jaw fell open. She dropped her wooden sword to the ground yet didn't flinch when it landed on her own foot. Her eyes widened even farther until the green was completely surrounded in white. Her face paled to a sickly grayish green color. She stared at nothing in the distance, yet her eyes fluttered back and forth.

"What's happening?" I glanced around but there was no threat. "Tegan, what's wrong?"

CHAPTER ELEVEN

TENNESSEE

"Tegan?" Cooper ran up to her and squeezed her shoulder. "Tegan, what's wrong?"

She didn't respond. Her head shook slightly and her lips moved, but no words came out.

Easton staggered into my line of view. He ducked down to get on her eye level. "Tegan, are you okay?"

Something brushed against my shoulder. It had long platinum blonde hair and smelled strangely of smoke. *Emersyn.* She pushed by the three of us and got right in her twin's face. "Tegan? Damn it, answer us."

"Is she having a seizure?"

"What did she say right before?"

"What did you do to her, Tenn?"

I flinched. My stomach rolled at the idea of being the cause of this moment. *Nothing. I didn't do anything.* I'd barely touched her. I'd only blocked her strikes. And it wasn't the first time I'd pulled the sweeping-of-her-feet move on her. In fact, I was the one who taught her how to do it. Besides, Tegan was tough. She could handle herself in a fight, even without magic.

Within seconds, everyone surrounded us, talking over each other. I moved closer. Her heart was pounding, and the vein in her throat throbbed. Goose bumps spread over her arms, under the sweat shimmering against her skin. Her beautiful eyes were open but not seeing anyone in front of her. If I hadn't known any better, I would've thought she was watching something with the way her eyes bounced around.

"Cooper, go into her visions," Bentley said from somewhere behind me.

I glanced over my shoulder and watched him push his way through everyone. His golden eyes sparkled with knowledge. He walked over to stand between his two siblings. It was eerie to see a child so calm when everyone else was panicking.

Cooper blanched. "What? I can't...do that. She's awake?"

Bentley waved his hand in the air then pointed to Tegan. "Yes, you can. Trust me."

Cooper cursed. "Okay, okay. I'll try." He squeezed his eyes shut.

I felt the push of his magic roll over me like a wave.

His Irish Spring soap scent tickled my nose. He mumbled something under his breath, and his fingers twitched. His eyes flew open, stretching wide until the whites surrounded his pale green irises. Just like Tegan's, they bounced back and forth like he was watching something. The two of them stood side by side like zombies. No one else spoke.

"Bentley..." I whispered as low as my voice could go.

"Wait for it," he whispered back.

It felt like an hour passed while we waited for *anything* to happen. But then, just as suddenly as it began, it vanished. Tegan and Cooper blinked rapidly and shook their heads. I held my breath. Something had just happened.

Tegan turned to face Cooper. "We have to go."

Cooper nodded. "Now." His voice was gravelly.

My pulse quickened. I frowned. "Why? What happened?"

Tegan licked her lips and met my stare. "Henley doesn't have much time."

"What?" Royce cried.

Deacon wrapped his arm around his cousin's shoulders. "What do you mean?"

Tegan glanced up at Cooper, but he stared at the ground in silence. She closed her eyes and shook her head. When she reopened them, I saw pain...and fear.

She cleared her throat. "They're planning something big and terrible. We need to get her back to our realm."

Royce groaned and buried his face in his hands. He mumbled a prayer in our ancient language. If it wasn't for his cousin holding him up, I wasn't sure he'd still be standing.

"How do you know?" Easton asked.

"Don't make her tell you." Cooper's voice cracked. He didn't look up.

I shuddered. Ignorance was bliss. I didn't want to know what they saw. Tegan and Cooper were the two people I trusted most, along with Kessler. If they said they knew, then I believed on faith.

"The quest starts now?"

Cooper nodded. He scrubbed his face with his palms. "Right now."

"I don't understand." Emersyn twirled her long hair between her fingers. "How is the quest related to Henley? Not that I don't want to rescue her."

"Your fate lies in the Book of Shadows." Tegan began unstrapping her training gear. "Our quest is to find The Book of Shadows. Inside it is the answer for how to save her."

"How do you know that?" Willow said with a small voice.

Tegan narrowed her eyes and looked around the

group. "I just do. I'm the High Priestess. It's time for you to trust me."

"She's right." Bentley rubbed his fingers over the prophecy lines on his arm. "We have to trust her. More importantly, those chosen must go now."

"Okay, you heard them. The Cards chosen, go home *now* and get ready." Kessler looked each of the selected witches in the eye. "Pack a bag of necessities, and make sure it includes ceremonial white. Meet at my house in forty-five minutes."

CHAPTER TWELVE

TEGAN

I sprinted up our driveway, unlocking the front door with my magic as we ran. Emersyn's footsteps echoed behind me. I raced through our house into our room without stopping to look for my parents. Part of me knew we needed to let them know we were leaving, but my brain was too preoccupied to tell my mouth to call out for them. I yanked my black backpack off the ground and dumped its contents on my bed. Notepads and pencils rolled across my sheets.

"Necessities. Necessities. Necessities. What in the hell are necessities for a quest?" Emersyn cried from somewhere behind me.

"I don't know?" I ripped my sweat-drenched shirt off and tossed it in the general vicinity of my bathroom. *Not like we were prepared for the last one.* I ran into the walk-in closet we shared and yanked clothes off hangers.

"Bring an extra set of clothes, and think about the things we did on our last quest. Nothing fancy or cashmere!"

Emersyn mumbled something, but I didn't make out the words. I pulled a black graphic T-shirt over my head. I wasn't even sure what it said since I'd grabbed it so fast. My concern was making sure my clothes covered the glyph on my chest and my shoulder since it was spreading.

I ran back into the room and tossed my sister her ceremonial white gown. "Here, we might need these."

"You'll need these, too."

I gasped and spun at the sound of my father's voice. "Dad? Mom. You heard?"

"I tried to call you on our way home," Emersyn said in a rush.

Mom stepped forward and dropped a duffel bag full of stuff at the edge of my bed. "We were on the phone with Kessler and gathering things for you since this is your first quest to actually prepare for."

"This backpack has a few weapons and such. Take it with you and use what you can. Share them with your Coven-mates." Dad pointed to the bag. "You'll also find some crystals, incense, a couple of wands, and some herbs—just in case. Your brother knows how to use it all. I've already told him you'll have it."

"Emersyn, sweetheart, I know you don't usually

wear these type of shoes." Mom walked over to my sister with a pair of steel-toed black combat boots. They were definitely made for function over any kind of fashion, but they'd be awesome to have. "But you're going into the mountains, so you're going to need them. So borrow mine."

"Thank you!" Emersyn flushed and tears filled her eyes. She took the boots and sat them on her bed. "I'm such a mess. I don't know what I'm doing here. What else do I need?"

"Here, I'll help you," Dad said with a smile. He gave me a wink as he passed.

I frowned and watched him walk over to help my sister pack. It was ludicrous to think it, but I wasn't sure when my father stopped helping *me* with stuff. Was I allowed to be jealous of the attention my father gave my twin?

"Tegan?"

I jumped and spun to find my mother waving her hand in front of my face. "I'm fine," I said automatically.

"Come here," she whispered and dragged me out of my room by my wrist. Once we were alone in the hallway, I realized she had something dark tucked under her arm. She pulled it out and held it out for me. "*This*, my darling daughter, is for you."

"No boots?" I said before I could stop myself.

She chuckled and shook her head. "You have boots. You *need* this."

I grabbed the black item. It was soft black leather that felt strong and sturdy under my touch, yet surprisingly lightweight. My eyes widened. "Wait, a leather jacket?"

"Not just any leather jacket. When I was your age, I wasn't a Card yet and my parents did *not* like your father, so I had to hide..."—she glanced around then leaned in closer—"the glyph. I had this jacket made—long story—to do just that. There are spells and charms on this to keep the wearer comfortable in any temperature, so you can always have it on. Also, to keep it lightweight so you can fill all the pockets with anything you want without being dragged down."

My jaw dropped. "Bad. Ass." I smiled and slid the jacket on. The leather was silky soft against my skin.

Mom reached out and tugged on the front of the lapel. "There are straps up here over the chest that will also cover the glyph, if need be."

"Mom..." I shook my head and looked down at the jacket. Every time I saw some new witchy object, it blew my mind, but a magical jacket was near the top of coolness. "Mom, thank you. This is perfect."

"You're very welcome, love." She cupped my face with her hands. It was such a motherly thing to do that it made my eyes burn. "Listen to me. Do not let *anyone* in Eden know about the glyph on your chest."

My stomach rolled and my mouth went dry. "Mom... would they really strip me of my Mark and my magic?"

She dropped her hands and took a step back. "Without hesitation or regret."

CHAPTER THIRTEEN

"Wait. We have our own plane?"

"Yeah. What Emersyn said." Deacon whistled and scratched the back of his head.

"Says the guy who drives a brand-new Porsche." Willow laughed.

"I'm rich, but I don't have a plane."

I rolled my eyes. "It's The Coven's plane. In order to keep the world safe from destruction, we have to be able to get around quickly, so we have a plane. One. Not a fleet."

"Hold up. Do Coven members get paid?" Tegan walked up on my right then blinked up at me with those long, black eyelashes of hers. "Is that a thing?"

"Yes." I held my finger up to stop her from asking more questions, and it took everything in me not to press it to her lips. "Let's save the world first, graduate high school second, then worry about getting paid third. Okay?"

"I wonder..." Royce turned his back to the plane and wagged his eyebrows. "How many Mile High meetings The Coven has had?"

A wave of heat rolled out of Tegan. She chuckled.

I refused to let myself look at her. This quest was already going to be disastrous. There were too many people, too many eyes watching everything I did. Before Tegan came into my life, I'd never understood when people said, "there was so much tension, you could cut it with a knife." Now I got it. I so, so got it. Whenever she was near me, my body temperature raised ten degrees. My fingers itched with the need to reach out and touch her, even just to hold her hand. I didn't understand how no one else had noticed yet. Every time our eyes met, we stared a little longer. Surely our auras were radiating wild energy levels, but still no one reacted. I was grateful...and confused.

Just keep a safe distance away from her at all times.

"Royce." Emersyn rolled her golden eyes and smiled. She smacked his arm playfully.

His smile faded. He shrugged one shoulder. "Henley would've said it, so I had to."

"Come on, guys, we gotta get moving." Cooper stomped past us with a hiker's pack on his back.

Emersyn leaned into Royce and wrapped her slender, pale arm around his waist. She whispered something to him, and he sighed but there was a small smile on his face. Deacon walked over and squeezed his shoulder. Emersyn glared up at him with more anger and distaste I'd ever seen in her eyes. Royce and Deacon, however, missed this entirely. If Deacon did something to piss Emersyn off, I wasn't surprised at all.

Up ahead, the plane door opened. A small flight of stairs were propped up for us to climb onboard. Walter, our pilot, stuck his head out to wave at someone behind me then disappeared again. Cooper ran up the steps. He'd been quiet since Tegan's visions, and it made me nervous.

"So..." Tegan's voice broke through my thoughts.

I looked down and met her gaze. Her pale green eyes sparkled in the afternoon sunlight. I waited for her to finish her sentence, but she just stared up at me under those black eyelashes. Up close, she had these adorable freckles on her high cheekbones that I wanted to count. She licked her lips, and it brought my gaze to her mouth. Her cheeks flushed a soft, rosy pink. The entire right side of my body was hot, like I stood in front of a fireplace. If I just leaned forward, I could kiss her. The idea filled my stomach with butterflies.

"So..." I said back, except my voice came out lower and rougher than appropriate.

"So..." She leaned closer, and her breath brushed over my shoulder. "Does this plane have a bathroom?"

"Um..." It was my turn to blush. A whole bunch of thoughts I shouldn't have been having flashed in my mind. I blinked and searched for words to speak.

Tegan rolled her eyes, but her entire face turned red. She shook her head and tucked her black hair behind her golden cuffed ears. "That is not..."

I shrugged. "Well..."

She buried her face in her palms. "I just said the first thing I thought of."

"And I make you think of airplane bathrooms?" I covered my mouth with my hand to try and hide my laughter. I failed.

"Oh my God." She groaned and hung her head. "I'm just... It's Royce's fault."

"What's Royce's fault?"

Tegan gasped, and if possible turned even redder. "Uncle Kessler. Nothing. Just...nothing. I'm gonna get on the plane now." She spun and sprinted for the stairs.

"What just happened?" my father asked.

I sighed and shook my head. "I have no idea."

My father nodded and stepped up in front of me,

blocking Tegan from my view. "Listen, I know you have to go, but...um...just...uh..."

I frowned and took a good look at my father. His blond buzz cut hair was overgrown and his jaw rough with a five-o-clock shadow. There were bags under his amber eyes I somehow hadn't noticed before. But it was the stuttering that filled my lungs with ice. My father was the picture of calm.

I cleared my throat. "Kessler? Are you all right?"

He grabbed my shoulder and hauled me into his chest. He wrapped his arms around me in a tight hug. After a few seconds, he stepped back and cleared his throat. "Come home to me, son."

Well...

Hell...

CHAPTER FOURTEEN

TEGAN

I should've waited for Tennessee to pick his seat first. Except I'd been so distracted by the elegance of the plane, I'd just taken the seat Emersyn asked me to. As a result, I spent the last seventy-four minutes trying not to look at him...while he sat directly across from me. Our plane wasn't like a commercial plane where all the seats were in rows. Oh no, this private plane had to have seats facing each other. Deacon and Royce took the two in the back, next to the bathroom. Willow and Chutney were in the pair of seats right behind them. Which meant there was only the small grouping of four seats up at the front. And somehow that ended up with Tennessee and I sitting at the windows staring into each other's eyes. Or desperately trying not to.

The sun setting outside my window painted a gorgeous picture of every shade of pink I'd ever seen. It was breathtaking to see it from above the clouds. Yet even still, I only managed a few seconds before I had to look back at *him*. My chest burned and my body was on fire. Sweat dripped down my spine. My mom told me the jacket would keep me comfortable, but I was starting to realize that only meant the outside temperature. Not the wildfire raging inside me. I peeked over and found his eyes on me. They were hot and intense. His chest rose and fell.

Why does he have to look so damn good all the time? I inhaled a deep breath and crossed my right leg over my left. My shin brushed the back of his leg. I exhaled in a rush. A hot electric shock shot up my leg. Tennessee arched one eyebrow at me like it was no big deal, but he clutched the armrests with both hands. His knuckles paled. The veins in his forearms throbbed. *Abort. Abort. Abort.* I flexed my leg out, and my boot slid under his knee. His lips parted and his chest rose.

My gaze met his and locked on. I didn't know what to do. I forgot how to move. The heat pouring out of his leg through his black jeans should've melted me into a puddle. I licked my lips and tried to think, but his pupils dilated and it did weird things to my insides. My whole body pulsed with energy.

"What the hell is that?" Walter shouted from the cockpit.

Before anyone could react, something slammed into the side of the plane. The world spun in slow motion. My purple-tipped hair flew into my face, robbing me of sight. The crystal hanging from my necklace smacked my jaw. For a split second, everything was clear and normal, but then the plane dipped to my left. The horizon became vertical. Emersyn smashed my hand against the armrest, holding on for dear life. Willow and Chutney's screams pierced my ears. Or maybe the screaming was me. I wasn't sure of anything anymore. My stomach turned and flipped each time the plane did.

I reached out in front of me—for what, I wasn't sure. My hair was wrapped around my head in a tangled mess. Tennessee's hands found mine in an instant. I recognized the softness of his skin and the tingle in my arms. His grip was strong and steady, and the only thing keeping my sanity in check. In the back of my mind, I knew this was happening really fast, but it felt like an eternity. The plane rolled at least one or two more times before we steadied right side up.

What's happening? I yelled to him with my mind because I couldn't get my mouth to work.

"Stay buckled!" Tennessee dropped my hand and jumped out of his seat. He threw open the cockpit door and raced over to Walter who was slumped forward but still clutching the steering wheel.

The plane dipped left again, and my head smacked against the window.

Tennessee grabbed the steering wheel and pulled it towards him until we leveled out. He ducked and looked out the front window, then spun around to face us with wide eyes. "Demons!"

"*WHAT*?!" someone behind me yelled.

"Walter! Is he all right?" Cooper shouted.

Tennessee crouched down and placed his hand over Walter's forehead. My soulmate frowned then looked over at us. With the hand not holding our pilot, he tapped his own chest and nodded his head to Walter.

Deacon cursed and sprinted into the cockpit. "I've flown before. Just get rid of those things while I try to keep us airborne." He dropped into the copilot seat and buckled in.

Something slammed into the top of the plane, and we dropped like that ride back at Hidden Kingdom. Chutney screamed. My stomach turned and my feet hovered above the floor.

Tennessee braced himself in the cockpit doorway. He looked over his shoulder. "You sure, Deacon?"

"You do you, buttercup, or I won't be able to!" Deacon shouted back. The plane surged forward. Deacon cursed violently. "Incoming in three, two—"

Dark objects flew past the windows and slammed

into the wing. Everything wobbled. Cabinets and drawers flew open, spilling their contents. *Demons.* Metal shrieked in protest. I didn't want to ask what it came from. All I knew was we had to kill these monsters before they killed us.

"Stay buckled!" Tennessee shouted over the pounding of demon feet outside the plane. "We flip again and we'll have broken necks. We have to use our magic *through* the windows before they work their way in and we all die."

"Ray of sunshine, you are!" Royce yelled from behind me.

"How do we do that?" I asked and peeked out the window.

The demons were a dark blueish-purple color that blended in perfectly with the setting sun. I couldn't tell what kind they were, or how many. All I saw were spindly legs with talons and wings thicker than our plane's.

"Like we always do." Tennessee's voice dropped low and gravelly. He raced over to the door we came in and looked out the window.

Purple magic swirled around his hands. His body shimmered then glowed like sunlight reflecting off metal. He raised his palms to the door and flexed his fingers. His magic shot through the plane door and blasted the demon trying to claw its way in. It shrieked and dropped out of sight.

I gasped and pressed my face to the window. *It worked!*

"MORE!" I copied my soulmate's move and placed my palms on the glass. My body lit up like a flashlight. I clenched my teeth and summoned my magic. It pulsed in my veins, roaring to life with eager excitement. *Where are you, demon?* I waited until one of them slithered into my sight, then pushed my magic out like I'd been taught. It hissed and rolled away. Black demon blood splattered over my window.

"Royce! Trap it with vines!" Emersyn shouted.

"I can't *create* them!" he snapped back.

Keltie's words echoed in my mind. *Your magic does not follow the same rules as your fellow elementals. You can create.*

"No, but *I* can." I closed my eyes and pictured Bettina's garden in her backyard. I imagined walking through it, taking in every different type of plant and flower. My hands tingled with warmth and energy, so I focused on that and pushed my magic out.

"Oh my *God*," Royce whispered. "Girl, what did you *do*?"

I opened my eyes and gasped. The entire floor was covered in roses and sunflowers, little daisies and tulips.

Bougainvillea vines crawled up the sides of the plane like something straight out of *Stranger Things*.

"ROYCE!" Tennessee shouted. "Use it!"

"On it!" Royce threw his hands in the air without unbuckling his seatbelt. His magic coiled around his body like pure yellow rays of sunshine. He narrowed his eyes, and his nostrils flared, then he pushed with his hands. "Hold on tight!"

My vines shimmered like crystals, then slid *through* the plane and pierced two demons like kabobs. Roses turned to torpedoes, shooting into demon flesh faster than I could track. Out my window mine and Tennessee's magic sliced demons like lasers. One of Royce's sunflowers cut through a demon's leg. It ripped off and smacked into the side of the plane.

The wing outside my window exploded. Flames of red and orange spilled out into the sky. I reached down and tried to unbuckle myself to get out of the flame's way, but my fingers trembled too much. The plane dipped. Fire raced up the metal wing, going right for me. I needed to move.

Emersyn roared like a lion in my ear. Her magic rushed over me in one massive hot blast so forceful my hair flew into my face. The flames were knocked aside then slid up and over the plane.

A demon screeched above our heads. The whole

plane rattled. Demon talons pierced through the side panels. Metal shrieked in protest as the door was clawed right off its hinges. The air pressure buckled. Wind rushed in and sucked Tennessee out into the open air.

"NO!"

CHAPTER FIFTEEN

TEGAN

"**N**O!" I screamed. *NO, NO, NO. NO!*

I shot my magic into my seatbelt and blasted it into pieces. *Not him. Not him.* Everyone was shouting behind me, but none of them were louder than the pounding of my heart. I had to get to him. I had to save him. I *had* to. I wasn't Superman, but I had to try to save him. Or die trying.

"Royce! Close the door!" Cooper shouted just as I got to my feet.

Out of the corner of my eye, I saw those flowers I'd summoned used against me. They surged together and sealed the open doorway. But that didn't matter. My magic could blast through them.

I sprinted into the cockpit. Deacon was shouting and cursing. His fingers were white from clutching the steering wheel so tight. I ignored that and dove for the metal drawer that read PARACHUTES.

"We lost a wing!" Deacon screamed and the plane wobbled.

I knew that was bad, except all I could think about was Tennessee. I had to get out there and try to catch him before he hit the ground.

Demon feet pounded on the ceiling. If I looked up, the metal would be dented in. Then the demon screeched. Black blood appeared over the side cockpit window.

I yanked the parachute out of its holding spot and strapped it on my back. I spun to run for the door when the plane toppled to the right. My balance faltered, and I dropped to the ground.

Deacon cursed. "Second wing is gone too! We're in a free fall!"

The plane tipped forward as we began to nosedive. I slid all the way into the cockpit and slammed my forehead against the metal controllers.

"What the *hell?*" Deacon inhaled. "*HOW?*"

I groaned and pulled myself up onto my knees...and choked on a gasp. Tennessee was crouched on the nose of the plane clutching to the windshield wipers and glowing like a supernova.

TENNESSEE! Tears pooled in my eyes. My heart

fluttered so fast black spots danced in my vision. *He's alive. He's okay.*

"Tennessee!" Cooper screamed, his voice cracking.

"*Not human!*" Royce yelled out, but I knew what he meant by it.

"How is he doing that?" Emersyn said with awe in her voice.

How is he doing that? I pulled myself up until my eyes met his. Then it hit me. *Magic.* Tennessee's elemental magic included control over air. He was literally using his magic to manipulate the air around him.

Wait a second. A crazy idea popped into my mind. It was crazier than trying to catch someone from falling out of a plane. But what choice did we have? Our plane only had half a wing, if even. Deacon was doing his best to keep up us airborne, but we were in a free fall. The clouds loomed far above us. We were screwed...unless this idea worked.

I took a deep breath so my voice would sound calmer and more confident, then I shouted with my mind so everyone could hear. *Everyone stay buckled. Deacon, hold us steady and bring us to the ground.*

Tennessee frowned. His long black hair flapped in the wind behind him.

"WHAT?" Deacon hissed. He looked up at me with wild purple eyes filled with guilt. I knew he'd blame himself for us dying in this plane. "HOW? We don't have *wings!*"

I turned my gaze back to Tennessee through the window. *Tennessee and I are gonna be your wings.* Tenn flinched and his eyes widened. I held my hands out to the side like they were wings and pushed my magic. The plane wobbled in a straight line for a moment then sank again. Tennessee looked side to side, then back at me. A wide, entirely evil grin spread across his face.

"Why is he grinning?" Deacon cried.

Fly with me, Tenn.

He nodded and mimicked my pose with his long, muscled arms stretched out on either side. His mismatched eyes held mine. *Together,* he mouthed.

Together. I took a deep breath and pushed my magic out. *You're out there to feel it, so you take lead. I'll follow. Deacon, bring us down.*

"Oh, sweet Jesus," Deacon mumbled. "Okay."

My eyes latched on to Tennessee's, and everything else disappeared. My fears dissolved. Whatever was about to happen was gonna happen. But we'd do it together. I clenched my teeth and pushed my magic out until I felt it brush against Tennessee's. My body tingled with awareness, like it did whenever he touched me. Warmth spread through my fingers and up my arms. I felt the heavy pounding of his heart like my head was pressed to his chest. His lips parted and his pupils dilated. He felt it too. My left shoulder twitched a split second before Tennessee's right arm dipped. I gasped. Somehow I felt him move before he actually did. My eyes widened.

Did our magic...

Tennessee's cheeks flushed the slightest shade of pink. His lips curved. He nodded.

Our magic connected and synced together. I hadn't known that could happen, and judging by the wild sparkle in his eyes, he hadn't either. I licked my lips and nodded. We needed to focus. We had a plane to land. We had seven lives to save. *Let's do this.*

His strength and confidence poured over me in waves. I flexed my hands and pushed with every ounce of magic I had inside me. Tennessee's body shined brighter, almost too painful to look at. But I refused to look away. My magic filled his veins. Rainbow mist coiled around his arms.

He looked down at himself then back at me with the craziest expression, like a kid locked in a candy store. I turned my power over to him, to guide us. Cool air rushed over my fingers and ripped through my hair. It wasn't in the plane. I was feeling what he felt. I stopped thinking. Stopped planning. I just let him be our eyes. He was the one out there in it. He was the one who knew how to use his magic. He was the Emperor, and now I knew what it felt like to be him. To be so sure of myself. To have no doubts in my abilities.

Doubt, fear, insecurities—they were all gone. My magic flowed sure and strong, like it was a true extension of myself. I mirrored every one of his moves without taking my eyes off his. I'd never felt so powerful. In the back of my mind, I knew I had more gifts, more *abilities*, technically more power than him...except now I knew I was capable of *more*. For the first time, I felt invincible, capable of taking on the world and winning.

Part of me registered the sounds of my friends freaking out in the back of the plane and the sight of land rushing up in front of us. But the rest of me tuned it out and relished in the power of my magic. The plane dropped low and wobbled.

"Goddess, please let me land this thing and not kill *anyone*," Deacon whispered.

I gasped. My pulse skyrocketed. We were about to try and land. If Tenn didn't hold on to something, the impact could... My stomach turned. I must've made a face because Tennessee frowned and cocked his head to the side.

Hold on. We're about to land. I'll guide us from here, I said to just him.

The muscles in his jaw popped, but he didn't drop his arms.

Tennessee, please. I can hold us. Please just hang on for impact. I clenched my teeth and steadied my arms.

He nodded and dropped his hands to the windshield.

The plane dipped, but I summoned my magic back to me and held on to the breeze carrying us down. The horizon was straight ahead. The ground just below. Up in the sky, the sun was still setting, but down on land, night had fallen. I couldn't see what lay below us, or what we could be about to hit. I let Deacon handle that. All I had to do was keep us steady. Air rushed up from our tail, and the whole plane trembled. I held Tennessee's stare. The light coming off his body lit up an empty field just ahead.

"Hold on! Dropping the wheels," Deacon yelled.

I didn't look down to see what he did, but I recognized the sound of the plane's wheels sliding out. We just had to hope the demons hadn't damaged those, too. The plane rattled. Lights on the dashboard flashed and flickered. Something beeped incessantly. I held my arms straight. My magic surged on. All I had to do was hold us steady.

"Tegan," Tennessee yelled through the windshield.

I gasped and looked back up at him. I hadn't even

realized I'd looked away. Our landing strip stretched out just behind him. It wasn't as flat as I'd like it to be. I wasn't even sure what I was seeing, only dark objects surrounded by more darkness. My heart fluttered. *Tennessee.* This was it. The moment was here. We would either survive this together... I cut that thought off. I couldn't even think the words.

Words. There were a whole lot of words I wanted to say to him if this was going to be my last chance, but they dried on my tongue.

Land rose up in front of us, and I spotted dozens of trees and boulders. Impact was not going to be smooth. If he held on, he'd be thrown off. Too many scenarios of equal awfulness flashed through my mind. Then I remembered some of the stunts he'd pulled during our training session earlier. Like Royce said, he was barely human. And he definitely didn't have to abide by the same laws of nature the rest of us did.

Tennessee...JUMP.

He didn't hesitate. He didn't pause to ask why, or how high. He just *disappeared.*

"Here...we...goooo..."

Deacon's warning came a split second before we made initial impact. I was so worried about Tennessee I hadn't paused to worry about *myself.* Without any kind of harness or seatbelt on, I had nothing to protect me. The force of our hit launched me into the air. My head slammed into the panel above me. Any control I had on the air snapped as I was thrown around the cockpit like a pinball.

Everything went dark, but I was still completely conscious. Pain lanced through my body. I hissed and cursed with each impact. My back hit the ground and knocked the wind out of me. I gasped and clung to the base of Deacon's seat. I coughed and tried to get oxygen in. Somehow I could control the air enough to fly a plane but not to freaking breathe. The plane bounced and crashed more times than I could count. When we finally skidded to a stop, I lay there gasping for air. Every bone in my body hurt. I just wanted to lay there until my brain stopped rattling in my head and my stomach quit turning. But I had to get up. I had to find Tennessee. I needed to find him.

Deacon coughed a string of violent curses full of relief.

I tried to sit up, but the parachute was still strapped to my chest. My fingers trembled. My heart pounded. *C'mon, c'mon, c'mon. I gotta get out there.* Tennessee had jumped before our first impact. I had to get to him. I needed to make sure he was okay. It took me a dozen attempts to actually unlatch the buckle. I was up on my feet before the metal latch clanked against the cockpit floor.

By the time I made it to the door, the rest of my crew was stirring. Emersyn groaned, and it was all I needed to hear to know she was alive. I turned to Royce's garden-built door, raised my hands...and nothing happened. My magic crackled like fairy dust around my fingers. It sizzled and popped then completely evaporated into thin air. *No, no, no.*

"Royce!" I screamed and pushed at the vines with my bare hands. "Royce, release them!"

Royce mumbled something but didn't move.

I glanced down and spotted Tennessee's sword lying off to the side. I picked it up with both hands, sliced through the vines just enough for me to wiggle through... and dropped a few feet to my knees on the ground below. I cursed and scrambled upright. My body screamed in protest, but my concern for Tennessee prevailed. Outside the plane was nothing but blackness. The night air was significantly cooler than the Florida heat I'd grown accustomed to.

"Tennessee?" I yelled and spun in circles, searching for any sign he was alive. "Tenn!"

My chest ignited with searing hot pain. I gasped. Tears rushed to my eyes. *Tennessee.* If my glyph burned, then he couldn't have been far. It hadn't burned when I first got out of the plane, which meant he was moving closer. I turned in a slow circle, scanning for any sign of him. It was too hard in the dark to tell which way we'd come from, and he could've landed anywhere. *Come on, where are you?*

Something moved in the distance. I spun toward it. I wasn't sure how I even noticed it, but somehow it stood out.

"Tennessee?" I shouted. It could've been a demon, but I moved toward it all the same. I had Tennessee's sword gripped tightly in my hand. Uncle Kessler had trained us for just this situation, fighting without magic.

A little white light illuminated the darkness. The lit-up box raised in the air until it illuminated a sharp jawline, high cheekbones, and the most beautiful pair of lips I'd ever seen.

"Tennessee!" I cried out and sprinted toward him. My chest burned hotter with every step I took. Tears threatened to pour, but I held them in.

I smelled his fresh rain scent a few steps before I made it to him. He opened his mouth to speak, still only lit up by his phone, but I didn't wait. I threw my arms around his neck and pulled him down to me.

"Tegan," he half whispered, half groaned as he wrapped his arms around my waist and lifted me off my feet. His fingers dug into my skin through my shirt. He buried his face in the crook of my neck. He whispered my name over and over, just loud enough for me to hear. He dropped me to my feet and pulled back.

A strangled cry left my lips, but I didn't try to stop it. He was alive. He cupped my face in his big, warm hands. I gripped the front of his shirt and yanked him down closer. Our lips crashed together in desperation and relief. There was a plane full of our friends who could report us and have our magic stripped, but in that moment, none of that mattered. My soulmate was living, breathing, and kissing me like I was the oxygen he needed to survive. We stumbled back a few feet, our lips still entangled.

"Tennessee," I whispered against his mouth.

"Tegan."

"Tennessee..."

"Tegan," he whispered, then pulled back. Even in the dark, his eyes sparkled as he looked down at me. His warm breath brushed over my face. "Are you okay?"

I didn't want to move out of his embrace, but I needed to check and make sure he was okay. It was too dark to see, so I slid my hands down his chest then back up. I patted his thick shoulders and biceps. "Are you all right? Are you hurt? Are you okay?"

"Tegan. Tegan," he said with a chuckle. His lips

brushed against mine again, then again. And again. He dipped my head back and deepened our kiss.

I melted into him and let his lips chase off all the fear surging to the surface.

"Tennessee?" Cooper's voice rang out, slicing through our little bit of Heaven.

He broke away from my lips then traced his fingers down my throat. In the light off his phone, I saw the grin on his face. "You are amazing."

"Me?" I chuckled and shook my head. "You're the amazing one."

He leaned in like he was going to kiss me again. I popped up on my tiptoes.

"Tennessee, are you out here?" Cooper shouted.

"TEGAN?" Emersyn screamed. Her voice was a few octaves higher than her panicked voice. "Tegan, where are you?"

Tennessee groaned softly and pressed his forehead to mine. "We have to answer."

I pressed my lips to his once more then stepped back. "We're here!"

"I'm okay," Tennessee yelled.

By the time we made our way back over to what was left of our plane, the others had climbed their way out. Six cell phone flashlights lit the faces of my extended family. We were sweaty and spotted with blood from that landing, but we were all alive.

Royce chuckled and shook his head. "Girl, what did you *do*?"

I blushed. "I don't know."

"That was amazing, you two non-humans." Royce sighed and scrubbed his face with his blood-covered hands. "Just wild."

Tennessee cleared his throat. "Deacon, man, that was some flying. Nicely done."

Emersyn sighed. It was almost a sound of annoyance, but I couldn't have heard it right. "Yeah, Deacon. That was impressive."

I looked over to our Devil who was leaning against the battered plane. "You'll have to tell us how you learned to fly like that."

"How's Walter?" Tennessee asked.

Deacon groaned. "He's breathing, but not very well. I called for an ambulance through the plane's radio. The local airport spotted us going down and sent help to our location. It should be here any minute."

"We need to be gone when it does."

Everyone gasped and turned to stare at our Emperor.

He just shrugged and shook his head. "You know I care, but Walter is beyond our help now. We can't afford the time it will cost us to get caught up with human

148

emergency services, especially without Kessler here to assist."

Reality settled back in. I nodded. "Henley needs us."

"We don't even know where we are," Emersyn whispered.

I frowned and looked around us. Sure, everything close by was drenched in darkness, but off in the distance, a soft golden color filled the sky. There was a city just beyond the black area we'd landed in. I squinted my eyes and tried to focus on the silhouette of the buildings.

"We don't have a way to get to Eden now," Willow cried. Soft, sky-blue mist swirled around her face as her magic lit up the night sky. "What are we gonna do, steal a car?"

"We can't go straight to Eden tonight. We need to find a safe place nearby here to rest."

"Tennessee..."

"Royce, I know." Tennessee sighed. "Trust me, I *know*. But Tegan and I both depleted our energy landing the plane. Deacon is hurting. You're hurting from your garden attack. Everyone is struggling."

"We can't make the trip to Eden like this," Cooper whispered. "We need to rest *now*, not in a few hours from now. Assuming we're somewhere—"

I gasped as realization hit me like lightning. I knew

where we were. The accident made my eyesight a little blurry, so it took me longer than it should have. I knew that skyline. I knew that salty scent in the air that wasn't quite fresh. I knew exactly where we were. More importantly, I knew exactly where we could go to rest.

"I know where we are," I said to the others. "Follow me."

CHAPTER SIXTEEN

TEGAN

I wasn't sure exactly how long it took us to walk there, I hadn't checked the time. But it felt like hours before I stopped in front of an old wooden house. I knew this street. I knew these massive trees stretching over the road like we were in a tunnel. I knew the white shimmer on the leaves wasn't water or snow, but light spilling off the moon above us. I knew where there were four hand-prints in the sidewalk and the giddy expression on my Dad's face when we'd done it. I knew why the street lamp was dented and how if you looked closely, I still had a scar from it on the back of my head. I knew why there was a bow tied to the power cable in between two houses. I knew there was the most wonderful cat named Freddy buried under the oak tree, because we always had to beg him to come out of it.

I knew every detail of the two houses in front of me.

If I closed my eyes, I could picture myself walking inside past the memories printed and hanging on the walls, and the ones we didn't catch on camera. I knew which door-frame had pencil lines with our names and dates scribbled next to them to mark our growing. I knew exactly which day my father included Bettina. I knew each and every spot the old hardwood floors creaked when you walked on them. I knew how to get onto the roof without killing myself. I knew everything about this place.

This was home.

So why didn't it feel like it anymore?

A few weeks ago, this was the only home I'd ever known. It was hard to think about who I was then, or what my life was like before I knew the truth. The weird thing was...I didn't feel sad looking up at my old house. There were countless cherished memories inside, but I couldn't say I missed it all that much. The only part of my old life I wished I still had was my best friend Bettina. Other than that, this house and this street no longer felt like *home*. But my new house in Tampa didn't either. I wondered if I had anything that gave me the comfort that *home* used to.

Heat rushed over my right side, and my fingers tingled. Tennessee's fresh rain scent washed over me. Warmth filled my body and I sighed. I peeked up and found his mismatched eyes watching me. Then it hit me. It was *him*. Somehow, in such a short amount of time, this handsome boy beside me had become *home*. He smoothed the cracks in my armor. He soothed the mess inside me. I'd known I was falling in love with him. I just hadn't realized the falling part was complete.

He cocked his head to the side and frowned. "You okay?"

I blinked and peeled my eyes off of him before someone else saw. My mouth was dry and my heart pounded in my chest. *Am I okay? No, not at all. Not really.* I was madly in love with him, and I couldn't do anything about it. I wasn't even sure if I could tell him, or if that was asking for trouble.

Trouble. I cleared my throat and led my crew up the walkway to the front door. We sounded like an army stomping down the quiet street. I raised my hand and knocked on the front door. It wasn't even ten o'clock, but I knew there would only be one person awake inside. The old house had such thin walls that I heard the television sound get turned off, then the soft thud of feet walking toward us.

The front door swung open, and soft golden light spilled out onto the stoop. A tall girl stood in the doorway with blonde hair falling in waves down to her shoulders. She frowned and took a step back. The front door closed a little while her gaze scanned the small army in front of her. Then she spotted me.

Her eyes widened, and a grin spread across her face. "TEGAN!"

She pounced on me before I had a chance to react. Her long arms squeezed me like a boa constrictor. A hot mess of a lump formed in my throat, but I smiled through it. I wasn't going to cry. Everyone would realize how close to falling apart I was.

"Surprise?" I said.

Bettina pulled back and wiped a tear off her cheek. "Oh man, I missed you so much."

"I missed you, too."

"Why didn't you let yourself in? Don't you still have a key? Never mind, just come in." She jumped back and gestured for us to enter. "What are you even doing here?"

I waved my arm and led them into the living room just inside the house. The walls were still that same strange mauve color I remembered, and the tan leather sofas still didn't match. I smiled. My Coven-mates were gathered behind me as Bettina joined us.

"Um, it's kind of a long story, but we need a place to crash tonight," I said.

"Obviously, *long story* isn't sufficient for... Wait...

Emersyn?" Bettina's eyes widened. She looked back and forth between me and my sister.

"Hi, Bettina." Emersyn waved but her gaze turned to me with uncertainty, like she knew this was not going to go over easily.

I know, I know. I'll handle it.

It was a good thing my twin was an overly friendly person who liked hugs as much as Olaf because Bettina didn't give her a chance to say no.

Then Bettina pulled back. "Wait, what? How? We got separated, and now you're here together? Am I dreaming?"

"Do you dream about Emersyn often?" I chuckled but my spidey senses were tingling. The questions weren't going to stop, except I wasn't sure how I was going to answer them. I cleared my throat and gestured toward my crew. "These are my friends, Cooper, Royce, Deacon, Willow, Chutney, and—"

"Oh my God, you're the hot guy!"

"Bettina!" I whisper-yelled but she didn't hear me, or chose to ignore me.

Her face paled. She turned her shocked eyes on me and pointed to Tennessee. "It's *him*! The hot guy from The Gathering!"

"Bettina..."

"The *hot* guy?" Cooper all but growled. "You met them?"

Oh no.

"I'm sure he doesn't remember me. He only paid attention to Tegan. Right, Emersyn?"

My face burned so hot I thought actual flames were going to pop out. *Oh my God.*

Emersyn covered her mouth to hide her chuckle and failed. "Um, I mean, considering what was happening and all..."

"Yeah, being all knight in shining armor and all." Bettina clapped her hands and laughed. "Tegan! The hot guy is in my living room?"

"Stop calling him that," I mumbled and buried my face in my hands.

This was bad. This was horrifying. This was potentially life-threatening. I'd never admitted out loud to anyone besides Emersyn that I thought Tennessee was good-looking. Sure, Henley assumed it, but I never confirmed it. If Cooper knew I was attracted to him, he might start watching me around Tennessee. Would my own brother tattle on me? Would he let mine and Tenn's magic be stripped? I chanced a glance up at my brother, and my stomach sank harder than the *Titanic*. His hands were in fists at his sides. His green eyes were sharp and narrowed on my soulmate's back.

I peeked up at Tennessee standing beside me. His eyebrows were raised and his jaw hung open. His cheeks were flushed. It was an expression I'd never seen on his face.

"I can't believe what's happening right now. I'm Bettina, best friend extraordinaire." She stuck her hand out in front of him and did this little curtsy. "It's nice to *officially* meet you, Your Royal Hotness."

"Oh my God, who *are* you right now?" I groaned. My best friend was a shy, quiet girl who never approached guys. Ever. And she most certainly never embarrassed me in front of one.

Tennessee made this little nervous laugh, and it was entirely adorable yet also mortifying. "I'm Tennessee..."

Bettina giggled and shook his hand. She looked to me and nodded her head in his direction. "You were right. Even his voice is hot."

"Umm..." Tennessee shifted his weight around and rubbed his face with his hand. His cheeks were definitely a solid pink now. "What?"

"*Bettina!* He can hear you!" I whispered. My entire face was on fire.

"Yeah, we all can." Deacon laughed behind us. "Please do continue."

"She has a point." Royce chuckled. "What else did Tegan say about him back then?"

"Oh my God," I whispered and stared at my feet. *Please let this end.*

"So you left The Gathering and talked about how hot he was?" Emersyn asked. "Like of all the things to discuss from that night, and you chose that? Did you even know his name?"

I hissed like a cat. "Emersyn. Seriously?" *Whose side are you on right now?*

"No, she didn't!" Bettina answered for me. "Maybe that's why the spells didn't work."

"SPELLS?" Everyone behind me repeated in unison.

"BETTINA," I yelled through clenched teeth. *What is happening right now?*

Tennessee cleared his throat. "Um, I'm sorry...what? You did...spells?"

I shook my head. "No..."

"YES." Bettina rolled her blue eyes. "We tried to find you using these spells we found online, and a few from Tegan's witchcraft books. Silly stuff. None of it worked—oh my God, is that how you found him? Did you keep doing spells? You always loved that stuff."

"Bettina, stop talking!"

"It's okay, Tegan. You're not the only one who thinks he's hot," Willow said in a soft voice.

"Yeah, Cooper, you should be used to it by now," Chutney added. "You know he's hot."

"Not helping," I whispered. Hearing other girls call my soulmate hot did not make me feel better about anything. My gaze turned to Tennessee, who was blushing a deep scarlet red and staring at the ground.

Cooper said something in our ancient language, but I had no idea what it meant. I was still learning it.

"What language is that?" Bettina asked. Her eyes narrowed and watched the rest of my group with suspicion. "I am so confused."

"I know…"

"You show up late at night with a group of strangers, none of whom are your father, needing a place to stay? That's weird, dude." She pointed one hand toward Emersyn, the other toward Tenn. "You being with Emersyn again is even weirder. But with Mr. Hottie, too? Dude, that's too much weird for me."

"Bettina, it's a long story…"

She scoffed. "Like I care? We've apparently got all night."

"Excuse me," Cooper whispered as he passed between me and Emersyn. He walked up to Bettina and stuck his hand out like he wanted to greet her properly. But the second she took it, her eyes rolled to the back of her head and she fainted.

"BETTINA!" I raced forward to catch her, but my brother had already caught her in his arms. "What the hell was that? Is she okay?"

Cooper placed her gently on the shaggy cream rug right where she'd been standing. "Yes, she's just asleep."

"*Asleep?!*"

He sighed and stood back up straight. "Yes, asleep. She was asking too many questions. It's against Coven law to tell Sapiens the truth, so I put her into REM cycle."

Fury surged to the surface. *How dare he!* I slapped him across the cheek with every ounce of strength I had left after the plane crash. It wasn't much, but the sound echoed through the room and I left a dark pink mark on his skin.

Tennessee jumped in between us. Emersyn gripped my wrist and pulled me back, like she knew I might actually hit him again.

"How *dare* you!" I snarled. "She's my best friend since I was five years old. I get to decide how to handle this secret, not you. You've had your secrets, darling brother."

Cooper opened his mouth, but Deacon beat him to it. "If I may? I'd like to offer my services here." He walked over and stood over my best friend.

I frowned. "Like what?"

He arched one eyebrow and pointed to his Mark. "Devil here. Persuasive speech comes with the territory. I do believe you're all quite familiar with how it works. Libby was far more gifted than I've had time to be, but if we wake her, I can simply tell her *not* to ask questions."

"That's..." Emersyn sighed and released my hand. "Actually a good idea."

"Thanks for the glowing review, Empress." Deacon rolled his pretty purple eyes. It was the first time he seemed to genuinely be annoyed with my sister. He shook his head and looked to me. "Well?"

Everyone turned to me.

I looked down at my best friend sleeping soundly on the floor. Part of me knew we could've just left her like that. Maybe it was the best idea. Just move her to the couch and turn the television back on, then we could crash in the attic and be on the road before she woke back up. She'd wake and assume it was all a dream. She'd call me and laugh about it. My stomach turned. I didn't think I could keep that kind of lie from her. If Deacon used his gift, she wouldn't know it, and I'd have time to come up with an approved explanation.

Stupid Coven laws. Who even makes this stuff? Rules written in a black-or-white manner never worked. Life happened in the gray areas. I agreed that in general, Sapiens couldn't know the truth about us, about the world, but I knew in my gut some could be trusted. Bettina could be trusted with it. *Maybe I should become Coven Leader so I can change these rules.*

"Tegan?" Tennessee bent down and scooped her into his arms. He carried her the few feet over to the sofa then put her down. He looked over to me. "What do you want to do?"

I cleared my throat. "Thank you, Deacon. That sounds like a great idea."

"Cooper..." Deacon wiggled his fingers. Red lightning sparked. "Please?"

Cooper rolled his eyes.

"Tegan?"

I jumped at the sound of her voice. Cooper hadn't even touched her to wake her. I walked over to the couch. "Hey, bestie."

Deacon knelt beside me. He gripped her elbow and helped her into a seated position. "Hey, beautiful."

CHAPTER SEVENTEEN

TEGAN

An hour later, I was still wide awake. My eyes burned and my body twitched from overuse, but I just couldn't fall asleep. Tennessee went into the kitchen to call Kessler and hadn't come back. There was no way I'd be able to sleep if he wasn't in the same room, not after we almost all died in that plane. I wished more than anything he could curl up on the couch and hold me, just so I'd feel his heart beating and know he was safe. But there was no way we could with everyone in the same room.

But he's not in the same room.

I sat up with the intention of going to find him, but my gaze landed on my sister. She was under a blanket in a lounge chair. Her long Rapunzel-like hair hung over the armrest and grazed the hardwood floors. I assumed she'd fallen asleep, but her eyes were open. They were dark and hooded...and sad. I threw my blankets off and jumped to my feet.

Emersyn's eyes widened. "Oh, you're awake?" she whispered.

"And so are you," I whispered back. I tiptoed over to her then dragged her off the chair by her elbow. She didn't fight me. "Come with me."

I led her out of the living room and down the hallway to the far side of the house to Bettina's room, careful to not step on the squeaky boards. I opened the door and stood aside for Emersyn, then closed it behind her. Before Em had the chance to speak, I ran over and turned the standing fan on. The lamp in the corner cast the room in a soft golden glow. The room looked exactly like I remembered. Bettina hated the mint-green paint her mother insisted on, so she covered it in pictures. I sighed and let the nostalgia seep in.

"Bettina's room?"

"Yup."

She narrowed her eyes and walked around, eyeing all of the memories on the wall. "So, what did you drag me in here for?"

I walked over to Bettina's bed and sat down. Turned out I still hated the quilt her mother made her use. "Em, talk to me. What's going on in your head lately?"

She dropped her gaze and nodded. I knew that look.

It took me until that moment to place it. My father had made the same face whenever I talked about Bentley's mother and sister back before the move.

She sat on the edge of Bettina's wooden desk and wrapped one arm around her stomach, the other one pressed against her chest. After a long, quiet moment, she closed her eyes and whispered, "It's just...I remembered you two being close at The Gathering... I know she's your best friend, and I have no right to be jealous..."

"Of course you do."

She spun around with wide eyes. "What?"

"Emersyn Howe Bishop." I smiled and shook my head. "You're my *twin*. Bettina has been my best friend for eleven years, but that bond didn't form overnight. After I used those spells to try and find Tennessee, I used them to try and find *you*. If there's anyone who should be jealous, it's Bettina, because though I love her, she doesn't mean as much to me as you do."

The bed dipped with Emersyn's weight, then she wrapped her arms around me. "I love you, too, twin." After a few long moments, she pulled back.

I watched her out of the corner of my eye. There was a conversation I'd been wanting to have with her, and it was the reason I'd dragged her into another room. I turned more toward her...and frowned. She stared out the window with her hand still pressed to her chest.

I ran through my catalog of memories, scanning through the images. Emersyn started acting weird once Deacon arrived. That was why I wanted to talk to her. It hadn't made sense. I couldn't think of a single reason for her to be so angry with him. But looking back, every time Deacon was around, my sister looked like he was physically hurting her. *Maybe he was.*

"Why are you looking at me like that?"

"Hold that thought." I didn't want to say what I was thinking if I was wrong. I reached into the inside pocket of my leather jacket and pulled out the Tarot deck. It could provide the answer I needed. Emersyn watched me like a hawk. I shuffled the deck and focused my thoughts on what I wanted the deck to show me. The cards didn't work within the same restrictions as normal tarot cards. These had magic.

What's on Emersyn's chest?

I fanned the cards out in front of my sister. "Pick a card."

She frowned. "I'll never understand the way your brain works." She waved her hands over the cards, then stopped over one and plucked it out.

I took it from her and flipped it over. Purple eyes the same color as my hair sparkled up at me. *Deacon.* His smirk was devious and confident, an exact replica of the one I saw in person on the plane. He held a bright red apple between his fingers. One of his eyebrows was raised, like he dared me to reach out and grab the fruit. At the bottom of the card, written in glowing red script, was *XV The Devil.*

"Which card did I pull?"

I turned the card around. Her eyes narrowed into little slits and her nostrils flared. But it was the way she gripped her chest that really told me I was right. The question I asked the cards could've been answered figuratively, as in what was weighing on her. Instead, it answered me literally. Or probably both, actually.

I tried not to smile. "Show it to me."

Emersyn's face paled. She shook her head. "Show you what?"

"Show me your chest, Em." I swallowed and pointed to my chest, right over the glyph.

When she just stared at me without moving, I leaned forward and pulled the collar of her white T-shirt down. *Boom, there it is.* Twinkling like a star on a cloudless night was a mark that looked eerily like a crystal was glued to her skin. The mark shimmered with light, like it was glowing from within. It was a soft blue color, like the sky just after sunrise. I recognized it immediately.

"It just showed up the other day, after that night we went to Hidden Kingdom. It looks like the demon scar on your chest from when we first moved here." Emersyn's heart pounded through the veins in her neck. She twirled her hair around her fingers nervously. "I kept meaning to show you, but everything has been crazy. I don't know how I got it."

"I do." I smiled and leaned back. "Why does Deacon annoy you so much?"

"I don't... It just...He's just..." She groaned and threw her hands in the air. "I don't want to like a boy!"

I giggled then threw my hand over my mouth. That was not the answer I expected.

"Don't laugh! I have zero interest in romance right now. Everyone keeps expecting such awesome things from me because I'm the Empress, and I supposedly have the most power after you and Tennessee, except I don't. I hate that everyone is depending on me when I can't deliver." She rubbed her face with her hands. My magic may have been on power-saver mode, but hers was soaring wild. "I need to focus on learning my power and knowing how to use it. A stupid, pretty boy with stupid purple eyes is *not* what I need right now. And he's just so not my type. Have you noticed how confident he is? Why can't I keep my eyes off him? Why does he stare at me so much? Why does he smile like that at every girl he sees? I don't know, and it drives me insane. Wait, how does this connect to the mark on my chest?"

I slid my leather jacket off then peeled my shirt off.

If I was going to show her, then I had to show her the whole thing. Or at least what it looked like at the moment, because it changed every day. I knew the second my sister saw it because she gasped.

"What...what the hell is that?" She leaned closer to look at it. "That is *not* the same thing I saw a few weeks ago."

I chuckled. "No. No, it's not. Yet, it is at the same time. I didn't know what this was back then, but after I blew up that fountain, Mom told me."

"Mom knows?" She pressed her fingers to my mark then yanked them back. "It's *hot*."

"You have no idea." I laughed, thinking of the intensity between Tennessee and me. "This mark is called a glyph, and it means that I have a soulmate."

"A *soulmate*?!"

I nodded. "Not every witch has a soulmate out there, so those of us who do are lucky—and cursed, I suppose. When we meet our soulmate, this glyph appears, and it happens immediately. It burns like hell, like someone lit a match on your chest."

"No," she whispered and shook her head rapidly. Tears pooled in her eyes. "No, no, no. You're not—you're not telling me that...that...that..."

"Deacon English is your soulmate."

She groaned and buried her face in her hands. "I

didn't ask for this."

I scoffed. "You think I did?"

"Wait." She looked up and frowned at me. "That means you have a soulmate. Who is—*oh.* Tennessee?"

"Tennessee." I nodded. I ran my fingers over the crystal-looking mark. "Yup."

"Does he have the mark too?"

"Yeah. It looks exactly like mine. Our glyphs are linked. Whenever he's near, it burns, though I'm told the pain is a temporary phase." I glanced down at my right shoulder. "You see these vine-like lines? They spread a little farther every day. Eventually they'll cover our entire right arms down to our fingers."

She traced the vines. "Why is yours pink and mine blue?"

"Mom says the glyph will change colors to reflect moods and stuff. She says it can even warn you if your soulmate is in danger or hurt." I looked down at my arm and tried to imagine what that would be like, to look down and know Tennessee was hurt. "Mine has always been pink, though, so I kinda assumed that's how they all started."

"Mine has always been blue," she whispered.

"Well, maybe that's because things are cold between you two?"

"And yours is pink because things between you and

Tenn are super hot?"

I blushed and bit down on my bottom lip. "Um...well..."

She rolled her eyes and smiled. "Oh, right, tongue down the throat. So things with him are...?"

"Great. Wonderful. Awful. Torturous." I groaned and pulled my shirt back on before someone came into the room. "At first, finding out we're soulmates made me feel better, like there was a reason I was so out of my mind for him, but now? It's just more torture. I'm forbidden from being with my *soulmate* until I'm middle-aged. If we break the law, if we get caught together, then we can get our magic stripped. No one can know, Em."

"Your secret is safe with me."

I reached out and squeezed her hand. "It's your secret now, too." I pointed to her chest with my other hand.

Her face fell. "Do you think Deacon knows?"

"Absolutely. That day we took him to Hidden Kingdom, he was asking all these questions about you. Totally makes sense now. He knows you're his soulmate, I don't have to look to know he has a glyph to match yours."

She cringed. "And I'm awful to him. It's just... I don't want this."

"Well, lucky for you, it's forbidden." I laughed for

her sake, even though it killed me inside. "I'm just telling you what it means."

"Thank you, Tegan." She sighed. "It's nice to know there's a reason for it all."

"You don't have to like him, but maybe it's worth getting to know—" I gasped and clutched my chest. *Tennessee.* It always burned more after we spent too much time near each other. I clenched my teeth and breathed through it.

"Tegan? Are you okay?" She exhaled. "Wait, does that mean he's nearby?"

I nodded. The hardwood floors outside Bettina's room creaked a second before the door flew open. Tennessee stormed inside with wild eyes. His hands were in fists at his sides, and the muscles in his arms flexed. His gaze swung around the room, then did a double take on me. His cheeks flushed.

"Hi," I whispered.

He sighed and his shoulders dropped. "Hi." His voice was rough and low.

I knew Emersyn was watching us, but all I could do was stare. My pulse quickened and my body temperature soared. The light from the lamp flickered. Still, I stared up at him. A muscle in his jaw popped. His lips had a little shine to them, like he'd just licked them. I jumped to my feet and walked forward until we were a few inches apart. That fresh rain scent of his washed over me, and all I wanted to do was bury my face in his chest.

His eyes scanned me over once before resting on my face. "You weren't in the room with everyone."

"You were on the phone." I grabbed a handful of his shirt and pulled him closer. The heat radiating off his body felt like a fireplace. "We're okay, though."

Emersyn cleared her throat. "Okay, I'm gonna go back and try to sleep."

Somewhere in the back of my mind, I registered the sound of the bedroom door closing, but all of my attention was on Tennessee.

I pulled him flush against me. "Hi."

He cupped my jaw and pulled my head closer. "Hi."

I licked my lips. "You okay?"

He brushed his thumb over my bottom lip. "No." He dragged my mouth to his.

A moan slipped out between our lips, and I didn't try to hide it. I'd been dying to kiss him for hours. I sighed and sank into his chest. His lips were warm and soft, but his kiss was hot and rough. The world around me disappeared. He fisted my hair and held me close while he kissed me senseless. I twisted my hands in his shirt and pulled him into me. I needed more. I needed him closer.

He angled my face to deepen our kiss, and we stumbled across the room until we crashed into Bettina's desk. My back smashed into the lamp and sent it flying to the ground, but I paid it no attention. I was lost in him. I threw my hand out to balance us. Papers and what felt like pens rolled off the surface. I didn't care. I'd clean it up later. All I wanted was more of this moment with him. I didn't want it to stop or end. His lips on mine was the only thing that kept me sane.

But then he was gone.

An ice-cold draft washed over me. I shivered. "Why?"

Tennessee was across the room, gripping onto the doorframe like it was the last life preserver on a sinking ship. His cheeks were flushed and his eyes wilder than I'd ever seen. "No. We can't," he said between labored breaths.

"Tennessee, please. Don't go."

"Cooper is going to be suspicious after Bettina's comments. He'll be watching. We *can't*." He closed his eyes and banged his head against the wall. When he finally reopened his eyes, they looked as broken as how I imagined mine were. "Go get some sleep, Tegan. We need your power restored."

Then he disappeared, leaving me grasping for solid ground all alone.

CHAPTER EIGHTEEN

"Wait, *why* didn't Kessler just send someone to get us? Eden isn't that far, is it?"

I sighed and turned to face Willow. The rest of our gang stood beside her, and judging by their faces, they wanted to know the same thing. "I had Kessler send help to follow Walter to that hospital. But it's too dangerous out here. I don't want anyone else leaving Eden. I can't have anyone else on my conscience, can you?"

Tegan shook her head. "No."

She hadn't looked at me since I'd left her in that bedroom the night before, but surely she understood why I did it. She *had* to. I forced myself to look away from her.

The sun had a warm haze that made everything seem a little fuzzy. The morning dew had yet to evaporate, so everything was a little wet, too. We stood in the

175

parking lot of an animal rescue center waiting for Bettina to come back with the keys to her father's work van. I wasn't thrilled about taking a Sapien vehicle into Eden, but desperate times meant desperate measures.

"Who's that?" Emersyn pointed behind me.

I spun around and spotted Bettina strolling across the parking lot with an unfamiliar guy. The dude had on a black beanie and dark-rimmed glasses. His hands were stuffed in the front pocket of his red-hooded sweater.

"Tegan?" I said.

"I don't know."

Bettina was full smiles when she bounced back up to us. "Hey, guys, this is my friend Dean."

Her friend smiled, but it didn't reach his eyes. He waved. "Hi. So, I hear you're trying to get into the mountains this morning...but...uh...her dad's van didn't want to start an hour ago when I tried to move it. We can try again, though."

One of us can make it start, right? Tegan's thoughts slipped into my mind.

I nodded. "Thanks, Dean. Let's give it another shot and see what happens."

I held my hand out for the keys, and Dean's eyes just about popped out of his head. I frowned. Dean's face paled. His gray eyes widened. He stared at my arm like it was going to bite him, then he met my stare. I opened my mouth to ask him what was wrong when he narrowed his eyes and scanned each of my friends' arms. His jaw dropped, but he recovered by wiping his face with his hands. His gaze met mine and held for an awkwardly long moment.

I frowned. "You okay, Dean?" *Do you know what our Marks mean?*

A light flush filled his cheeks. He nodded. "I was just thinking...why risk getting broken down in the mountains where there's no cell service and stuff, right?"

"We have to get there, though."

"Well, I have a van full of supplies that need to be dropped off at our other location. If you promise to drop the van off once you get into town, then I'd be happy to let you borrow it." He pulled a piece of paper out of his pocket and held it out. "Should be right on your way."

I frowned and took the paper. The address listed was in Eden. The name on the receipt read Constance Bell. Also known as one of the two Coven Leaders. *I think you do know, Dean.*

Dean cleared his throat, then he bowed his head ever so slightly. "What do you say?"

I had no idea who this Dean guy was. I'd never seen him before, but he definitely knew what the Marks on our arms meant. I nodded. "Deal."

He smiled and this time it wrinkled his face around

his gray eyes. "Follow me." Without another word, he turned and walked across the parking lot.

I waved for my crew to follow. "Let's get going."

Tenn?

I froze at the sound of her voice in my head and not for the first time wished I could respond to her in the same way.

"I can't believe you're leaving me again," Bettina mumbled once everyone else had left.

Can I have a second to say bye to Bettina? I won't tell her anything, I promise.

I glanced over my shoulder and met Tegan's gemstone eyes. They were sad and wistful, like she thought she had to say a permanent goodbye. Bettina fiddled with the frayed hem of her shorts and stared at the ground. Cooper had warned Tegan she couldn't tell her friend the truth, but I didn't see why that meant she couldn't tell her a lie. Hell, we'd been doing just that to Tegan for her entire life. If anything, she'd earned the right to keep her one Sapien friend. Especially since Bettina was at The Gathering and never had her memory swayed.

"Florida is gorgeous in the winter, you know."

Tegan's eyes lit up. *Can she?*

I winked then turned to catch up with the others. By the time I got over there, Deacon was already in the driver's seat. Dean stood in the open doorway pointing toward the dashboard.

"Uh, boss?"

I groaned. "Royce, for the last time." I loathed when they called me that.

"There's nothing in the van."

I frowned and peeked inside. Sure enough, the inside was completely empty, not even a seat or stray box. There weren't even windows. It was like a jail cell on wheels. Willow and Chutney climbed in and propped themselves up against the far wall.

"What are you thinking?" Cooper leaned against the open door. "Suspicious, no?"

"He said there were supplies to deliver, but there's nothing inside." Royce rolled his sapphire eyes and shook his head. Ever since Henley was taken, he'd lost a little pep in his step. And he'd taken to wearing all black, except unlike me, it seemed he was dressed for mourning. "I'd say that's suspicious as hell."

Emersyn pushed past us and stepped inside. She crouched in the middle of the van and raised her nose in the air...then sniffed. She turned her champagne eyes back to us and shrugged. "Smells like dogs."

Royce scoffed and rested his forehead against the side of the van. "Where's Tegan? She's good at not believing a word people say."

"Maybe he has to go get the supplies still?" Willow asked, though she didn't seem concerned at all. She was huddled up next to Chutney looking half asleep.

"Nope, supplies are all here," Dean said, suddenly behind me.

I must've made a face because his smile vanished.

He held his hands in the air. "Constance called me this morning and told me The Coven was in town and to keep an eye out in case I could help you. Although I never expected to get the chance, so this is cool."

"You know who we are?" Cooper asked.

"He saw our Marks." I held my hand out to our new friend. "Thanks, Dean. We'll return the favor one day. Oh, and keep an eye on Bettina for us."

CHAPTER NINETEEN

TEGAN

My dad used to take me camping in the Smoky Mountains once a month growing up, even if it was just one night. It was kind of our thing. He always said he wanted Bentley and me not to be afraid of the wilderness but to welcome the comfort nature could give us. It was on one of our mountain adventures that I was first intrigued by witches. I thought it had to be real, because the forest around me felt more alive than the bustling city of Charleston.

Guess it all makes sense now.

The crazy part about our drive into Eden was that I recognized almost every part of it. I knew exactly where we were. My father must've wanted us to know where Eden was even if he couldn't tell us. Eden was the homeland for witches. The location had moved a few times in the millenniums since Adam and Eve fell from the

Garden, but it was always a safe place for our kind. Nothing could hurt us inside Eden. No demons, no fairies, no living or dead creature from another realm. Sapiens couldn't even find it if they wanted to.

The drive was as gorgeous as I remembered, too. Narrow, winding roads tucked away between peaks and valleys. Rivers and creeks rippled in the distance just out of sight. Every shade of green a person could think of danced by, flowing in the wind. I spent most of the drive crouched between the driver's and passenger's seat because the only windows were up there, and I wanted to *see*. But mostly because Tennessee was in the back and I just couldn't handle being locked inside a small space with him after the way he'd kissed me the night before. Butterflies bounced around in my stomach at the thought of it.

"Okay, this is it. Turn here." Cooper pointed out the passenger window. "Then park right up at the front of the building."

Deacon whistled. "This place looks exactly like I remember."

"Yeah. Time doesn't really show around here." Cooper leaned over the seat and looked at the rest of our group. "Tenn, you want to take lead on this?"

Tennessee mumbled something under his breath, but he climbed to his feet and moved to the sliding door.

He took a deep breath then pulled the handle. Bright light spilled inside, blinding me from seeing anything outside of the van. I blinked and glanced away. When I turned back, Tennessee was out of sight. I meant to scramble to be the first one out of the van. I wanted to see Eden. I'd been dreaming about it for weeks. Except now that we were here, my body froze. One by one my Coven-mates hopped out until I was left alone inside.

I didn't know why I was so nervous. These were *my* people. They were supposed to have my back, just like Dean. But I couldn't help but wonder what they'd think of me. Would I live up to the former High Priestess? I'd heard wonderful things about her. Would they like me at all? *What if they see my glyph?* My pulse quickened and my palms got sweaty. If The Coven Leaders found out about my soulmate glyph, would they strip my magic right then and there? Would they search everyone else just in case?

A tan hand with two shimmering silver rings gripped the edge of the van door. I knew who it was without his *IV* Mark. Tennessee leaned inside the van, and his mismatched eyes found me immediately. "Coming, Kitten?"

I smiled and heat rushed to my cheeks. He called me that on purpose. I crawled to the edge of the van then knelt right in front of him. I placed my hand on his chest and almost sighed at the warmth of his skin seeping through the cotton.

He ducked his head down to meet my eyes. "Talk to me."

"What if they see?"

He smiled and took my chin between his thumb and pointer finger. "If Cooper or Kessler haven't figured it out, and they see us together every day, then there's absolutely no reason anyone else will. We just need to be careful and behave ourselves while we're here." He tipped my head back and pressed his lips to mine.

He pulled away far too soon.

I groaned and licked my lips. "Is that what you call behaving ourselves?"

His heavy gaze dropped to my lips, and then his mouth was on mine again. His fingers dug into my jaw, pulling me in. He brushed his tongue against mine, and all of my control snapped. I grabbed his face with both hands and yanked him closer. It was stupid and reckless to be kissing him like that in the very place we could have our magic stripped, but I couldn't stop myself. Every time he touched me, it got harder and harder to stop. Maybe it was because we had to hold back every day, or maybe it was because we'd almost died. All I knew was the silky feel of his hair tangled around my fingers and the gasps for air we took from each other.

He jumped back and cursed a line of words I'd never heard him say. His face was flushed and his lips were red. He closed his eyes and shook his head. "Maybe we better stay away from each other until this is over."

I nodded even though it killed me inside to agree. We couldn't get caught. I loved him more than anything else, which was why I couldn't ask him to give up his whole world for me. That wasn't the way love was supposed to work. Happiness wasn't supposed to come at a cost. No, if we were going to be together before we were middle-aged, then the rule was going to be changed. And now I knew what I was fighting for once we closed the gaps. I had to focus my efforts on that for now, but after Samhain, my own battle would begin.

I took a deep breath then jumped out of the car. I'd lost my backpack in the plane accident, but it didn't matter. I had everything I needed on me. My Tarot deck and cell phone were stuffed in the inside pockets of my leather jacket, along with some of the crystals my father gave me. My mother's white-hilted dagger was strapped to my right thigh, ready for action. And Keltie's jewels were still wrapped around my ears and finger.

Without looking back at my soulmate, I stomped forward to catch up with our friends who were standing in a circle up ahead. The brick building just behind them sprawled out on both sides with EDEN-BURG EST. 1693 carved into the bricks above the doors.

Tennessee walked silently behind me. Only the heat of his aura told me he was there. When we approached the group, Royce turned to look at us.

I smiled and forced a laugh I prayed they believed. "Sorry, Keltie's ring slid off, so I had to find it."

"Well, well, well," an older man with a thick salt-and-pepper beard said with a cocky grin on his face. "Tennessee, you seem to be having many problems lately, don't you?"

What the hell? I frowned and glanced back at my soulmate, but Tennessee just narrowed his pretty eyes. His lips pressed together in a firm line.

"You jealous?" Deacon snapped.

The big guy in the red-and-black-plaid shirt step forward with his chest puffed out. "Excuse me?"

"I could arrange some problems for *you* if you're jealous." Deacon leaned forward and narrowed his purple eyes into slits. His voice was silky smooth and dangerous. "It's kind of what I'm good at."

The other man raised his bushy eyebrows. His brown eyes were as wild with anger as the energy pouring out of him. "Are you threatening me, boy?"

"Keep bullying our Emperor, and you'll find out."

Deacon leaned back on his heels and crossed his arms over his chest. Red lightning flashed in his eyes.

In that moment, I understood why the Goddess chose him...and it made me smile.

The man arched one eyebrow at Tennessee. "Got the Devil on your side, do ya'?"

Tennessee grinned the most devious, mischievous smile I'd ever seen from him. "We have a job to do, Timothy. Let's shelve this adorable rivalry for the time being."

Timothy? My eyes widened. This big, burly man with a bad attitude was our Judgement Card? I looked down at his left arm, and sure enough, there was the *XX* Mark. *Wow.* I never would've expected such open hostility from a Coven Leader to one of its own. Especially Tennessee. But then his words registered. *Rivalry.* Timothy knew the throne really belonged to Tennessee. That had to drive him nuts.

The double doors behind him flew open, and a woman ran out. Her blue eyes were wide and her skin pale. The heels of her flats clacked against the sidewalk as she ran over. She narrowed her eyes on the big guy with an attitude. "Timothy, we talked about this."

He snarled without taking his eyes off Tennessee. "You're not the boss of me."

"No, but keep it up, and he may be," she snapped.

Timothy's face paled. He spun toward her. "Excuse me?"

She put her hands on her slim hips and arched one blonde eyebrow. "Did I stutter? Perhaps you forgot that The Coven is a team, not a dictatorship. We work together, not bully our own."

"Listen here..."

"No, *you* listen. Coven Leaders can and will be changed out at its own discretion. Do you really think they'll pick you over him?" She nodded her head in Tennessee's direction with a smug smirk on her pretty face. "Keep it up and I'll hold a reelection right now."

Timothy glared at Tennessee a few moments longer. "I'm going to check on Walter," he grumbled. Without another word, he pushed past us and stomped out of sight.

"That man. I don't know what has gotten into him." The woman sighed and pushed her sandy blonde hair out of her face. "Tennessee, I'm sorry."

He smiled. "Thank you. That was quite the defense. I'm not sure I deserved it."

"Of course you do," Emersyn snapped. Her golden eyes were narrowed and watching Timothy's back as he walked down the sidewalk. "That behavior was rude and unprovoked."

I adore you, twin. So feisty.

"You see, Emperor. I believe we discussed this before." The woman chuckled and shook her head. But then she looked at me, and her eyes sparkled. "High Priestess, Empress, it is an honor to meet you. Welcome to Eden. I'm Constance Bell."

My sister shook her hand first. "I'm Emersyn. Nice to meet you."

I held my left hand out, and she shook it immediately. I looked down and spotted her *XI* Mark on her arm. *Justice.* My jaw dropped. "Constance? As in our Coven Leader?"

"For now, at least." She smiled a warm, friendly smile and nodded. "Come, Kenneth is waiting for us."

CHAPTER TWENTY

TEGAN

Constance led us inside the brick building and out the back doors. We followed in silence, just the thud of our footsteps hanging between us.

This was what we left Tampa for. The quest. The first line of the prophecy said *Where only Eden and the chalice knows.* That meant we were officially starting. There was no more prepping or planning, no waiting around. This was it. Now we just had to hope Kenneth knew where we were supposed to start. Because no one else knew, and Henley couldn't afford to wait.

We walked across a massive courtyard with a sprawling green lawn and oak trees around the edge. There were benches and picnic tables along the sides, but they were all empty. At the other end of the courtyard, a brick building stood basking in the sunlight. It looked like something you'd find in England or France. It had to be three or four stories high, but it was hard to tell with the tall, arched windows. The glass panes reflected the cloudless sky.

Thirty feet later, Constance pushed through the grand glass doors. The bright daylight cast everything in a white shine. After a few seconds, it settled and I gasped. The entire back wall was made of glass, and it overlooked a gorgeous mountain-scape that had to be breathtaking in the fall. In the middle of the room, there were a dozen sofas and lounge chairs, all in varying shades of brown leather and condition. But none of this was what captured my attention.

It was the books.

I almost squealed in delight. *It's a library!* Along both sides of the room, there were three floors, lined with racks of books. The mahogany wood, vaulted ceilings, and dim golden light from the lamps made it feel like we'd stepped through a time portal. I wanted to spend hours and hours in there just discovering all the material.

"Wow," I breathed.

"Oh, this is just the academic section for Edenburg students. Wait until you see the *fun* parts." Constance chuckled and waved us along.

She led us around the corner and up a wooden spiral staircase. The floor creaked and groaned under our weight. When we made it to the top, we found the most elaborate attic I'd ever seen. It stretched the entire length of the building. The ceilings were vaulted with mahogany wood. There were different levels with stair-cases leading up to balconies and more books. There were no lamps in sight, only floating orbs of shimmering golden light. *Magic.*

Books floated around the room, from desk to book-shelf. There were quills with long feathers scribbling on parchment. A fireplace at least ten feet wide crackled from a nook off to the left. In front of the fireplace, a cauldron sat with bubbling liquid inside and a spoon stir-ring itself. In the far corner, an entire wall was stacked with long swords that seemed to be from different eras.

"What is this place?" Emersyn whispered.

Heaven.

"My home," an unfamiliar male voice said from somewhere above me. The man walked down a flight of stairs and stopped just beside me. He had long, wavy silver hair that shimmered in the light like liquid metal. His beard was scruffy, with hints of black mixed in. He held his hand out in front of me. Behind his glasses, his eyes were such a pale blue they almost looked white. "Hello, I'm Kenneth. And you are?"

I shook his hand and smiled. "Awkward." *Wait. No. Crap.*

"Fantastic." He threw his head back and laughed.

He shook his head then turned to the others. "Ah, Tennessee, how are you doing? It's been too long."

Tennessee gave Kenneth one of those standard dude half hugs. "I believe the appropriate phrase would be *hot mess*. How about yourself?"

"A mess has never stopped you before." Kenneth's smile faltered. He walked over to a desk covered in a mountain of open books stacked on top of each other and sat down. "Things have been stressful since the solstice, as it has been for you. Emersyn, Tegan, Deacon... welcome to The Coven, to our crazy little family."

"Thank you," Emersyn and Deacon said in perfect unison.

Emersyn blushed and looked away from him, but at least it wasn't a scowl like usual.

"Please, have a seat. Let's get started."

I cleared my throat and moved closer. "My brother said he's been in contact with you?"

Kenneth nodded. He crossed one ankle over the other and scratched his beard. "Bentley is a smart kid. I know Cassandra would be proud of his selection. Yes, I've assured our young Hierophant that I'm always available to him. We were just discussing the prophecy a few moments ago."

So he knew exactly who I was when he asked. Nothing was going to go unnoticed here. I shook myself and joined the group. My first instinct was to stand beside Tennessee, but after the van incident, I knew he was right. We needed to stay away from each other. I forced myself to sit in the chair a few feet over. It was the farthest I could be without offending Kenneth.

Cooper cracked his knuckles. "What do you make of the prophecy?"

Kenneth picked up a pipe off the desk and rolled it between his fingers. "*Where only Eden and the chalice knows, your fate lies in the Book of Shadows. Between the balefire, the runes shall dance, from within the cauldron comes your chance.* I have to admit, it's one of the heaviest prophecies I've seen. Tell me, High Priestess, what do you make of it?"

I took a deep breath. "Obviously we're looking for the Book of Shadows. From what I know, there are spells inside we need both to get Henley back and close the gap in Salem. Some visions were shown to me, but they're not...not in context."

"I had a feeling you'd say as much. Once you find the book, you'll have a whole new project on your hands." He cocked his head to the side and watched me. "I hope you realize this?"

I nodded. "I do. I will be seeking your assistance, if that's all right?"

"I look forward to that." He smiled at me. "Tennessee, penny for your thoughts?"

Tennessee rubbed the back of his neck. "The chalice is something specific, isn't it?"

Kenneth exchanged a guarded glance with Constance. She sighed. He tapped his pipe on his desk. "We can't protect them any further."

"I know, I know." She turned and paced in front of the window. "Tell them."

"I have a bad feeling about this," Royce mumbled and sank down to the ground at the base of a bookshelf.

"You're all familiar with the chalice the Goddess used to create our species, right?"

Tennessee paled. "We're looking for *that* chalice?"

Cooper cursed.

Royce groaned. "This is definitely not good."

I'd heard that story recently, once my parents were able to teach us some of our history. When the Garden of Eden fell, the Goddess created our species by mixing her blood with that of an angel's and a human's in a holy chalice. It was quite literally where we were born.

"I didn't realize this was a cup we actually had," I said.

"We don't," Tennessee answered.

"Was it lost like the Book?"

Emersyn stopped braiding her hair halfway down.

Her face paled a little and her eyes stared into space. "Or like the Hierophant's locket?"

Tennessee sighed and leaned against a wooden railing. He crossed his muscular arms over his chest. "Both. Neither."

Deacon cursed. He ran his fingers through the longer blond strands of his hair. "I agree with Royce. This doesn't sound good."

I doubted the chalice was lost like the Book. That wouldn't make sense to send us on a quest to find two impossible-to-find things. To find the locket we had to —*ooooh.* "It's a quest within a quest. Isn't it? Like Leyka and the sirens."

"That sounds fun." Deacon leaned his head against the rack of books.

"No, no, no." Royce buried his head in his hands. "That was awful. That was how...how..."

"How we lost Libby," Cooper finished for him in a low voice. He was a few feet behind Tennessee, sitting at one of Kenneth's desks.

There was a moment of silence where we all just looked around at each other. This was my family. I'd already said goodbye to one of them. I'd be damned if I did it again anytime soon. The same mistakes couldn't happen this time. We had to be more cautious and careful. We had to watch each other's backs.

I cleared my throat and returned my attention to our Hermit Card. "Kenneth, please. Continue?"

Kenneth rubbed his face with the hand not holding the pipe. "The originals had the chalice, but with the Goddess's help, they hid it where it would be almost impossible to find. In a place where only those worthy of finding could ever do so."

Tennessee cursed.

Cooper groaned. "Tenn, what do you know that we don't?"

"I know..." He sighed, like he couldn't believe this was the conversation at hand. "I know they hid it in the Old Lands."

My stomach turned. My magic prickled with awareness, like a threat had just walked into the room. Maybe it had. "What are the Old Lands?"

Tennessee just shook his head. To anyone else, he probably looked annoyed with all the questions, but not to me. I saw the anxiety rolling under the surface.

Kenneth took a puff off his pipe then exhaled a large cloud of white smoke. It twisted and swirled until it formed a row of mountain peaks. "There are areas of this world that are hidden from the rest."

Constance walked over to stand beside him. "The Old Lands belong to the Creator."

Kenneth nodded. "The Old Lands are cloaked from

the human eye and tucked away deep inside the world's largest mountain ranges, the Smokies, Rockies, Himalayas, and so on. Not much is known about them, because not many return once they go in."

"So obviously that's where we have to go," Royce mumbled.

Kenneth pulled his pipe out and exchanged an alarmed glance with Constance. "You have to go to The Garden of Eden."

Silence.

I blinked and shook my head. "I'm sorry, what?"

"As in...*the* Garden of Eden?" Cooper's face paled, and it made him look even more like my father. *Our* father.

Kenneth nodded.

Whoa. Wow. Holy crap. The Garden of Eden. My mind went utterly blank. I didn't even know how to think of that place.

It took me several attempts to get my mouth to form the question on my mind. "How do we get there?"

"I have no idea." Kenneth shrugged, and for the first time since I'd met him, he looked as perplexed as we felt. "Witches have tried to travel there, but they've never returned. Let me get you something. Hold on."

"You guys have to know the Old Lands follow their

own rules." Constance fiddled with the globe on Kenneth's desk. I meant to gauge her facial expressions, but my eyes were locked on her soulmate glyph covering her fingers. "We've only barely explored it, but we know modern technology doesn't work. There are creatures you've never faced before, maybe even never heard of before. I wish I could give you examples, but I simply don't know either. And the magic there... It's ancient. As old as the world itself. We have no idea exactly what you'll find."

I looked around at my crew and saw all of my own fears staring back at me. We were scared. Of who would make it home alive. What we'd have to do to ensure that. What would happen if we failed. Was there even an option of failure? If no one had ever returned, then I got the sinking impression that no, there was no failure. There was success...and death.

I hated that so many people I cared about were there with me. My brother Cooper, even though I was still mad at him. My twin. I'd only just found her. I couldn't fathom losing her. But the worst was Tenn. I hated that he was part of this death quest. The world needed him alive. *I* needed him alive. The idea of living without him was just a black hole of pain. Yet at the same time, I was glad he was with me. If there was even a sliver of a chance I wouldn't survive this journey, I wanted to have him by my side while I could. I just wished I could *be* with him.

Kenneth walked back over with something in his hand. He held it out to me. "High Priestess, you are the keeper of things."

My eyes widened. I reached out and took the object from his hands, ignoring the way my fingers trembled. The object was about the size of two baseballs, and weighed about the same. On the bottom, the surface was an inch thick of solid white stone, almost like limestone. On top were clear quartz crystals in varying size and shapes. It actually looked like a crown glued to a rock. Raw energy like I'd never felt tingled up my arms.

"What is this?" I asked.

He scratched the back of his head. "There's a path inside the Old Lands that is protected by the Banished One. We only know he's dangerous and not exactly human. This is a piece of that land. In order to get to The Garden of Eden, you must begin there. You'll have to track its origins."

"How do we track it?" Cooper asked.

"Well, Cooper, I'm afraid that's not an easy answer either. We've got a few different spells or rituals you can test out, but like Constance said, the magic of the Old Lands is older than us." He went back over to his desk and shuffled through some of the books.

I stared back down at the crystallized Earth in my palms. It was warm and soothing to the touch. The longer I stared, the more colors I saw reflecting in the crystals. An image popped into my head of another piece of crystal. It, too, tingled like electricity in my arm and radiated warmth. I owned a lot of crystals, and since becoming a witch, I'd had my hands on hundreds. But none of them felt alive like this one. Except one. Something told me it was ancient magic too.

I looked over at Tennessee and found him staring at the ground, lost in thought. His arms were crossed over his chest. He really was beautiful.

"Why are you staring at Tennessee like that?"

I jumped at the sound of Chutney's voice. Tennessee's gaze turned to me, his stare hot and intense.

My cheeks filled with warmth. I shook my head. "I was thinking about George."

Deacon frowned. "Who's George?"

Tennessee's eyes widened. He stared for a moment then dug into his pocket. George was the pendulum Tennessee had attained in a quest right before I met him. Tenn pulled the blueish colored crystal out and held it by the silver chain at the top. Purple mist billowed from the stone and swirled around it like a protective force field, or a snake. After a moment, it swung back and forth. I knew without asking that he'd asked our question silently.

He looked over at me and grinned in a way that made my toes curl and butterflies bounce around my stomach. "Brilliant. George can lead us to the entrance with the crystal."

"That's excellent," Constance said with a relieved smile that made me nervous.

"But there's one more thing you must do before you leave." Kenneth sat the books down. His gaze traveled around the group, one at a time. "You must perform a Binding Ritual."

CHAPTER TWENTY-ONE

TEGAN

"Constance." Kenneth turned toward her. "It's time."

I frowned and looked over at our Justice Card. Her sandy blonde hair was tied up in a ponytail so tight it pulled the muscles in her face a little. The blue of her eyes looked like an aquamarine crystal. They were soft and delicate, but heavy and weary. Being the Leader of The Coven probably weighed on her. I wanted to stare at her soulmate glyph and inspect every inch, but that would draw way too much attention and this was *not* the place to do that.

"I'll get it," she whispered then walked to the other side of the room.

Kenneth cleared his throat. He gestured for Constance to set a cauldron on the desk right in front of him. Smoke billowed out the top. "This potion was designed to bind witches before they entered the Old Lands. The magic in there is *alive*. If you find yourself lost, you may never find your way out again."

Constance turned to face us. "You *must* stay together. It's the only way you'll make it back out. That is why She has chosen so many of you for this quest. It will take all of you."

I swallowed down the rush of anxiety threatening to spill out. I had to keep myself together. The room fell silent around me, but I could've sworn I heard the pounding of my friends' hearts. I glanced over my shoulder at them. Their faces were white and their eyes wide. No one spoke, because we all knew we *had* to do this. I turned back to our elders.

"Unfortunately, Constance and I cannot be present in the room while you perform this ritual, or else we will be bound as well." Kenneth waved his hand over the cauldron, and the smoke spilled over the edge. The purple glow grew brighter, turning his silver hair as violet as mine. He raised his left hand up, and something shimmered like glass. "Tennessee, will you lead them?"

"Yes," Tenn answered without hesitation. His voice was strong, steady, and full of that confidence I'd grown used to seeing in him. He stepped up and let Kenneth place the dark object in his palm. "Constance, on your way out, would you mind?"

I frowned. That was the vaguest request I'd ever heard. Did she mind *what*?

But Constance smiled and nodded her head once. She raised her hands in the air, palms up, then rolled her fingers in a wave. The air crackled with new energy. Little balls of varying size and color rose from the ground and tabletops. One hovered in front of my face about the size of my fist. It was light pink with smooth sides and rough edges. *Crystals.*

Constance turned her gaze to Tennessee and held it. "I loan to you my crystals from earth. Guide them while your circle is in birth." She winked at my soulmate, then stepped through the doorway.

"Find us in the courtyard when you're done." Kenneth nodded then left us alone.

The rest of us spun to face Tennessee. Not for the first time I recognized how beautiful he was. In the soft golden glow of the candlelight mixed with the flickering light of the fireplace in the distance, his skin was tanned and smooth like honey. His long black hair fell in perfect waves past his jaw. He was gorgeous, but dangerous. His aura radiated power so strong it was almost visible to the naked eye. If you stood close enough, you could feel the strength of his magic, even when he just stood there.

"Where would you like us, boss?" Royce said in a soft voice.

"This is an altar cloth beneath us, used for circles. I need all of you to stand in the middle." He waited until we were in place, then he nodded. With the dark object cupped in both palms, he walked a circle around us along the edge of the carpet. "I cast this circle round and round, to follow me as I walk this ground. Come with us where we go today, protect us while we move through the fray."

The crystals surged forward and followed him like a shadow. When he reclaimed his spot among the group, the stones continued to fly around us. They moved faster and faster until they were a white blur.

"Now, everyone stand in a straight line in front of me, with Tegan first, then Emersyn." His voice was steady and calm, like he'd done this a million times. "Cooper, my brother, please take the end since you know how to do this?"

Me first? My heart skipped a beat. I had to remind myself this probably had to do with the strength of my magic and not his personal affection for me. Still, that rational thinking did nothing to prevent the warm blush in my cheeks or the sudden unevenness of my breathing. He was just *so close.* The air smelled like fresh rain, and it took everything inside me not to lean forward to let his breath brush over my face.

"Of course." Cooper inclined his head then moved to the opposite side of the carpet.

Tennessee took the dark bowl-like object in his hand and dipped it into the cauldron. When he pulled it back out, neon purple liquid dripped over the edge. He brought the object to his mouth and took a sip. His lips lit up the same bright purple as the liquid from the cauldron. The glow spread to his cheeks, down his throat, then all the way to the tips of his fingers.

He raised the little bowl up to me. "Take a sip, then pass it along."

I nodded and took the bowl. Part of me was a little nervous to drink something that glowed. Hell, I had no idea what was in the potion. But I trusted Tennessee. He was my soulmate. Anything that hurt me would hurt him too. I brought the bowl to my lips and drank. It felt like liquid sunshine seeping straight into my bones. Warmth spread through my body with the purple glow. I held the bowl behind me for my twin to take while watching my body change colors. I felt light on my feet, like if I jumped, I might not come back down.

Tennessee held his hand out, and the bowl flew up behind me and into his palm. He sat it on the desk beside the cauldron then turned back to us. "This next part we do in pairs. Emersyn turn to Royce, Willow turn to Chutney, and Deacon turn to Cooper."

A firework exploded in my stomach, then rained butterflies. I bit my bottom lip and tried to focus on breathing. We'd agreed to stay away from each other while in Eden because we couldn't keep our hands—or lips—off each other. Yet he wanted me to give him my undivided attention in a circle for a ritual. *I can do this. It's totally fine. No one will notice. Just stare into his eyes like you always do—wait, maybe not quite like that.*

"Now raise your arms and cross them at your wrists like an x in front of you." Tennessee's deep voice sucked me out of my mental tailspin.

I nodded and held my arms like he'd asked.

"Okay, now hold hands."

My eyes widened. *Hold hands?* I tried to remember a time when Tennessee and I had held hands, but my mind was struggling to think properly with him standing so close to me. I licked my lips and opened my hands. I looked up and found him watching me. His eyes sparkled against the potion's purple glow. He crossed his arms then slid his palms against mine. I wasn't sure how we were supposed to do it, but our fingers intertwined. We gripped each other tight, our eyes locked. His skin was hot to the touch, and I wanted to wrap myself in it. My chest burned that familiar burn; it was almost comforting now.

Purple mist swirled around us, twisting and turning

through our arms. I peeled my gaze off his to watch the spell. Inside the violet smoke was a white cord. It slithered out of the cauldron like a snake. I glanced up at Tennessee and he winked.

"By knot of four, this power we store," he chanted. "By knot of five, our spell's alive."

There was a tug in my gut. The cord shot up and wrapped around our hands, tying our wrists together. The cord bound us to each other so tight I couldn't pull away. It tied a knot under our hands then slid over my shoulder toward Emersyn. I watched it repeat the same knots around Em and Royce's hands. Their fingers definitely were not intertwined like ours. Tennessee's gaze tingled against my jaw. I turned back, letting myself have an excuse to stare at him.

Something happened whenever we were this close. The rest of the world always disappeared. Tennessee's lips moved, except I couldn't hear his words over the heavy thumping of my heart. My chest grew tight, like I wasn't breathing. Maybe I wasn't. I leaned into him until the tips of our noses brushed. I wanted to close my eyes and lose myself in the moment, but I knew there were too many witnesses in the room. Instead, I held his stare, memorizing every fleck of color in his mismatched eyes.

Cooper chanted something, but he was too far back for me to hear. The purple mist lightened until it was gone, like a vacuum sucking up powder. The white cord shimmered gold and radiated heat...and then it was *gone*. The crystals crashed to the hardwood floor.

"So...was that it?" Royce asked from behind me. "We done?"

Tennessee gasped and jumped back, without letting go of my hands. It was only then I realized just how close we'd been standing. A cold draft swept over me from the loss of his body heat. My head spun from lack of breathing. I blinked and waited for the world to right itself.

"Yeah, cousin. No big deal, right?" Deacon chuckled.

Tennessee squeezed my hands. He leaned forward and pressed a quick, soft kiss to my knuckles, then pulled back. His fingers slid out of my hold, and I almost whined in protest.

He cleared his throat and looked away from me. "We better keep moving."

WE FOUND Constance and Kenneth standing in the courtyard just outside the library.

Constance cleared her throat and smoothed the front of her white shirt down. "Come. You don't have time to waste." With that, she turned and led us across the courtyard.

No one asked where we were going. We knew. We may not have known where they were leading us, but we knew our destination. The Old Lands to find the Garden of Eden. It seemed wild that all of this was to find a book, even though I knew how valuable the Book of Shadows was. Bentley had told me himself before I left. He said the only way we could close the original Gap in Salem and fulfill the prophecy before Samhain was to find the Book. He wasn't sure what was in it that we needed. That part was on me. In the back of my mind, I kept wondering what spell I'd have to perform for Keltie. There was no tricking the Fae. I would have to come through on my promise, and it scared me more than I wanted to admit.

A loud bell chimed from nearby. Moments later, a horde of people practically ran out of every door in sight like a stampede. *Students.* They looked about my age, some younger, some older. They all laughed and talked with the people around them...until they spotted *us.* It was like everyone saw us at the exact same moment. A hush echoed through the crowd. In an instant, several hundred eyes were on me. I glanced left and right only to find the same slack-jawed expression. Eyes of every color widened. Fingers pointed. Mouths were covered.

Tennessee raised his right arm in the air and flexed his hand. The air warped around his fingers. It was subtle though. If I hadn't been looking, I would've missed it.

I frowned and looked around. I knew what he was doing. I knew what the hand-in-the-air thing meant. He was calling his sword, except I had no idea where it was. I hadn't seen it since I used it to slice open the garden door on the plane. Every time I asked someone how it worked, they just shrugged and said, "Tennessee isn't human. We stopped asking how."

I bit my lip and waited. A few seconds later, there was a swooshing sound as something shimmered through the clouds. His sword slammed into his right palm with a soft thud. All without him breaking his stride. He twirled the hilt around in his hand, like they were greeting each other.

And then I heard it.

Emperor. All around the crowd the word *Emperor* bounced in hushed voices.

I smiled and looked up at my soulmate. He marched in front of us, right alongside Kenneth and Constance. Right where he belonged. He stood tall, with his shoulders back and his head held high. His long black hair rustled in the mountain breeze. Pride bloomed inside me. I didn't understand why he didn't want to lead. He was *made* for it. It was natural for him.

"Okay, this is as far as we can take you." Constance stopped and turned toward us. She pointed behind her. "This is the path that will lead you to the Old Lands."

I frowned and followed her point. My stomached dropped. It was something straight out of a horror film. A black wrought iron gate separated the school grounds from the wilderness. The archway had runes etched into the metal in silver and gold. It loomed like a gate into Hell itself. Behind it, the path was only paved a few feet, then it disappeared into a cloud of fog. My mind flashed memories from the Gathering and sent my pulse into overdrive.

"Use your pendulum to guide you to the Banished One. May the Goddess be behind you, and the Heavens on your side." Kenneth placed one hand on Tennessee's shoulder and squeezed. He leaned in and whispered something so low only Tennessee could hear. Then he looked to the rest of us. "Remember, you were chosen for a reason. Stay together, stay strong."

CHAPTER TWENTY-TWO

TEGAN

I lost cell phone reception at quarter till four. My phone stopped working at two minutes after six. As in entirely refused to function. Couldn't slide it open to the home screen. Couldn't power it off. Couldn't turn on the flashlight. It was stuck. According to my phone, time just stopped. The sun kept dropping, but my clock remained the same.

The trees stood too tall to see the sun or the moon to track the time. Darkness fell upon us far too soon. The flashlights we packed were supposed to last for sixty hours, or something crazy like that. I kept telling myself that running out of battery was a product of the Old Land's ancient magic and *not* because we'd been walking that long. Without artificial lighting or the moon's guidance, we only had the glow of mine and

Tennessee's bodies. And we tried not to use it. We didn't know if our magic would be depleted faster there as well. We had to conserve everything.

Including our strength. My body ached in places I never knew could hurt. The bottoms of my feet burned and pleaded for me to sit down, to relieve the pressure. Everything around us looked the same. Part of me wondered if we were walking in a circle. The *only* thing that gave me hope that we hadn't already failed was the blueish-colored crystal dangling from Tennessee's fingers. Somehow the pendulum was its own light. It shined like a Christmas light in the dark.

It was difficult to see Tennessee with his black hair and all-black attire, although the same could be said about me. Unlike the rest of us, his steps made no noise. His breathing was calm and steady. He moved like a black leopard, a shadow in the dark. The purple crystal amulet in his dagger shimmered a subtle glow, but it barely stuck out of his boot enough to see. I knew his sword was gripped in his hand, but the black crystal hilt and black hematite blade were as invisible in the night as he was. For the first time since we met, I understood Emersyn's fear of him. He was elusive and dangerous, the perfect camouflaged weapon among shadows.

Without the binding spell, I wouldn't have known

he was there at all. That spell allowed me to feel my friends' presence without seeing them. I couldn't tell what they were feeling or thinking, thankfully. But I felt every step they took. If someone stopped for even a second, it tugged in my stomach. I gripped my mother's dagger in my right hand and held it at my side. My fingers itched with the need to pluck the other dagger from my thigh holster, but with that hand I held Chutney's.

I expected her to be terrified, but she was the most at ease. All around us, animals stirred and went on with their lives. We couldn't see them, but we heard them. The clawing of their nails against tree barks. The gnawing on leaves. The hissing. The growling. Every sound sent a chill down my spine.

Chutney squeezed my hand and stopped walking.

STOP. I whispered into my friends' minds. We froze in place as a unit with our weapons raised and ready for use. Chutney's magic allowed her to speak with animals, and she heard their thoughts in her mind. It didn't take long for us to realize why she was chosen. When she heard something coming near, she let me know by squeezing my hand, then I'd tell everyone else. That was how we chose to talk to reduce the evidence of our existence.

A large shimmering gold lion with wings on its back and talons on its feet stomped into our pathway.

Willow, now.

Willow was becoming a bigger asset with each animal interaction. She raised her hands just inside my peripheral vision, and the air around us sparkled like glass. I had no idea what she made the creature see, but it hissed and fled. Chutney tugged my hand and began walking again.

Continue, guys.

The path we were on wasn't so much a set path but slightly less wild than the rest. We ducked under branches and climbed over fallen trees or random roots. In the dark, I couldn't be sure what anything was. The pendulum swung in a leftward angle. We followed it around what appeared to be the biggest tree I'd ever seen in my life until everything around us flattened out. For the first time since we left Eden, we were on level ground with open air around us and a perfect crescent moon above. There was just enough light off the moon to see we'd found a clearing of some kind. It was a small circle, maybe thirty feet across, with trees lining the perimeter like skyscrapers.

Tennessee's pendulum spun in a circle.

Emersyn made a little whimper noise behind me. I knew what she was seeing. This was far, far too similar to the Gathering for my comfort. That night had been terrifying to live through, but looking back at it, knowing what I did now, only made it more frightening.

Are we here?

"Yes," Tennessee whispered.

Great. Now what? I asked on everyone's behalf.

Tennessee scowled and shoved the pendulum back in his front pocket. "We're supposed to find the Banished One here," he whispered back.

"I don't see anyone else." Willow clung to Chutney's arm.

"Doesn't mean we're alone." Tennessee narrowed his eyes on the edge of the clearing and walked forward.

A blast of hot energy hit my back. My eyes widened, and I stood tall. I glanced over my shoulder but found only darkness. We had no idea who or what the Banished One was, but it was here...and it was watching. Almost like it was waiting for something. But I had no idea what it would be waiting for—*unless...maybe it wants the crystal?*

I reached into the inside pocket of my leather jacket and pulled out the massive chunk of raw quartz crystal. Its energy tingled against my palm then shot up my arm.

Acting on an impulse I couldn't identify I walked to the edge of the clearing where I felt the heat coming from and knelt down. I set the crystal on the ground and nodded to the dark.

"Tegan, what are you doing?"

I don't know.

The darkness *moved.* That heat I felt intensified and slammed into my face. Without standing, I crept backward. Chutney gasped a split second before a massive pair of scarlet red eyes appeared from within the dark. Tennessee shouted something, but it was too late.

Something huge and black shot out from the trees and slammed right into my stomach. The wind was knocked out of me. Black spots danced in my vision. My back hit the dirt, and I slid across the clearing. There was yelling and shouting, except everything sounded fuzzy and faraway.

I clutched my stomach and rolled to my side, trying to get up and failing. My face smashed into cold dirt. I coughed and coughed until my throat burned and I gagged. I ran my hand under my shirt, sure I'd find a hole in my body and gallons of blood, except I found neither. I shook my head to clear the fuzziness, but it wasn't working. Everything seemed to be happening far away. I closed my eyes and summoned my magic. *Heal me. Heal me. Heal. Me.*

I opened my eyes and choked on a gasp. Standing between me and my Coven-mates was a twenty-foot dragon as black as night itself. Its wings stretched up and over its head, blocking my view of the moon above. It turned and whipped its tail through the clearing. Tennessee jumped over it like he was playing jump rope on the playground. Deacon tackled Emersyn to the ground just as the tail swept over their heads. I got up on my knees.

Royce yelled and waved his arms. A long branch jumped out from within the trees and wrapped itself around the dragon's tail. It thrashed and hissed. The three spikes on the end of his tail would slice through the tree in no time. We had to act fast. I just wasn't sure what we were supposed to do. Something told me killing the creature wasn't a good idea.

The dragon roared, and the ground trembled beneath us. I glanced at Tennessee. He was glowing and held both his weapons at the ready, but he wasn't using any magic. His eyes were locked on the beast.

He doesn't think we should kill it either. Except, if killing it wasn't the plan, then what was?

The dragon lowered its head. Smoke seeped out from its nostrils. My stomach rolled. I threw my hand up and pushed my magic out just as the creature spit a stream of fire right at my friends. The flames hit my magic and shot up to the sky. The dragon didn't notice its failure. It turned and spit stream after stream. I threw my energy into the center of its fire. I'd never tried to control fire like this, but I managed to force each of the flames away from my friends.

Tennessee's eyes widened. He dropped to his knees and crossed his arms over his face. A little tornado of wind wrapped around him, blocking the flames from touching him.

None of this mattered. The dragon just kept shooting. We were going to run out of energy long before it ran out of fire.

Emersyn growled like a lion and jumped to her feet. Her long blonde hair whipped around her pretty face. Her golden eyes burned like the sun. She leapt in front of the flames with a ferocious scowl on her face, and then she...*inhaled*. With her arms raised, my sister sucked in each and every flame. Once they were gone, she stepped forward and gave the dragon a taste of its own medicine. Fire shot out between her lips and slammed into the dragon's side.

The dragon jumped back and shook its head.

"STOP!" Chutney shrieked. She sprinted to the center of the clearing. Blood dripped down her forehead and her jeans were ripped at both knees, but her light blue eyes were wild. "Stop! Don't hurt him!"

"Don't hurt *him*?" Royce spun on her. "He just tried to cook us!"

Chutney's curls bounced as she ran up to Emersyn's side. "He doesn't mean to hurt us. Stop fighting him. Royce, release his tail!"

"Are you nuts?"

"It's not trying very hard to kill us, Royce. Think about it." Tennessee dropped his arms and stared up at the creature.

"Then what did you call all of *that*?" Royce snapped.

"A test." I climbed to my feet, still holding my stomach. "As usual, I'm never ready for them to start."

The dragon turned its bright lava-red eyes on me. He snorted and a puff of smoke left his nose. He tugged at the branch holding his tail, and it snapped like a piece of silly string, like it wasn't actually ever restraining him. He whipped his tail over our heads to the edge of the clearing. The three-spiked tip scooped me up and carried me to the center where my friends were. Tennessee's gaze scanned me up and down with a deep scowl.

I took a deep breath and smiled up at the dragon. "Thank you."

"*See*," Chutney snapped. She moved to stand right in front of the dragon. "I'm Chutney of The Coven. A prophecy from the Goddess requires us to seek the chalice inside the Garden of Eden."

No one else moved or said a word. We all watched silently while our Fool talked to it.

Chutney nodded but then her eyes widened. She blinked. Before we could ask, two glowing orbs the size of basketballs appeared at the dragon's feet. One was sea green, the other sky blue. *Kinda like Tennessee's eyes.* The orbs hovered above the dirt. A cold chill slithered down my spine and I shivered. This wasn't good. I knew enough to know this dragon was presenting us with a choice.

"Chutney." Tennessee's warm, silky voice broke through the silence. "What is going on?"

Chutney cleared her throat. "He says he had to test us to make sure we were worthy. Now that we've passed, he can offer us a ride to the entrance of the Garden of Eden."

"At what cost?" Deacon asked with a frown. His purple eyes were narrowed on the orbs.

Of course the Devil knows there's a cost. That almost made me smile.

"A choice." Chutney took a deep breath. "Choose an orb, or we have to turn around and go home. And please, don't make me explain what will happen if we refuse an orb."

Tennessee nodded. He moved forward until he stood right beside Chutney. "What does each orb offer?"

"The blue grants us safe passage to the Garden of Eden and back out of the Old Lands. But once we step back into the world, memories will be stripped from each of us. There will be no warning, and no choosing which to give. They will just be *gone*." She shuddered. "The green one severs our binding spell and nothing else."

CHAPTER TWENTY-THREE

TEGAN

My heart sank. What a choice to make. The blue one would almost guarantee everyone returned home alive and well, but at the cost of memories. I thought back to all the books I'd ever read where memories were taken as tokens... All of the memories were significant ones. It wasn't like giving up bad ones. Hell, it wasn't like choosing what you could stand to lose. But the whole reason we did the binding spell was because of how easy it was to get lost.

"Okay." Tennessee's voice was calm and steady. He nodded then stepped forward and snatched the green orb out of the air.

I sighed with relief. If there had been a debate, I wasn't sure how the outcome would've looked. I wanted everyone to survive the quest. Of course I did. But there was *nothing* in the world I'd ever sacrifice my memories for. It wasn't about the magic or the powers. It was about the people. I'd only just gotten my mother, sister, and older brother. I didn't want to lose them.

I refused to lose Tennessee.

"DUDE."

"What the hell, man?"

"Tenn, you didn't even ask us!"

Tennessee turned back to face us with his head held high, but his eyes were dark. "None of you know what it's like to live without your memories. I do, and I wouldn't wish it on my worst enemy. I would rather die than sacrifice my memories of you."

His eyes met mine, and warmth spread through me faster than a wildfire. I held his stare and nodded. *Me too,* I said to only him. There was so much more I wanted to say, except there were too many eyes watching us.

Cooper pushed past me. He walked up to Tennessee and squeezed his shoulder. "We'll just have to take extra good care of each other until we get home."

The dragon dropped down to its belly.

"Okay, he says to climb on his back and he'll fly us down." Chutney bounced forward and stepped onto the dragon's tail. He raised it up for her to slide into the spot right behind his head, between two massive spikes. "Come on. Load up."

"Shotgun!" Willow yelled and sprinted forward. She used his tail to get on.

Royce sighed and walked up to the dragon, then glanced over his shoulder. "Hey, Superman and Super-girl, you two get the back."

Tennessee shook his head and laughed. "Fine."

Emersyn climbed on behind Royce, with Deacon and Cooper in line behind her. I walked up to the dragon then stepped onto his tail. I rode up then climbed into the small space behind Cooper, in between two spikes. It was a tight squeeze, but at least I'd be secure. I didn't know what I expected a dragon's back to feel like, but I was surprised to find it was a lot like riding a horse bareback. The spikes were cool to the touch and smooth like stones. Up close, his scales were soft like raw silk and the purest black I'd ever seen. There wasn't even a hint of another color in there. If I could've bottled it, I would've painted my entire house with it.

In my peripheral vision, Tennessee rode the tail up and slid into the space behind me.

"Okay, hold on! We're taking off now," Chutney yelled from up front. "He says he flies uber fast, so don't freak out."

The dragon flapped its wings, and we rose into the air. It was at that moment I wondered how he was going to take off in such a small space. He flapped his wings over and over until we were at least twenty feet above ground, and then he shot straight up into the sky. I gasped. Willow screamed. The world passed by in a gray blur. In the flash of a second, we were soaring above the pine trees and cruising through the mountains.

Tennessee's hands landed on my hips and pulled. My back slammed into his chest. I exhaled in surprise, but then his arms wrapped around my waist and all of my concerns disappeared. I smiled and sank into him, letting the heat of his body burn away all of my fears. The smell of freshly fallen rain filled my nose and I sighed.

His lips brushed against my ear. "I couldn't risk losing you."

Goose bumps spread across my body. My pulse skyrocketed. I licked my lips and looked up at our friends, but they were all white-knuckle gripping the dragon's spikes so they weren't paying any attention to us.

I smiled and grabbed his forearms, then squeezed. "Me either," I whispered back.

He sighed then dropped his face to the crook of my neck and kissed my throat. I slid my hands into his and held on. The view beneath us was gorgeous and breathtaking. I meant to watch...but Tennessee had never held me like this before, like we were an actual couple. I closed my eyes and let myself enjoy the heat of his skin and the strength in his arms.

"Hold on! We're landing!"

I groaned and squeezed Tennessee hard enough to leave a bruise. It was too soon, too fast. I needed more of this moment, of the peace it provided.

"Tegan, *look*," Tennessee whispered in my ear.

At his urging, I opened my eyes. It may have been summer in the real world, but in the Old Lands, the mountainside was a sea of deep reds and oranges. The sky was a vibrant blue despite the heavy fog. The lower we dropped in between two mountains, the thicker the fog got.

"Wait, why is it daylight?" I asked.

Tennessee chuckled and it vibrated against my back. "I have no idea. I guess the Old Lands like sunshine better?"

Weird. I braced myself for my ears to pop, but it never came. As soon as the dragon landed, cold air brushed over my back. I frowned and looked around. Tennessee stood on the ground. He raised his left hand in the air, and his dagger flew out of his boot and into his open palm. He nodded then tucked it back in his shoe. He lifted his right hand and smiled up at us. I threw my leg over the dragon's spine and slid down his scales until my boots hit the dirt with a thud. There was a soft whooshing sound, and then Tennessee's sword was in his hand.

He shrugged. "Wasn't sure if that would still work down here."

I rolled my eyes and smiled. *You and your tricks.*

I distracted myself from the heat in his eyes by surveying the world around us. It was beautiful. The trees towered over us in all their colorful glory. I was half tempted to pluck a few red leaves to bring home, but I figured that was a horrible idea in the Old Lands so I stuck my hands in my jacket pockets to resist the urge. The grass below my feet was thick and soft, the perfect lawn for cloud gazing.

"Chutney, ask your dragon friend where we go from here," Cooper said without turning around to look at either of them.

"Dragon friend?" Chutney shook her head and crossed her arms. "He has a name."

I frowned and looked up at our new friend. "How rude of us for not asking. I'm sorry. What is your name?"

Chutney giggled, which seemed a weird response to my question.

The dragon curled its wings in and rolled his shoulders. A shadow swirled around him like a tornado. When it vanished, a man stood in the dragon's place. Well, not a man. He looked to be about our age. He wore nothing but low-slung black jeans and some kind of charm on a necklace. He had short jet-black hair and sapphire blue eyes. Actually, he looked kind of like Royce with the most epic deep tan ever.

The guy smirked and waved. "Hello, I'm Lonan."

"Oh my God, you're a human!" Emersyn's jaw dropped.

"Well, no more than you, Empress," Lonan said with a wink.

Royce mumbled a string of gibberish mixed with curse words.

"You know who we are?" I asked.

"Yes and no, High Priestess." He walked forward until he was in front of us. Then he turned back around. "May I just say, Empress, that was badass. I've seen all kinds of tricks from witches, but never has someone spit my fire back at me."

Emersyn blushed bright red. "Thanks?"

Lonan laughed and shook his head. "To answer your question, Emperor, your magic will work exactly the same here. Only the human technology and such does not."

"Wait, wait." Cooper waved his hands. "How do you know who we are but we didn't know shifters even existed?"

Lonan frowned and stared off into the distance.

"Perhaps if you survive this quest, we can discuss all of this, as friends would. For now, just know I am far from the only shifter in the world, though I am one of a few who know of your existence."

Tennessee nodded. "*When* we survive this, we'll talk. Thanks for your help in the meantime."

"You're welcome. We're on the same team after all." Lonan began walking backwards. "Now come. The Garden of Eden awaits you."

He led us into the thin space between two stone cliffs. No one spoke. To my surprise, the dark pathway was only ten feet long. The tunnel opened up into another clearing, this one surrounded only by stone slates that were part of the mountain. The light in the clearing was darker, like the soft reddish glow of the setting sun. A soft fog lingered in the air.

I stepped forward, and something cracked under my boots. I frowned and looked down, then gasped. The ground was littered with dead leaves...and human bones. I spun in circles, but everywhere I looked, I found more and more bones.

I cleared my throat. "Um, guys...do you see what I see?"

"Where *are* we?" Emersyn asked in a soft voice.

"This is the entrance to the Garden of Eden." Lonan gestured ahead of us. "It's right through there."

I followed his point, and my jaw dropped. A waterfall about ten feet wide fell straight out of the sky. There was no pool at the bottom, though. There wasn't even water. It just disappeared into the ground. I moved forward until it was right in front of me, but even with squinting my eyes, I couldn't see beyond it.

"These bones are witches," Tennessee said from close behind me.

I glanced back and looked to where he pointed with his sword. "How do you know?"

"The weapons have our runes carved into them."

"Not everyone is worthy of entering." Lonan sighed. "You aren't the first group of witches to try, but you *are* the first to choose the correct orb."

Royce gasped. "Wait, we chose correctly?"

Lonan narrowed his eyes. "Well, *he* chose correctly. You see, there is no arguing here. Only the worthy may enter. But if the worthy are bound within a binding spell and still choose to go in...well, the rest of those they're bound to die. Instantly. What you're seeing here are the witches who chose to sacrifice themselves so that their worthy counterparts could enter."

Everyone turned wide eyes to Tennessee.

He scratched the back of his neck. A soft blush covered his cheeks. "I did not know that."

Cooper shook his head. His green eyes stared at a

skull right in front of his feet. "Yet you always lead us the right way."

"All right, well, it's time I leave." Lonan stepped back and stretched his arms. "Good luck. If you manage to make it to the ledge...look for me. I'll fly you back to Eden. If not, well then, I'll see you on the other side someday."

Without another word, he squatted down then jumped straight into the air. Black wings shot out of his back. In a dark flash, he was back in his dragon form and flying away from us. We all watched in silence until Lonan was out of sight...then reality set back in.

"We made it to the Garden of Eden," I whispered. I turned to face the waterfall with a knot in my stomach. "Now how do we find out who's worthy of entering?"

"I tell you," an unfamiliar male voice said from out of nowhere.

CHAPTER TWENTY-FOUR

TEGAN

I gasped and jumped back. A man shimmered into existence right in front of me, or at least I assumed it was a man. He was taller than Uncle Kessler's six foot five. His eyes were white and surrounded by gold irises. He had some kind of metallic material wrapped around his hips. But none of that was what captured my attention. He was completely covered in a vine-like tattoo. Over his bald head and down all of his limbs. My eyes widened. While I watched, the vines changed colors and moved like they were alive. Directly over his heart on his chest was a huge crystal-looking mark that sparkled like it was three dimensional.

I've seen that before.

Unable to stop myself, I glanced up at Tennessee. His eyes were already on mine.

"Who...who are you?" Emersyn asked in a soft voice.

I peeled my eyes off my soulmate and returned my attention to the unknown man. He cocked his head to the side and arched one eyebrow. Wings as white as snow shot out from his back. They had to be six feet long. They looked soft. I had the ridiculous urge to touch them.

"You are an Angel." Tennessee's voice was reverent and gentle.

"I am Gabriel." He smiled, and it seemed genuinely kind. "The messenger."

I bowed my head. It seemed the appropriate way to greet an Angel. "It is an honor to meet you, Gabriel. I am Tegan Bishop."

"Thank you, although I know who you all are."

"You do?"

He didn't smile any more than he was, but his eyes twinkled a little brighter. "The creator sees and knows all. Let us not delay your quest. You are at the entrance to the Garden of Eden. Please, speak your intentions."

I glanced around at my friends, but they all looked to me, even Tennessee. *Well, I am the High Priestess.* I licked my lips and took a deep breath. "We are seeking our lost Book of Shadows. Inside it are the answers we require to finally close the gaps in our dimension. We were given a prophecy by the Goddess that says 'Where only Eden and the chalice knows,' which we have reason to believe means *the* holy chalice."

Gabriel nodded. He crossed his arms over his chest. "Your Book of Shadows was not lost."

A chorus of gasps and mumblings sounded behind me, but I ignored them.

"I'm afraid I do not understand."

"It was not lost. It was taken by Heaven because your species no longer deserved it." He narrowed his eyes and looked to each of us, as though challenging us to disagree. "Your ancestors became too dangerous with what they did in Salem, and to that innocent tribe not far from here. So we took it. Since then, many have tried, but none have been worthy of reclaiming it. Now it is your turn to try."

I bit down on my lip to stop myself from asking too many questions. The last thing I wanted to do was offend an Angel of Heaven. Except we needed to know how to reclaim it.

"*How* you reclaim it, young High Priestess, has already been told to you in your prophecy." He waved his hand in the air, and the words of our prophecy appeared in glowing gold letters. "This does not lead you to the Book's location, but the path to prove that you deserve it. Succeed on this quest, and I shall return the Book to you."

"That sounds fair and reasonable." I took a deep breath, then pointed to the waterfall. "We have to start with the chalice which is inside the Garden, correct?"

He nodded.

"Okay, so let's go find it." Willow took a step forward, with Chutney right on her heels.

"Stop." Gabriel stepped in front of them. "An Angel of the land must grant you entrance with a token."

"But we don't have any tokens," Willow said in a small voice. "Do we?"

Cooper shook his head. "How can we get tokens?"

Gabriel shook his head. "You cannot. You are not worthy."

My heart sank. Had we gone all this way just to be rejected at the door? I couldn't fathom the idea that the Goddess wouldn't have seen that we weren't worthy. There had to be something we missed. I gnawed on my bottom lip.

"Excuse me, Gabriel." Emersyn raised her hand. "If we leave here today and come back with a token, will we be permitted then?"

"Technically, yes. But as your High Priestess was just thinking, your Goddess wouldn't have sent you here if none of you were worthy." He turned to look me straight in the eye. "You and your Emperor may continue on to the chalice."

My Emperor? What does that mean? Does he know? Wait, he said what I was just thinking? Can he hear my thoughts? But then his words registered.

"Wait, we can go in?" I looked up to Tennessee to see if I'd heard that correctly.

Tennessee's jaw was slack. He stared at the Angel a moment then shook his head. "I'm sorry, Gabriel. I mean no disrespect, but why are Tegan and I worthy but not the others?"

The Angel shrugged, a small smirk on his face. "Ask my brother Leyka."

My eyes widened. "Leyka?" *What? How? I don't understand.*

Gabriel walked up to the two of us and waved his hand. Both mine and Tennessee's left hands rose up. Gabriel waved his fingers over the backs of our hands. Our skin shimmered with golden dust then darkened until it was black. I gasped and pulled my hand back to get a closer look. There on my skin was a lotus flower outlined in black. *What?*

"Your tokens." Gabriel stepped back to stand beside the waterfall. "You must enter now. Your friends and your belongings will have to wait here for your return."

"Thank you." Tennessee turned and walked over to Cooper. He handed his sword to my brother, then plucked his dagger from his boot and gave that over too.

Next he reached into his pockets and turned over his cell phone. He froze, then pulled George out of his pocket. He turned to Emersyn. "Empress, please hold on to this."

Her golden eyes were wide as she nodded. "Of course."

I took a deep breath and unstrapped both dagger holsters from my thighs. I shoved them in the inside pockets of my leather jacket. The idea of handing over the Tarot deck made my skin crawl, but if Tennessee could let go of George, then I could do the same.

I slid my leather jacket off and held it out for my sister. "Watch this?"

Emersyn gripped the jacket. "You're coming back for this."

"Of course," I promised my twin.

What can go wrong in the Garden of Eden?

CHAPTER TWENTY-FIVE

TENNESSEE

I t took everything inside me not to take Tegan by the hand to walk through the waterfall and into the Garden of Eden. Cooper was watching. Everyone was watching, even the Angel Gabriel. *Who might be listening to this right now.* After everything she and I had been through already, there was no way I could hold her hand and have it look natural. But then I remembered why we did the binding spell in the first place. If there was even the slightest chance we could be separated going through the waterfall, I didn't want to risk it.

I looked down and found her gnawing on her bottom lip. It seemed to be a new nervous tick of hers. I held my elbow out and smiled. "Ready?"

A light blush touched her cheeks. She smirked then slid her hand into the crook of my elbow, then looked up into my eyes and nodded. "Ready."

I moved to the edge of the waterfall. Water droplets splashed onto my face.

One, she said in my mind.

Two.

Three.

Without hesitating another second, I stepped into the waterfall. The moment the water touched us, Tegan gripped my arm with her other hand. I reached over and covered both of hers with mine. Then the water was gone. I looked down to dry our clothes only to discover we weren't wet.

"We're *in* the Garden of Eden."

I nodded and looked around. I hadn't put much thought into what it might look like, but it definitely wouldn't have been what I saw before me. The ground beneath our feet was light gray cobblestone. The pathway cut through white sand that stretched on in both directions as far as I could see. The sky was such a faint blue it looked white. Up ahead, the cobblestones turned into a small set of stairs. At the top, a chalice sat sparkling like glitter.

We raced forward, all but sprinting up the stairs. When we got to the chalice, Tegan dropped my arm and took the holy cup between her two palms. She moved it around, inspecting every side. It was the most extravagant thing I'd ever seen. The gold metal was speckled like glitter and sparkled like a disco ball. All over the chalice were little crystals in all kinds of bright rainbow colors. It was exactly the kind of thing a person would picture in their mind for a holy chalice.

I frowned. It was a little too perfect. Too obvious. I glanced around us again. There was nothing but us, the chalice, and the entrance a few feet back. Could it really have been that easy? Was the only issue a matter of being worthy enough to enter? It didn't make any sense. If there was anything I'd learned in my life as Emperor, it was if something seemed too easy, then it usually wasn't over.

"This can't be it," Tegan said.

I sighed with relief. I loved when we were on the same page. It confirmed what I was already feeling. "It can't be this easy."

"You're right. It's not." Gabriel appeared in front of us, on the other side of the glittery chalice. "Very well done. You will find many chalices within the Garden, but only one is holy."

Tegan set the chalice down on the stone pedestal. "How will we know?"

Gabriel raised both hands then pressed a finger to our chests, directly above the crystal in our glyph. "This is your guide."

I opened my mouth then shut it again. There was

too much to say, yet nothing at the same time. An Angel telling me to follow my heart was both predictable *and* surprising.

Gabriel dropped his hands and stepped to the side of the pedestal. "Nothing here will harm you, unless you drink from the wrong chalice. Good luck. Heaven is with you."

And then he was gone. I looked back to the waterfall to get a glimpse of our friends, but nothing was visible through it. When I turned back, my jaw dropped. Gone was the white desert and blank sky. In its place was...paradise, of every kind. Everywhere I looked, there was something to see. Sprawling mountains with high peaks and waterfalls gushing from their sides. Luscious green grass and trees of every shape and size. In the distance, I spotted lakes with glass-like surfaces reflecting the white puffy clouds above. There were spots of color and light. I wanted to discover all of it.

"Well, shall we follow the yellow brick road?" Tegan asked.

I smiled and looked down at my soulmate. It was unreal to think that we were together in the Garden of Eden. Alone. Where humankind began. The holy land. Pride swelled inside me. I didn't understand why or how Leyka had decided we were worthy, but all the worry over my oath to him disappeared. *Well, mostly.*

"Tennessee?"

I blinked and shook my head. "Sorry. Yes, let's do this." Then I did the thing I'd been dying to do for weeks —I reached down and took her hand in mine.

We walked along the cobblestone pathway until it turned into bright green grass. I resisted the urge to take my shoes off. Barely. Birds chirped in delight as they flew over our heads. Rabbits and squirrels chased each other across our path. Butterflies fluttered around my face. The warmth of the sun on my skin was soothing while not being too oppressive.

Everything around me was absolutely beautiful, but I couldn't keep my eyes off Tegan. I didn't know if it was knowing we were truly alone and the freedom in that that made her more breathtaking than I'd ever seen...or if the Garden's sunshine made her skin glow a little warmer and her eyes sparkle a little brighter. Or maybe it was both. Maybe I just hadn't let myself truly look at her for a while. We walked in silence, hand in hand.

It was the weirdest thing...but it was comfortable silence. Pleasant. I didn't feel any pressure to think of something to say to her. I wasn't worrying what she might say to me. We just walked together, watching the Garden around us. Well, at least she did, I mostly watched *her*. I couldn't help myself. The smile on her face was too wide, the flush in her cheeks too pink.

If there were chalices around, I didn't see them.

Then she stopped. She stepped up to me and rested her chin on my chest then batted her long dark eyelashes. It was adorably distracting. "I said, we've reached a fork in the road."

I smiled and kissed her forehead. But then her words registered. I pulled back and frowned. Sure enough, just behind her head I spotted an intersection of sorts. Off to the left, the grass faded into golden sand with soft ocean waves rolling onto the shore. To the right, there was an intricate archway made of limestone that was covered in flowery vines, and beyond it a thriving garden of vibrant flowers beckoned us in. Up the center, the path disappeared between the trees and led into the tall mountains basking in the sunlight. Each option looked inviting.

"What do you think, High Priestess?"

"The beach. It seems the best place to look for a chalice. We both have water gifts. We both worked with Leyka and Keltie near water. Plus, it's where I feel strongest."

"Then let's go that way."

"But what do you think?"

"That you're brilliant." I shrugged. "Your reasoning is logical and exactly what I would've said."

She smiled and shook her head. Her long black hair blew in the wind behind her like a cape. I tightened my grip on her hand and led her toward the ocean. The truth was, the water *was* both our elements. More so than any of the others. I, too, felt my strongest near it. Especially the ocean. The salty air and rhythmic pulse of the waves soothed me more than I could ever put into words. And the Garden of Eden's beach did not disappoint.

The white sand was soft and powdery. The water was calm, with only small waves rolling into the shore. I'd seen many oceans in my short life, but I'd never seen the colors that vibrant. At the shore, it was almost entirely transparent, with just a hint of green. The Caribbean had taught me why it was called sea green, but this was definitely the birth of the name. There was aqua, then turquoise, then the richest blue I'd ever seen.

Tegan giggled beside me.

I looked down. "What's so funny?"

"Nothing. It's just..." Her cheeks flushed a deep pink. "Your eyes are like this ocean. The most beautiful sea green and the most breathtaking ocean blue. Just like that."

"Tegan..." My cheeks turned warm, and I knew I was blushing. I'd been complimented many times by girls, and guys, but only she had the ability to make me blush.

She shrugged. Then her eyes widened and her jaw

dropped. She pointed out into the water. "Look, a chalice!"

I followed her point, and sure enough, she was right. A white chalice floated on the ocean's surface, blending in with the breaking waves. "Nice call."

We raced ahead without letting go of each other's hands. I didn't stop to take my shoes or clothes off, and neither did she. We'd both be able to dry ourselves on command. The water was the perfect temperature, cool enough to be refreshing but warm enough to be enjoyable. It almost made me want to stop and appreciate it. Almost. When we got up to the chalice, I discovered it wasn't floating at all. There was a stone pillar holding it in place. The chalice itself was made entirely of white seashells.

I reached out and picked it up. And felt *nothing*. I frowned.

"What's wrong?" Tegan whispered against my shoulder.

"I just... Shouldn't I feel something when I hold the holy chalice of the heavens? The Goddess created an entire species out of *this* and yet—"

"I know. That's what I keep thinking. It may not be a witch's tool, but there should be an aura, some energy transferred upon holding it. We should feel..." She closed her mouth and stood up tall. "Oh my God. That's it. We should be *feeling* our way through this."

I looked down at the chalice with the ocean rolling under it. "We've been thinking our way through this. We *thought* the ocean was a good idea for a list of reasons, yet none of them were a feeling." I cursed and set it back down.

"We need to relax. We need to take a step back to reset. We're not acting like ourselves."

"Exactly. Relax." I nodded and stared out at the horizon. If there was ever a place to chill out, we were in it. We needed to relax. To stop thinking. Stop stressing. Just let the ocean smooth everything out. I took a few deep breaths, but it wasn't helping. I rolled my shoulders and wiggled my fingers. *Relax. Just relax. I'm relaxing. I'm not thinking about this quest.*

Something smacked into the backs of my legs and swept my feet out from under me. I flew back and dropped under the water. It wasn't easy to catch me off guard. I stuck my feet into the sand and pushed out of the water. My weapons were back outside the entrance, but I had my fists and magic. I raised my hands, ready to fight, except there was nothing in sight.

A wave of water crashed onto me like a miniature tidal wave. *What?* I stumbled back a step, though only from surprise. A warm current slid between my legs and wrapped around my ankles. I frowned and kicked my legs. *What is that?* I hadn't expected to be attacked inside the Garden of Eden. Gabriel said nothing would harm us.

Something moved in my peripheral vision. I spun around and was splashed in the face with water.

Tegan giggled and it sounded a little evil. "I don't think I've ever seen you look so confused."

"I don't think I've ever seen you smile that wide," I whispered before I could stop myself.

If possible, her smile widened. She stared out at the now setting sun. Her black hair was the only dark spot in a world of vibrant colors. "Being alone with you soothes me. I love it."

"I love *you*." I slammed my mouth shut. *Oh God. I did it.* I said those three little words.

Tegan spun around so fast her hair wrapped around and smacked her in the face. She didn't notice. Her light green eyes were wide and staring up at me.

Oh God. My stomach turned.

It was too late. There was no taking them back. I loved her, and now she knew. *What if she doesn't feel it back yet? What if it was too soon?*

She opened her mouth, and I stopped breathing.

CHAPTER TWENTY-SIX

TEGAN

Did he just say that? Or did I imagine it? I hadn't expected him to say it. Of course I loved him, too. I'd already come to terms with that after the plane crash. But what if that wasn't what he said, and I made things weird by saying it? I needed to be sure. He was a private person.

"Say it again," I whispered. I held my breath and waited. His long black waves flapped in the breeze. My fingers itched to touch the silky strands.

He closed the distance between us then cupped my face with his hands. He leaned down. His ocean-colored eyes twinkled. "I love you."

Tears pooled in my eyes. My heart thundered in my chest like it was going to explode. I swallowed through a lump of emotion in my throat. The heat of his skin against my face lit my body on fire. "I love you, too."

The smile he gave me took my breath away. His eyes sparkled like diamonds. He sighed. "You don't know how long I've wanted to say that."

My jaw burned from grinning. "I might be able to guess."

I grabbed a fistful of his shirt and pulled myself up until his lips crashed into mine. He tightened his hold on my face. My body went into sensory overdrive. All I knew was *him*. The smell of fresh rain. The taste of salt-water on his lips. The sound of our ragged breathing. The feel of his fingers pressing into my skin. Even with my eyes squeezed shut, my mind replayed the look on his face when I said the words.

He slid one hand back and fisted my hair, angling my face up to deepen our kiss. His tongue brushed against mine, and I melted into him. I wasn't sure what the noises leaving my throat were, but I was helpless to stop them. I just needed more of him, and I needed him closer.

His words echoed in my head. *I love you. I love you.*

I pushed his shirt up, breaking our kiss long enough to pull it over his head. There was a flash of tanned skin pulled tight over muscles that I wanted to ogle, but he gripped my waist and dragged my lips back to his.

I sighed against his mouth and wrapped my arms around his neck. We stumbled and moved through the water, though I couldn't have said which way. Water splashed us. Waves rolled against our legs. We paid no attention. All I knew was *him.* He slid his hands in a scorching hot path down my sides and then slipped *under* my shirt. I gasped. Something cold brushed over my face, but I ignored it. His hands on my bare skin were the hot lava to the volcanic eruption threatening inside me. I hadn't realized we'd moved until my back slammed into something hard. I bit down on his bottom lip and groaned in pain.

He pulled away to look at what we'd hit, then shrugged. "Just the pedestal."

"Oh," I said with a nod. As long as it wasn't a demon or dangerous animal, I didn't care. I grabbed onto the vintage key hanging from his leather cord necklace and pulled him back to me.

But instead of kissing me, he pressed his forehead to mine and sighed. "Tegan, we— Wait, what's that?"

I frowned and leaned back, only to find his eyes locked on my chest. When I looked, I discovered I stood only in my bra. That something cold must've been my shirt. Heat bloomed in my cheeks. I chuckled. *Why does he look so confused?* "Um, they're called...?"

"What?" He scowled and looked farther down. His cheeks turned bright red, and he looked away, shaking his head. A small chuckle left his lips. "No. No, not *those*."

That shouldn't have disappointed me. *Wait, then what is he looking at?* I looked down at my chest. At first I didn't see anything different. My soulmate glyph looked like ink against my fair skin, stretching all the way to my right shoulder now. The pink heart-like crystal in the middle of my chest pulsed like it usually did when he was near.

Wait. That was definitely not normal. It flashed neon pink, echoing my heartbeat. But then it *moved*. After lighting up the center, it rolled over to my shoulder like a wave crashing on the beach. It repeated the pattern.

Tennessee's tan fingers came into view as he ran them along the glyph lines. "Doesn't feel any different, does it?"

"Only when you touch me," I whispered. Goose bumps that had nothing to do with the flashing glyph spread across my bare skin.

He chuckled then tapped under my chin.

I opened my mouth to say something I shouldn't have when I realized his glyph was doing the same thing. "Tenn, *look*. It's the same."

He looked down at his own chest and frowned. "It's

not the same, though. Mine is flashing from my shoulder to the crystal, and yours is going the other way."

My eyes widened. He was right. Our glyphs were both flashing the same neon pink color in the same direction, yet in opposite directions from each other's. "What does it mean?"

"Tegan…" Tennessee gripped my elbows. "It's *guiding* us."

CHAPTER TWENTY-SEVEN

TENNESSEE

I'm such an idiot.

Of course Gabriel hadn't meant to follow our hearts. I rolled my eyes at my own stupidity. Even when he said it, I thought it sounded like a weird thing for him to say. I should've listened to my own instincts. I should've thought about his word choices. He wasn't being sentimental or cheesy. He was literally telling us how to find the holy chalice. *By following our glyphs.*

I ran my fingers over her skin. "Look at the way these are flashing, like neon arrows."

Her eyes widened. "You think they'll lead us to the chalice?"

I shrugged. "I think I know why Leyka chose us."

She spun around so she was facing the same direction as me, then looked down at her chest. Sure enough, the flashing switched directions and matched mine. She ran her hand over her chest, and I looked away.

*Um, they're called...*Warmth filled my cheeks again just thinking about that. I hadn't been looking. I hadn't. But now it only made me *want* to, like being told not to push the red button. I cleared my throat. *Focus, Tenn.*

"It's leading us off the beach?"

I held my hand out and summoned a current to carry both our shirts back to my hand. "Let's follow it and see." I slid my free hand into hers and led the way toward shore.

The water didn't slow us down like it would've with other people. It made me weirdly happy that Tegan and I shared it as our elemental magic gifts. Sure, we also shared Earth and Air, but there was something different about Water. Maybe because it was a force of its own, too.

When my feet hit dry sand, I stopped and looked down to my chest. That neon pink light flashed from my shoulder to my chest. I tucked our shirts into the waistband of my jeans and pulled Tegan to our left. Down the shoreline a bit, the world kind of vanished. Either the Garden of Eden ended there, or we somehow would have to go *down*, though both seemed equally unlikely.

"Are you holding my shirt ransom?"

I frowned and glanced over my shoulder as we

walked. "What? No. Why— *Oh*. Um." I probably should've given hers back to her, but I was preoccupied.

Tegan chuckled. "It's okay. You can admit it. You like seeing me in just a bra."

I gasped and froze. "No. Tegan, that's not—"

She interrupted me with a kiss. When she pulled back, her eyes twinkled mischievously. "Gotcha. Come on, let's follow our love light." She winked and tugged me along.

We walked in silence, with only the soft crashing waves beside us. At first glance, the drop-off had seemed far down the beach, but we reached the edge in only a few minutes. Either my depth perception was off or...*something*. I shook those thoughts away and frowned. In front of us was nothing but white, puffy clouds and what appeared to be a spiral staircase, though I could only see the first few steps. After what we pulled with the plane, we probably could've walked *on* the clouds, but the light on my glyph rolled in a downward motion.

One of the things I loved the most about Tegan was her bravery. She'd narrowed her eyes in suspicion of the suspect staircase, yet she said nothing. She knew we had to follow our guide, so there wasn't much sense in complaining. The stairs were made of a light gray, smooth stone that matched the walls which closed us in.

It seemed like we descended in a dozen circles before a flat surface finally found us again. My first instinct was to peek at my glyph, but then I realized there was only one path. Straight ahead.

There was some kind of haze or mist blocking my view, so I had no idea what we were heading into. It was unnerving, but then again most of my life was. I swallowed through a rush of nerves then led us forward. With every step, the stones under our feet grew paler and softer until they were nothing but powder, or sand. The stone walls smoothed. We followed the path around a corner and I paused.

Somehow we were at the bottom of a canyon. The walls and ground were the same shade of orangeish clay. I reached out and dragged my fingers along the walls. They were warm and soft, yet unyielding. The valley we were in was more like a trench. The sky was so far above us it was only a sliver of blue. The canyon walls swooped low and stuck out over the pathway. In a few places, we had to duck down.

I had no idea how long we'd been in the canyon trench, but when it finally opened back up, the sky had darkened. To our right, stars twinkled against a navy-blue sky. The moon was full and shining its light down through tree branches. To our left, the ocean was calm and flat, only the tiniest ripple of waves. The sun hung low, half sunken beneath the horizon. The sky around it...took my breath away. All I could do was stare. Every shade of orange, pink, and purple swirled together in perfect harmony.

"Wow," Tegan whispered. "I wish I could take a picture of that."

I nodded. It was a good thing Gabriel made us leave our cell phones, or otherwise I wouldn't have been able to resist the urge.

Pride swelled in my chest. Tegan and I were chosen to be here, in the Garden of Eden, witnessing the most beautiful sunset in the world. I didn't know what we did to deserve it, but I was thankful. Tegan sighed and leaned against my arm. My body filled with warmth, like sitting in front of a fireplace on a cold winter's night. I felt lightweight, like I could float away from all of my stress and problems. I wanted to sit right here forever.

I gasped and shook myself. I blinked over and over until whatever haze had washed over me vanished. I looked down at Tegan still leaning into me. Her eyes were half closed, and there was a small, satisfied smile on her face. Her chest rose and fell softly. I pressed my fingers to her throat. Her pulse was so soft it took me several seconds to even find it. Meanwhile, her eyes stayed locked on the setting sun. My pulse quickened. I had no idea what was happening, but I knew I had to

260

stop it. I wanted to use my magic to snap her out of it, except I wasn't sure what could be trusted to use. Her eyes closed a little farther, and panic surged inside me. I did the only thing I could think of.

I kissed her.

Sparks of electricity shot through my body, tingling down my limbs. Tegan gasped and jumped back. Her green eyes were wild and bright. A swirl of rainbow mist coiled around her fingers. She glanced around, looking for a threat.

Finally, her gaze found mine. "What the hell just happened?"

I raised my palms. "I have no idea. Some kind of ancient magic."

She frowned and pointed to her left. "That sunset?"

"Let's not look at it anymore, okay?"

"Agreed." She licked her lips and tucked her hair behind her ears. The golden cuffs Keltie gave her glistened as bright as the sun. "Never thought I'd fear the ocean over the forest."

I frowned and looked down at the glyph on her chest. With the setting sun, her fair skin was the same soft rosy pink as Cassandra's favorite glass of wine. I smiled at the memory, but then forced myself to concentrate. The vines of the glyph etched into Tegan's skin illuminated from the center crystal out to her delicate shoulder. I glanced to my left and found the forest she referred to. The same one I'd seen the moonlight peeking through just mere minutes ago.

There were no artificial lights in the Garden of Eden, so all I could see were the line of palm trees separating the beach from the forest. Behind them was utter darkness with the exception of the moon's glow lighting up the tops of the trees. It looked like there was fresh fallen snow. I took a few steps forward then held my left hand out behind me. Tegan grabbed it without hesitation. The pink light flashing on our chests lit up the darkness like a Las Vegas billboard.

I frowned as Tegan's words from before dawned on me. "Love light?"

"Took you long enough." She scoffed. "Yes, *love light*. The glyph is a symbol of our love, and it's lighting up."

We couldn't see a damn thing, and the flashing wasn't helping. I kept reminding myself we were in the Garden of Eden. Nothing was supposed to harm us. But after whatever that was with the sunset, I wasn't so trusting.

I cleared my throat. "Okay, well, when we get back, let's call it something else to the others."

She mumbled something, but I didn't try to decipher it. I found the more we discussed how forbidden we were or about the law that prevented us from being together, the angrier she grew. Libby was right after all. Pushing Tegan away could've been catastrophic. But the path we currently walked was fraying with every step. She was going to snap. I was sure of it. I just wasn't sure *when* or *how*.

The ground lit up under my feet. Instead of darkness, I found a luminescent blue. With every step I took, the light returned. Curiosity urged me to stop and look, but my instinct told me to keep going. A blast of light slammed into my back. I spun on my toes only to find it was just Tegan.

She held her glowing hand out to the side and waved it around. "What is it?"

I sighed. Tegan had always been a curious cat. I couldn't blame her, but then again, it tended to lead her into dangerous situations.

My spine tingled. Every nerve ending in my body screamed for me to keep moving. "I don't know. Come on. We have to keep moving."

"Tennessee, just *look* at it for a second," she whispered. Her green eyes were wide and shimmering under her body's glow. She took a few steps away from me, walking straight into the darkness. "What is it?"

I frowned and followed after her. She stared ahead like there was a sparkling, dancing leprechaun in front of her instead of...well...*nothing*. "Tegan, it's nothing. Let's keep going."

"*Nothing?*" she hissed and waved her hands in front of her. "How can you say *that* is nothing? It's definitely something. Just tell me."

"Tegan, I only see pitch-black." A cold chill slid down my spine. Whatever she saw, I didn't. I cleared my throat. "What do you see?"

Her eyebrows rose. She opened and closed her mouth a few times before words actually came out. "I don't understand. It's like that Aurora Borealis thing in Norway I've always wanted to see, but it's floating up from the ground into the sky. Like smoke or something. There are these little shapes, almost like people. They remind me of the spirits I saw at The Gathering."

CHAPTER TWENTY-EIGHT

S *pirits.* Fear prickled my neck.

Tegan was the Aether Witch. I didn't fully understand what it meant, but I knew she had a deeper connection to the world than any other witch. *Can she see spirits we can't?* I didn't know, and I didn't have anyone to ask. We were in the Garden of Eden, so if she saw spirits, then there was only one place I could think of them going. And although I hoped to go there one day, I didn't want it to be for several decades.

Tegan reached her hand out into the darkness, and a sense of déjà vu washed over me. It was like in the Strait of the Dead, but it still made no sense.

"Tegan, no." I jumped forward and wrapped my arms around her, trapping her hands down at her sides. I leaned in with my lips pressed against her ear and whispered, "Tegan, come back to me."

She wiggled under my grip, fighting to get away from me. I kept saying her name, begging her to hear me through whatever hypnosis she'd fallen under. Words left her lips, but they were soft and not in any language I'd ever heard before. Whatever was happening in this holy land, it affected Tegan more than me. I had to break her of it somehow.

Think, Tenn, think. The answer that popped into my head made my stomach turn. Using my magic on my soulmate felt like a violation of our bond.

"I love you. Please forgive me," I whispered as I summoned my magic.

She may have had more gifts than I did, but I had more natural power. A gust of wind answered my silent call. It slammed into us head-on. Tegan's hair whipped around my face. I willed the wind to wrap around her ankles like a lasso then yanked back. She dropped to her knees. The ground beneath her surged with blue illumination. The wind spun her around to face me and I gasped. I sank to my knees in front of her and cupped her face. She kept whispering in that weird language. But that wasn't what scared me.

It was her *eyes*. They were white as snow with golden rims and irises.

"Haven," she whispered over and over.

What the hell? Her eyes matched the Angel

Gabriel's. Was she seeing some haven of the Angels? I wasn't sure. *This is not normal.* "Tegan. Tegan, come back to me."

No response. I pushed my magic out until I felt the strength of the Earth, then called it toward me. The energy was raw and cold, like deeply buried dirt. A thick vine covered in wide leaves and little white flowers wrapped around Tegan's head like a blindfold. Her grip went slack and her words died on her tongue. For a moment, she just froze, then she tried to throw her hands up toward her blindfold. But my wind was too strong. She wobbled side to side, then tipped forward until her palms landed flat on the ground.

Two big splotches of blue light lit up under her hands, and it didn't stop. It shot out from us like a wildfire, illuminating a massive oval shape. My jaw dropped. I'd heard stories long, long ago from a crone who visited Eden back when I was a child. She'd told me about the rumors of the Garden of Eden and what it looked like. What was supposed to be inside it. One of those things was the Lake of Holy Water. Back then, I'd assumed it was nonsense. No one had seen inside *the* Garden...but now, looking at my surroundings with new light, I realized she described it perfectly. Like she'd been here herself.

Holy Water keeps what isn't welcome. That was

what she'd said to me. It hadn't made sense then, but it did now. There was no way a person could swim in the lake and survive. The power inside would consume them. Yet there Tegan and I sat in the middle on our knees...on the surface. If we hadn't both been gifted with Water as one of our elements, we would've died almost instantly. And in the darkness of the forest, even I hadn't seen it coming.

Leyka knew though. My worry over my deal with the Angel returned tenfold. *He knew.*

"Tennessee?"

I gasped at the sound of her voice. I'd been so lost in thought I'd almost forgotten. I shook myself and looked down at her. "Tegan? Are you with me?"

"Of course I'm with you," she whispered. She reached up and tried to grab the vine. "What happened? What is this? Why can't I see?"

"Let me." I gripped her wrists then willed the vine to unwrap itself. It slithered away, back into the darkness. "Okay, it's gone."

She opened her eyes, and they were back to her natural peridot-colored light green. She blinked a bunch of times before her gaze landed on me. "Tenn?"

I sighed with relief. That weird entranced version of her was gone. "Hi."

"Hi." She smiled for a second before it faltered, then narrowed her eyes. "Where are we?"

I scratched the back of my neck. "I think this is the Lake of Holy Water."

Before she could respond, the lake surface rippled and sent little vibrations shooting up my legs. I frowned and looked down just as a black line shot through the space between us. Just after it passed us, the water split open, parting like the Red Sea. At first it was just a black hole, but then the blue illumination slipped over the edge and lit up a narrow staircase.

My stomach dropped like we were on a rollercoaster.

"We have to go down there," Tegan whispered.

"I know." I got to my feet then held my hand out for her.

She took it without hesitation, and it made my heart soar. *Focus, Tenn.* Her hand was soft and warm against mine. I tightened my grip on her then took the first step down. We didn't speak as we descended, not that there were words to say. When we got to the bottom, there was nothing but more blackness. *Maybe it's a trick?* Except the stairs were still there waiting for us.

I sighed and ran my hands through my hair. "This makes no sense."

"We both need to work on our insecurities about

being confused," Tegan mumbled as she stepped away from me. But she didn't let go of my hand. She walked forward, her eyes on the ground. "I was worried about my deal with Keltie before, but now I'm really concerned."

"I was just thinking the same about Leyka. They didn't choose us by chance."

Tegan shook her head. "Exactly." She pointed to the ground in front of her.

I narrowed my eyes and stared at the spot, but I saw nothing. "I don't see anything."

"But *I* do." She pulled me closer so she could squat down without letting go of my hand. With her free hand, she traced her finger along the black ground. "I have so many questions, except we can't even ask because no one can know we're soulmates."

She wasn't wrong. I kneeled beside her. "What do you see?" I, too, had many questions. Except I feared there wasn't anyone who would know the answers even if we *could* ask.

Tegan raised her left palm and held it open a few inches over the ground. Her rainbow-colored magic swirled around, then turned into little grains like dirt or sand. It dropped to the ground. She waved her fingers, and the grains moved until they outlined the shape of a lotus flower. The black lotus flower Gabriel had shown us before reappeared on the back of her hand. Little white beams of light shot up from the ground, peeking through the lotus she'd outlined.

The ground gave away in the shape of the flower, sinking farther and farther into darkness. The light grew brighter and thicker until we had to shield our eyes. When it suddenly vanished, I peeled my hand away. My jaw dropped. Sitting there in the place of the mark only Tegan could see was a chalice.

"Tennessee..."

"I see it."

It was about a foot tall and radiated clean energy. It was bigger than I expected, yet smaller at the same time. On the side of the chalice, there was a round purple crystal, and on either side of it were two purple half circles. Then two quarter circles. *No. This is the moon phase.* Similar to the Crones' symbol. The chalice itself was a shiny, metallic color that was both gold and silver at the same time.

"This is the one," Tegan whispered beside me.

"Yes." I nodded. I couldn't have said how I knew exactly. It was simply being in its presence. I felt its power seeping into my bones without even touching it. I turned to look at her. "Nothing here will harm you unless you drink from the wrong chalice."

Her green eyes sparkled as she stared up at me. "We have to drink from it."

"Together?"

She nodded. "Together."

We reached out with the hands not holding each other and picked up the chalice at the same time, our fingers overlapping. My magic surged with power like I'd been plugged into an energy source. Together, we raised the cup to our faces. I looked inside and wasn't at all surprised to find that blue luminescent water shining up at us. I had no idea what was going to happen after we drank Holy Water, but we didn't have a choice.

On three, we drink together, Tegan said into my mind.

I nodded and licked my lips.

One.

Two.

Three.

We tipped the chalice and let the glowing water fall into our mouths. I had no words to describe what it tasted like. It was warm and cold. Soothing and stimulating. Sweet and sour. My eyes rolled. Pain shot through my head and down my spine. It was like the worst case of brain freeze I'd ever experienced. My vision blurred until everything went white. I couldn't see what was around us, couldn't feel the ground under my feet. All I felt was Tegan's hand in mine.

Let it in, Tenn. Stop fighting it.

I frowned at Tegan's words. I hadn't realized I was fighting something. *Am I?* The white energy burned. I just wanted to shield my eyes from the intensity, but I couldn't feel my body.

Tennessee. Take a deep breath.

I did as she asked. Then I felt it. I *was* fighting something. There was a barrier between me and the white energy. I took another deep breath then exhaled everything. *Let it in,* I told myself and pulled back on my magic. The brightness faded slowly until I found Tegan kneeling in front of me.

She smiled wide. "Hi."

"Hi," I whispered back. I blinked and looked around. We were in the same place, crouched at the bottom of a staircase in the middle of the Lake of Holy Water inside the Garden of Eden. Except now I saw something I hadn't before. "Do you see that?"

"Where only Eden and the chalice knows," Tegan said softly. She stood and took a step forward. "I think this is going to lead us to the next step."

This was a silver glitter path that started under the chalice and spread up the staircase. I stood and walked to the edge of the stairs. "Well, let's not waste any more time." I gripped her hand and took the first step.

"*Take it with you,*" a voice whispered in my mind.

I froze. My pulse quickened. The hairs on the back of my neck stood up.

"Tennessee..."

"Please tell me you heard that too," I said without moving or looking back.

Tegan sighed. She squeezed my hand. "It's a test."

"Yes." I glanced over my shoulder at her pretty face. "I think I've seen enough of the Garden of Eden. You?"

She nodded and ran up the stairs, dragging me along with her. When we got to the top, the water surged around us. It rose up and trapped us in the middle of a tunnel of water. I pulled Tegan to my chest. Her bare skin pressed against mine and sent a wave of heat through me. For the first time that I could remember, fear simmered below the surface. I wasn't used to not being in control of water. Gabriel said nothing would harm us unless we drank from the wrong chalice, but I couldn't help but wonder...*what if we drank from the wrong one?*

Tegan squeezed me tight. She kissed my chest, right over the glyph that bound us.

And then it was gone. The Holy Water was nowhere in sight. Above us, the sky was a glorious, cloudless blue. We stood on green grass. In front of us... was the waterfall.

"Let's go save the world," Tegan said with a wide grin. She stepped forward.

I yanked her back. "Maybe we should put our shirts on first?"

CHAPTER TWENTY-NINE

TEGAN

Oh my God. My shirt. Heat burned my cheeks. Tennessee grinned and slid my black shirt over my head. I put my arms through while smiling up at him. Most guys would've tried something or made me feel uncomfortable. But not Tennessee. I'd been in front of him in only my black bra for hours and hours, yet I'd managed to forget. It was a testament to his love and respect for me, or the way Uncle Kessler raised him—or probably both. And he was all mine. Out of all the guys that could've been my soulmate, I really won the lottery.

He tipped my chin up. "What are you thinking about?"

My smile widened. I no longer had to lie or pretend with him. As long as no one else heard, I could be honest and tell him what I was feeling. "I was just thinking how lucky I am to have you as mine."

His mismatched eyes twinkled. He leaned down and pressed his lips to mine then pulled away far too soon. He took my hands in his and squeezed. "I love you."

My pulse skipped a few beats. I'd never get used to hearing it. "I love you, too."

"I wish we could announce it to the world."

I nodded and stepped back, letting distance pull my fingers from his hands. "But we can't. And we have a job to do."

Several jobs, actually. Rescue Henley, close the Gap in Salem before Samhain, and fight the Coven leaders on their stupid no-dating rule. For now, that last one would have to wait. Once we proved ourselves, they'd have to give in. *Right? Right.*

"Tegan?"

I frowned and looked around. Tennessee wasn't in front of me anymore. He stood over in front of the waterfall, waiting to rejoin our friends. I walked over to him, but I had to take one last glance at the majestic sight that was the Garden of Eden. There was no reason to believe I'd ever see it again.

"Are you okay?"

No, I don't think so. Something happened to me here, and I wasn't sure what. It shook me to my core. I had a feeling I would have nightmares about it. There would come a point in time when I'd need to talk about it, but it wasn't that day yet. I cleared my throat. My eyes were glued to the ocean twinkling in the distance. "What happened in the Garden of Eden..."

"Stays in the Garden of Eden. It's between us." He pressed his finger to my jaw and forced me to look at him. The kiss he gave me was soft and sweet, but full of passion and conviction. "I promise."

"Thank you. Now, let's go find our friends." I wrapped my hands around his forearm and held on tight. There was no way I was risking getting separated.

When he nodded, we stepped through the waterfall together. A blast of cold air brushed over me, and then we were back in the place we'd left our friends.

No one noticed our arrival. Willow and Chutney were propped up against the stone on the far side of the little space with their eyes closed. Royce sat beside them with his head between his knees while he tugged at the long black strands of his hair. Deacon and Cooper were lounged in the middle on the dirt ground sharing a bag of chips. Emersyn was off to the side with her back to me, braiding her long hair.

Deacon picked up a new bag of chips and started to open it. "What's the next line of the prophecy?"

"Between the balefire, the runes shall dance," I answered.

Potato chips exploded into the air. Deacon cursed and grabbed his chest. "Don't *do* that."

Cooper spun around with wide eyes. He looked back and forth between Tenn and me. "You're back?"

Emersyn jumped to her feet and captured me in a bear hug. She squeezed me tighter than I thought was possible for her. "That was the longest five minutes ever." She stepped back and smiled.

"Five minutes?" Tennessee repeated.

Cooper scratched his head. "Em was counting since our watches don't work."

I looked up at Tennessee, but the scowl on his face told me he was as surprised as I was. *How is that possible?* So much happened inside, too much for only five minutes. We'd watched the sun set, even. The images popped into my mind, and I panicked to make them go away. Except then I remembered what I saw in the dark, and my body turned to ice. I shivered and looked back to Tennessee. His eyes were already on me. There was too much emotion in them with other people around. I forced myself to look at the ground. The silver glittery path stretched out across the little nook we were in.

"Well, it was a lot longer than that for us." Tennessee's voice was low and rough. He cleared his throat. "But it doesn't matter. We have to keep moving now."

"Wait, did you find the chalice?" Emersyn asked. She slid my leather jacket off her shoulders and handed it to me. "Well?"

I took my jacket and put it on, trying to decide how best to answer the question. They deserved to know most of the truth. "Yes, we found the chalice. It is guiding us with this glittery pathway here."

They all frowned. Royce and the two younger girls had joined us.

"Tegan, they didn't drink from the chalice, so they can't see it," Tennessee whispered to me. He held his hands out, and his magic pulsed through the air. His sword and dagger flew from their spot on the dirt into his palms. He stuffed the dagger in his left boot and slid the sword into the holster on his hip. "You guys are going to have to trust us on this."

I reached into my jacket pockets and pulled out my two daggers then slid them into the holsters on my thighs. We had no idea what we were going to find, so we had to be ready. I followed the glittery path to the same narrow gap between the stone slates that we'd entered through and paused. I glanced over my shoulder. "Stay together. Be prepared for *anything*."

I didn't hesitate another moment. There were too many thoughts and questions in my mind to stand still. I had to keep moving. We had a job to do. I followed the glittery path between the slates that reminded me now of the clay cavern in the Garden—

Let's stop that train of thought right now, m'kay? I refocused on the path under my feet. Once we emerged into the little clearing Lonan had dropped us in, the path curved to the right and dipped between two towering pine trees. It appeared we were going back into the forest.

"Tenn, Chutney? Care to join me up front?" I paused just outside the tree line. It was daylight still, so the sun shone through the trees enough to see, but I wanted to be safe.

The burn in my chest flared a little hotter, and then I smelled his fresh rain scent. A split second later, Tennessee walked by me. His fingertips brushed over my hip just enough to make my heart flutter and my thoughts muddled.

He paused just in front of me and turned around to face us. "Chutney, this time stand behind Tegan. I need her to make sure we stay on the path. Coop, you still good to hold up the caboose?"

"You got it."

"Wait!" Emersyn dug into her jeans pocket, then pulled out a blueish crystal. She held her hand out, and the stone dangled from her fingers. "Don't forget George."

Tennessee smiled and took his pendulum from my sister. He quickly slipped it into his pocket then turned and waved us along. I followed in line right behind him, but after a few steps, we were side by side. It felt weird to not hold his hand, but there were too many eyes on us. *Save the world, then break the law.*

No one spoke as we walked through the forest so that Chutney could hear if something was coming. Although I suspected everyone's nerves were a little on edge. Mine were shot.

The forest thrived all around us. The trees towered so high above us I couldn't even see the tops. Little bits of blue sky poked through the branches and leaves. Streams of sunshine looked like spotlights. The air was warm and fresh. I sighed and let earth's energy calm me down with every deep breath. I closed my eyes. *Wait.* My eyes flew open. I remembered feeling that same kind of peace inside the Garden of Eden. I didn't know if this was more of the same magic, or if I was just on edge and paranoid. Either way, I forced my eyes to lock on the glittery walkway the chalice had given us.

Time and distance ceased to exist for a while. We walked up and down steep hills, curved around stone mountainsides, and climbed over fallen trees. The weird thing was my body didn't hurt like it had before the Garden of Eden. My magic sang in my veins, waiting patiently for me to call on it. My legs didn't burn, and my feet didn't throb. I didn't look back at anyone else, but their ragged breathing told me they were struggling. Yet I wasn't. Tennessee never did. I wondered if drinking the Holy Water had given me strength? If so, how long would it last?

"Heads up, guys," Tennessee whispered through the silent wilderness. "We've got another steep decline. There's a cliff on the right, so use it."

I turned and pressed my back into the cold rocky mountainside, then shimmied down the pathway. Emersyn cursed and it was enough to make me look. She'd slipped but Deacon caught her. She smiled and her cheeks flushed as she clung to his arm and continued down. I smiled. Deacon had a long road ahead of him with my sister, and it had nothing to do with the law, yet every day he seemed to make her smile at least once. So I prayed there was hope for them.

Something sparkled above me. When I looked, I found a blue dome hanging over and around us. *Willow?* I looked back, and sure enough, the same blue-colored smoke swirled around her fingers. *So that's why we haven't seen any wildlife.* I chuckled and turned to refocus my sights on the glittery path, then gasped.

"Willow, drop the dome," I whispered. *Please let this be an illusion.*

But it wasn't. Willow's blue dome faded away, and I faced the same thing I saw a moment before. Utter blackness. The glittery path was the only thing I could see, and it disappeared a few feet ahead. My pulse quickened. Adrenaline rushed through my body. I'd seen darkness like this before. I took a step closer. There was a wild energy around us, like static electricity waiting for something to spark it to life.

"Tegan, wait."

At the sound of Tennessee's voice, I froze, though I hadn't realized I'd moved forward. I blinked and licked my lips. We couldn't wait. Henley was in another dimension being tortured by demons. We didn't have a moment to lose.

I raised my hands and willed my arms to glow. White light shined around me. I spun in a slow circle until I spotted a pillar standing just off the glittery path. I hurried over, anxious to get to the next step. My eyes widened. *A torch?*

I raised my hand and summoned my magic. Heat bloomed in my stomach. A ball of fire flickered to life in my palm. I shot my fire forward. The torch surged with flames. That electric energy tingled with awareness, biting at my fingertips.

"Emersyn, come up here," I said.

"Why is *fire* my thing?" my twin whispered as she

joined me, though I doubted anyone else heard her. She narrowed her eyes on the lit torch like it had spread a nasty rumor about her through school. Before I could ask what was wrong, she stepped up to the torch and blew on it.

The torch exploded like a firework. Little balls of fire the size of golf balls soared through the air, splitting through the darkness. They fell to the ground, and flames shot up over our heads. My breath left me in a rush. The fire spread out ahead of us as far as I could see. I looked down at the glittery path and found it stretched a few feet into the flames before vanishing. Our pathway was in the middle of a fire tunnel.

"We are not walking through that, are we?" Chutney whispered from close by.

Then it hit me. *"Between the balefire, the runes shall dance."*

Tennessee sighed. "It's as bad as I thought it would be. Let's get it over with."

I nodded. "Emersyn, why don't you take the lead since you're our fire breather. I'll be right behind you."

Emersyn bit her bottom lip. The flames reflected in her wide eyes. Then she nodded and pushed her shoulders back. She took one deep breath then charged forward. I followed behind her. The glittery path was gone. We were on our own. The ground, sky, and everything around us was blacker than night. All I knew was darkness and fire. The flames swayed like palm trees in a storm. Little sparks flickered on the ground. Red glowing mist seeped out of nothingness all around us. I glanced left and right, but it surrounded us. It grew taller than a person, then swirled and shifted until it made shapes. *No, not shapes. Runes.*

"The runes shall dance," Tennessee whispered. His voice was loud, but it felt far away.

The runes wiggled and swayed, moving around the flames like people dancing around a bonfire. It reminded me of The Gathering. It also reminded me of the spell Tennessee and I had performed by the lake back at home. The energy between the balefire was dark and ancient.

"Tegan!" Tennessee yelled.

I spun toward the sound of my name, but his voice was too far away. Emersyn still stomped ahead in front of me with her arms stretched out like she was petting the fire. To my right, Cooper and Royce were frowning and looking side to side.

Where is he? A shadow passed in front of my face. I gasped and moved toward it, but it ran between the flames. It looked and moved like a person. It moved like my soulmate. No one moved like him. *Tennessee?* I had no idea what he was doing over there.

The shadow spun around and waved its arms over its head frantically. "Tegan! Over here!" His voice was high and clipped, a tone I'd never heard from him.

I sprinted toward him. I'd never seen him panic, and it sent a wave of fear rushing through my body like ice. Flames popped up from the ground in front of my path. I cursed and leapt around it, barely missing the fire. The shadow jumped and waved me on, but when I took another step, it *vanished*. I gasped and skidded to a stop. It was gone.

"Tennessee?" I shouted.

No one answered. I spun around to ask my friends if they could see him and choked on a gasp. They weren't there. No one was. Sweat dripped down my neck. My hair clung to my skin. My heart pounded so hard in my chest I thought it might break out. I turned in circles, searching for any sign of my friends, but all I found was fire and darkness.

CHAPTER THIRTY

TEGAN

No. No, no. This isn't happening. I stumbled forward in the direction I thought I'd come from, though there was no way to be sure. It didn't make any sense. One second I was surrounded by my friends, and the next they were gone. Or maybe I was gone. Maybe when I stepped off the pathway— *Oh no.*

That was why we needed the binding spell. Kenneth told us if we got separated, we might not ever be found again. The realization brought tears to my eyes and pain to my chest. But I wouldn't cry. I had to fight my way out of whatever this was. If I was worthy enough to enter the Garden of Eden, I had to be capable of beating it.

I pushed my hair out of my face and off my neck. I kept moving forward, praying I was headed in the right direction. With every step I took, more voices whispered through the darkness. I froze at each one, except none of them were Tennessee. They weren't any voices I recognized. Male and female voices screamed through the darkness, calling out names. I kept moving. They cried out for help, but I couldn't see any of them. I looked and looked as I walked, yet still, there was nothing. I didn't know what this place was, but I knew if I didn't find my way out now, I would be another invisible voice begging for help that would never come.

Pain flared in my chest. I hissed and stumbled a few feet. The pain grew hotter and more intense. My vision went blurry. My mouth watered like I was going to be sick. I pressed my hand to my chest and yanked it away. It burned to the touch.

I smiled. *Tennessee!* I screamed out for him with my mind. He was close. My glyph only stung when he came near. I took a few more steps, and the pain grew worse. *Yes.* I was going in the right direction. I clenched my teeth and sprinted forward. My pulse skyrocketed. The pain grew so intense I struggled to breathe. I ran but my legs were heavy and weak. I didn't stop. I ran until I slammed into a solid black wall.

I crashed to the ground, rolling over and over. When the world finally righted itself, I opened my eyes and found the most beautiful face staring down at me. *Tennessee.* His hair was disheveled and falling into his face. His eyes were wild and full of more heat than the fire dancing around us.

I took a shaky breath and tried to calm my racing heart. "Hi."

"Hi." He grinned and it took my breath away. He got to his feet then pulled me to mine. Once I was upright, he scanned me up and down. "Are you okay? What happened?"

Willow ran up beside him. She smiled and wrapped her arms around me for a hug. When she pulled back, there were tears in her eyes. "We thought we lost you, too."

"What the hell is going on?" Deacon groaned from Tenn's other side. He must've walked up while I was hugging Willow. He shook his head and looked around with wide, violet eyes. "One second you were there, and the next you're gone."

"I heard Tennessee calling for me and I saw like the shadow of him, but he was far away... I don't know. I just panicked and ran toward him and then..." I shook my head. "When I turned around, everyone was gone. I was alone in the dark with just the fire. There were other voices calling out for people, but I couldn't see them. It's like some twilight zone kind of thing."

Deacon's eyes narrowed on me. "Did you recognize any of the voices?"

"No."

Deacon cursed and scrubbed his face. He turned away from me, mumbling to himself.

"How'd you find your way back?"

I jumped at the sound of Willow's voice, too distracted by Deacon's behavior. I rubbed at my chest and looked up into Tennessee's eyes. "I felt..."—*you*—"something."

A muscle in his jaw flexed as he stared down at me. I knew him enough to know he was holding back whatever he was thinking and feeling. His nostrils flared, and he looked away. He shook his head just enough for me to see. It was the same face he made that day after I went to Hidden Kingdom without him, without anyone else besides Emersyn. He was mad at me, and I couldn't blame him. I was almost lost.

I grabbed a fistful of his shirt and tugged. *I'm sorry. I just ran to you. I panicked. I didn't think,* I said into his mind.

His eyes found mine again. He nodded and wrapped his fingers around mine. "You're safe now. That's all that matters."

"*All that matters?*" Willow shrieked. "Everyone else is gone!"

"Wait, *what?*" I spun around and realized far too late that there were only four of us standing there. I'd been so caught up in my fear, and in Tennessee, that I hadn't noticed no one else greeted me.

Deacon paced behind us while pulling on his hair.

Oh God. My stomach turned. "Where are they?"

"I was hoping you could tell us," Tennessee whispered. "You were the first to go. Then it all happened so fast, and they were just gone."

But I found my way out, so it was definitely possible. I turned my attention to Deacon. His cousin was out there, except so was his soulmate.

Deacon.

He froze and turned toward me with a frown.

Deacon, did you see which direction Emersyn went?

He nodded.

"Willow, hold on to Tennessee." I grabbed Tennessee's hand and dragged him over to where Deacon stood. Willow bounced after us, but she was holding on. I slid my hand into Deacon's and squeezed. "No one let go."

Deacon, move toward the direction Em went in until your chest burns.

He stood tall and looked at me with a guarded expression.

Relax, I know about it. Your secret is safe with me. Right now, I need you to use it to find my twin. Okay?

He licked his lips and nodded. "Okay."

I glanced over my shoulder at Tennessee. He winked and gave me a smile. I sighed. At least he realized what I was doing. Poor Willow definitely had no idea.

We walked together, the four of us linking arms for several feet before Deacon gasped and froze in place.

Deacon, is it burning?

He nodded but didn't look at me, his eyes locked on the fire.

Good, now slowly take one step forward. I tightened my grip on both his and Tennessee's hands.

Deacon's eyes went wide. He snarled and hissed.

I knew what he was feeling. The soulmate glyph was desperately burning through the magic of the Old Lands.

Deacon threw his free hand up in the air. The Devil's red lightning shot out of his fingers. "Give her back," he growled into the darkness.

The flames parted, and Emersyn dropped to the ground at our feet.

"Emersyn!" I screamed in relief.

She coughed and pushed herself up on all fours. Her hair was wild and tangled, and for some reason, smoking at the ends. Deacon reached down and pulled her up on her feet. She jumped forward and wrapped me in a hug. When she stepped back, she turned her eyes to Deacon and placed her hand on his chest.

"Thank you," she whispered.

Deacon blushed. "You're welcome."

I released Deacon's hand then grabbed my twin's. "Em, hang on to Deacon. We can't get separated again."

She didn't hesitate to take her own soulmate's hand. The two of them exchanged some kind of glance I couldn't quite see, but then she turned her attention to me. "Where are the others?"

My heart sank. Royce, Chutney, and Cooper were still lost to the darkness. I gnawed on my lip trying to think. Emersyn and I were lucky enough to have soulmates we could detect. There would be no beacon to guide the others. I'd known to follow the pain, but I couldn't even be sure my twin knew. If Deacon hadn't commanded—

I gasped as an idea popped into mind. "Deacon, command the balefire to give them back."

His violet eyes widened. "Like I did for Emersyn! Why didn't I think of that?"

Because these gifts are new to you, too. I thought it, but I didn't say it. Deacon's power of persuasion came with the Mark, but he'd only just gotten a taste. *You got this.*

Deacon closed his eyes and took a few deep breaths. When he opened them again, little red bolts of lightning flashed through the whites of his eyes. He looked at each of us, then turned his stare to the fire. With one hand raised out to the flames, he yelled, "Release your captives!"

Fire surged higher. The flames turned from orange to red, to purple, then to white. The ground rumbled under our feet. We still only saw blackness. The fire hissed and crackled like someone had poured water on it. White smoke billowed from within the darkness, rising into the black sky.

Chutney was the first to pop out. She was screaming, with tears streaming down her face. Willow gasped and dove for her. Deacon shouted with his magic, demanding it to listen. The flames shot out toward us, and Royce rolled like a tumbleweed right into Deacon's feet. Deacon yanked him up by his collar without pausing his commands. Smoke surged thicker, then it popped. Cooper ran for us with his swords raised. Em and I gasped and dove for him.

Then the ground opened up under our feet and we fell.

CHAPTER THIRTY-ONE

TENNESSEE

My back slammed into something hard. Sharp pain shot through me. I tried to shout, but the wind was knocked out of me. Black dots danced in my eyes. I gasped for air, and it took way too long to get in. My pulse pounded in my veins. Between that and the high-pitched ringing in my ears, I couldn't hear anything else around me. I tried to move, but the world spun and my shoulders felt glued to the ground, or whatever I'd landed on. I closed my eyes and counted to three.

When I opened them, the world stopped spinning, but nothing made sense. Stars twinkled against a dark blue night sky. The moon was a massive golden orb staring down at me. Thick gray clouds swirled into view, blocking patches of the moon's light. Or was that smoke? I squinted and tried to discern what I was seeing. The

last thing I'd seen was the darkest black and raging fire...
then we fell.

We. We fell. Where are they? My pulse quickened to
a speed I was sure wasn't healthy. I had to get up. I had
to find Tegan. My chest burned, but I couldn't tell if it
was *her* or whatever was hurting. I wasn't even sure what
I hurt. I just knew it throbbed.

I took a deep breath. Then another. Then two more.
I summoned all the strength I had and tried to roll to my
left. Pain like I'd never known exploded in my shoulder.
I shouted a string of violent curse words I'd never used.
The ground rumbled under me.

"Tennessee!"

Tegan's beautiful face came into my view. Her green
eyes were wide and bouncing around. Her lips moved
faster than I'd ever seen her speak before.

She leaned down and whispered to me, "No. Don't
move, love."

"Is everyone all right?"

I recognized Cooper's voice, though I couldn't
see him.

"Cooper, get over here!" Tegan screamed. Her face
was pale. She wiped the back of her hand over her forehead, and it left a streak of blood. "Cooper!"

"What's wrong? Who is— Oh, God." My adoptive
brother's face finally came into my view. His green eyes

perfectly matched his sister's. His jaw dropped and his face went pale. His gaze seemed to jump around at something below my face. "Okay, okay. It's okay. We can fix it."

"Fix what? What's wrong?" Royce loomed above them, his black hair blending in with the night sky. His jaw went slack. He smiled but it wobbled. "Hey, how's my favorite non-human?"

I frowned. Something was wrong. I wasn't an idiot. I knew the pain in my shoulder connected to the horrified looks on their faces. A bunch of equally awful scenarios flashed through my mind. I groaned. "What is it? Just tell me." I hated how weak my voice sounded.

Cooper whispered something to Royce, who nodded and disappeared from view.

I cursed. "Talk to me. I am alive down here." *I am, aren't I?*

Tegan smiled and brushed my hair off my forehead. *We know you're alive, love. We want to keep it that way.*

I frowned. That did not make me feel better at all. I must've made a face because she shook her head.

There's some kind of...unidentified object protruding from your left shoulder. There's a lot of blood, but it's nowhere near your heart.

I sighed and it brought a whole new wave a pain.

"Get. It. Out. Of. Me," I hissed through the torture.

Cooper's face reappeared. "Hey there, brother. So this is going to hurt like hell, but we need to lift you off this...*thing*. Okay? Can you handle it?"

"He's not human. He can handle anything, right, boss?" Royce's wide smile was back on.

"Yes. He can handle it." Tegan nodded. "I'll give him air. Y'all get him off *fast*."

"Wait!" Emersyn jumped into view right between her siblings. She raised her hands over my head. Something dark was wrapped around both fists and stretched in between. She brought it down to my lips. "Bite down on this so you don't jack up your teeth and jaw."

A belt. Brilliant. I opened my mouth, and she slid it between my teeth. It wasn't until I bit down on the warm leather that I realized how much it was going to hurt if she thought I needed a belt.

Tenn, look at me, Tegan whispered in my mind.

I blinked and met her gaze. Her eyes were calm and steady.

You tell me when you're ready.

I inhaled a deep breath through my nose then nodded. No need to stall. It would only make things worse.

She smiled down at me. *I love you. One...two...three...*

Agony. Blinding, hot agony. I couldn't have said what happened or how, but the next thing I knew, I was sitting up against the cold earth mountainside. I spit the belt out, and it dropped to my lap in three pieces. *Oops*. I leaned my head back and just focused on staying conscious through the pain. Something squeezed my shoulder and I flinched. When I looked down, I found it was a shirt wadded up against my shoulder. Blood poured down my chest, making my black shirt cling to my skin.

Cooper crouched down in front of me with a dark strap in his hand. "Tenn, you okay?"

I exhaled. "What the hell did I land on?"

Royce chuckled and rubbed his face. With his other hand, he pointed behind him. "The only time I see something get the best of you, and it wasn't even preventable. Some kind of tree branch or something."

I looked over to where he pointed and found Tegan standing there. She squatted down in front of a large, pointed end of something white...and covered in what had to be my blood.

"It's not a tree," she yelled back without turning.

Emersyn crouched beside her. She shook her head and looked around. "Whatever it is, there is a lot of it around here."

Tegan reached out and grabbed the object at the bottom. Orange flames flickered between her fingers. A second later, she stood up tall with the object in her hands. She turned and walked over to where I was propped up. Her eyes were narrowed and her eyebrows scrunched down low. She pursed her lips and glanced around before looking at me. "It's a *bone*."

My jaw dropped. I frowned as she dropped to her knees in front of me and held out the object. I took it in my right hand and held it up to my face. It was thick like my forearm, and solid white. It had to be a foot long. She was right. It was definitely not a tree. I looked around our surrounding area, and my stomach turned.

I cursed. "It *is* a bone."

"Why did you cut it off?" Deacon leaned over and wrapped another belt around my shoulder in a makeshift tourniquet. "Couldn't you tell it was a bone before you did?"

Tegan sighed. "Because we don't have the ability to heal him here. What if Katherine needs to know *exactly* what impaled him? I'm not taking that risk. So I cut the damn thing off."

The ground trembled under us.

"Tegan, it's okay. We get it. Don't bring the mountain down on us," Willow grumbled.

"I... That's not me," Tegan whispered.

Their eyes turned to me.

I frowned. "I didn't do that."

"GET OUT! GET OUT! GET OUT!" Royce screamed from out of sight.

"Royce, what's—"

A loud roar ripped through the night, cutting Deacon's words off. The ground shook like an earthquake. Royce flew through the air and slammed into the side of the mountain.

CHAPTER THIRTY-TWO

TENNESSEE

"ROYCE!" Deacon screamed and raced over to where his cousin lay in a motionless heap on the ground. He dropped to his knees. "He's breathing! Royce, c'mon, bud, wake up!"

There was a shriek like something from an alien movie, and it echoed around us. The mountains trembled. Rocks rained down on us. I grimaced as one hit my shoulder. I needed to move. Whatever tossed Royce was going to attack the rest of us. Deacon was still trying to wake him, but Royce wasn't budging.

"Whoa, whoa, whoa, what is that?" Deacon scurried backward, but thick black vines coiled around his legs. He swatted at them, but they spread up and trapped his hands against his body. "Get it off me!"

Cooper sprinted over with his daggers at the ready. As soon as he got close, he started slicing through the vines, but each time he chopped one, two more popped up from the ground. "What the hell?"

"Cooper, *move!*" I shouted, but it was too late.

The snake-like vines grabbed ahold of his dagger and pulled him face-first into the dirt. Cooper rolled to his back. "Stay back or we'll all get trapped!" he yelled to us as the vines wrapped around him like he was being mummified.

Damn it. I clenched my teeth and summoned my magic. A gust of wind swept under my legs and hauled me to my feet. My left arm was strapped to my chest in a makeshift sling made of belts. I held my palm out and called for my sword. The cold black crystal hit my palm in seconds. I ran to the middle to where Tegan and Emersyn stood with their weapons drawn.

"Guys, what's happening?" Chutney cried from right behind me, her breath brushing over the back of my arm.

Willow stumbled back and bumped into Emersyn. "What is it?"

"*Where* is it?" Emersyn muttered. Her golden eyes were narrowed and staring straight ahead, like she was daring whatever it was to come out and get her.

"Where are *we*, is my question." I frowned and took my first look around.

We were in some kind of valley. What I thought was mountainside was really just cliffs that towered several stories over us. The walls were rounded and smooth. Heat burned through my shoes. I bent down and touched the dirt. It was hot. Smoke seeped out from all around us, billowing up and out of our valley then pouring into the sky. I had no idea how deep the space was. The far side was cloaked in shadow. Bones of varying shapes and sizes littered the floor. Except they were different from the ones outside the Garden of Eden. Those had been perfectly intact, like the victims had simply fallen asleep and never woke. These were torn apart and tattered...like something had ripped them apart.

I spun in a circle, trying to make sense of where we were and how we got here. There was no staircase, no ladder, no bridge hanging over. It was like we were in the bottom of a bowl.

Oh no. My stomach turned and my pulse quickened. I licked my lips and looked around with new light. I knew where we were. *"From within the cauldron, comes your chance."*

Emersyn gasped and spun around in circles. "No, no, no. That is *not* how I thought that line would turn out."

"JUMP!" Tegan screamed.

I leapt into the air without hesitation, then used my Air magic to keep me up.

Willow and Chutney shrieked. I spun in time to watch the vines coil around their legs. They screamed and sliced their daggers through them, but the more they chopped, the more the vines grew.

"Don't cut it!" Tegan yelled at the girls.

Willow grabbed Chutney's arm and dragged her toward the back. The vines slithered after them like snakes, nipping at their ankles. The girls ignored Tegan's words and kept chopping them off. They jumped onto a boulder and huddled together, like they thought they'd be safe there.

I summoned a gust of wind and flew over. The girls screamed and swatted at the growing vines with their bare hands. The more they struggled, the faster the vines spread.

"Stop moving!"

They gasped and looked up to me with wide eyes, but they froze. The vines stopped growing instantly. They were thicker than my arm and black as night. They wrapped around the two girls like a bug in a spider's nest.

My eyes widened. The vines' job wasn't to kill its victims, just *trap* them. *The bones.* Realization hit. I reached out and gripped the vine in my right hand. I squeezed and pulled, but with one hand, I wasn't doing much.

"Don't cut them!" Tegan shouted again.

I looked over at the sound of her voice and found her hovering above the ground with Emersyn hanging on her back like a pet monkey. It didn't make any sense. Why did the vines grow faster if you cut them off? Were they like a weed? If so, that was a part of Earth. Tegan and I should've been able to manipulate them.

I yanked on the vines with all my strength. "How do you suggest we free them if not by cutting them? We don't know what this creature is—"

"It's a *hydra*!" she hissed. "We have to fight the monster, not the vines!"

I spun around to face her. The shadow moved behind her. I blinked. "I thought hydras were water creatures?"

Tegan scoffed. "What part of the last few days have you forgotten?"

She had a point. Nothing was playing by the rules as we knew them. *From within the cauldron comes your chance.* That was the last line of the prophecy. The last step to proving we deserved to get the Book of Shadows back. We weren't going to do that standing back and waiting to be eaten. I flew forward to the center of the cauldron.

"What are you doing?" Emersyn screeched.

"If our task is to kill this monster, then let's get it over with before it eats our friends for dinner." I adjusted my grip on my sword. *Why do I have to be one handed for this?* "It's now or never."

I called on my magic and let it simmer in my veins a few seconds before I shot it straight into the darkness. Green lightning struck the shadow. The animal roared. The force of its breath slammed into us like a brick wall. We flew backward and rolled. I cursed in agony each time my shoulder hit the ground. When I skidded to a stop, I scrambled back to my feet and raced forward.

The hydra leapt into the light. Its massive body was dark green and slimy, like algae in a canal. It towered over us on four legs and with three giant dragon heads. Six red, beady eyes narrowed on the three of us standing below it. It hissed and spit fire from each head.

Emersyn and Tegan threw their hands up and shielded us from the flames. The hydra shrieked. It whipped its tail. I felt the air pull away from me just before the spiked tail slashed across the space. Tegan and I jumped over it, but Emersyn wasn't so lucky. The tip of its tail slammed into her stomach and threw her back into the shadows behind it.

"*EMERSYN!*" Tegan screamed.

The hydra spit fire again, but it had nothing on Tegan's power.

She flicked it away like it was nothing. "EM!"

"I'm okay!" Emersyn shouted back, though we couldn't see her.

"Tegan, we need a plan. We have to kill this thing. It's just *playing* with us right now." I moved closer to her. "You've read books on these things, so how are they killed?"

She sighed and shook her head. "All I can think of is Hercules. He chopped each head off then lit it on fire to stop it from growing back."

"Okay, so we do that."

She scoffed. "He's *Hercules!*"

I grabbed her elbow and turned her to face me. "And you're the most powerful witch in the world. You've got the next strongest two by your side. You flew a damn plane with no wings."

She stared at me a moment, then nodded. *Emersyn, Tenn's gonna fly you onto its back. When a head is chopped off, you burn the wound,* she said into our minds.

"WHAT?" Emersyn mumbled something about us being out of our minds. "I can't create fire, Tegan!"

"No, but I can." Tegan growled and spun back to face the hydra. She shoved her daggers back into her thigh holsters, then wiggled her fingers. Two big balls of fire flickered to life. She waved her right arm in a giant circle then pulled her elbow back.

I gasped. She'd made a bow and arrow out of flames. I grinned. "That's my girl," I whispered before I could stop myself.

She peeked over her left shoulder at me and winked. *I'll distract. You chop. Em burns.*

I nodded and turned toward the monster. All of its focus had turned to Tegan's weapon of flames. I pushed my magic out until I sensed Emersyn's aura, then scooped her up into the air. To her credit, she didn't scream in alarm. She didn't make a sound. When she landed on the hydra's middle neck, she looked every bit the raging Empress. Her hair whipped through the air. Her golden eyes were wild with raw, hot energy.

"Light 'em up, Kitten," I whispered.

Tegan shot arrows of pure fire right into the hydra's face. It snarled and hissed back. She fired arrow after arrow. I flew forward until I was under its body then slithered up its arm until I was behind its head. I looked to my left at the neck in the middle and found Emersyn's eyes on me. She held her arms in the air, and flames coiled around her hands. She nodded. Tegan's flaming arrows slammed into the hydra's neck.

I flew up behind the head but stayed close so the others wouldn't see me. The neck had to be six feet wide. At least. Maybe with two hands I would've been able to manage it up close, but definitely not with one. I shot myself into the air far above it.

Don't mess this up now, Tenn. I tightened my grip on my sword then dove full speed at the hydra like a torpedo. The world blew by me in a blur, but all I focused on was my target. I swung my sword through the air in an arc and brought it down on the monster's neck. I pushed all of my strength and magic into my blade. It sliced through like the thing was made of butter.

The hydra shrieked and flailed around. Blood gushed like a fountain. The severed head plopped to the ground and rolled to Tegan's feet. Emersyn threw her flames at the open wound.

I grinned. *Yes! Yes, we did it!*

But the head on the far side dipped down and spit water onto Emersyn's flames. The fire sizzled into smoke. The neck thrashed around until two new heads grew out of it. Now there were four heads. My pulse skyrocketed. I looked down at Tegan and found her wide-eyed and frozen in place.

Now what? I mouthed.

Something grabbed my shirt and yanked me back. I realized too late what had happened. The hydra's sharp teeth sliced into my skin. I thrashed and sliced my sword through the air, except it was too far out of my reach.

Green and blue lightning flashed from my sword and smashed into the monster's neck. It growled and snapped its head. The pressure of its teeth lifted, and then I slammed into the dirt. My bones rattled. The air was sucked back out of my lungs. I rolled to my side and coughed.

The severed head moved, drawing my attention. At first I thought it might reattach, but those thick vines shot up from the ground and wrapped around it.

My stomach turned. *Is it going to eat its own head? Wait. Move, move, move,* I yelled to myself. I tried to push myself up, but I ended up in barely a crawl. My body was numb and tingling from the hips down. I tried not to think about what that meant as I scurried to get up. It was too late. The vines sensed my presence and snatched me up like the others.

I froze in place, knowing it would stop spreading if I stopped moving. Only my neck and right arm remained free. Tegan was still shooting her flaming arrows at the monster. Emersyn shot thick blasts of fire into the monster's sides with one hand. With the other, she pulled the smoke from the cauldron walls and whipped it around the hydra's heads. It coughed and blinked, like it couldn't breathe through it.

TENN, are you okay? Tegan screamed into my mind.

"Yeah," I yelled back. But I wouldn't be for long if we didn't figure out how to kill the thing. "Give me water!"

She flicked her hand back, and a massive ball of water rolled to a stop in front of me. I wasn't sure what water would do to a hydra, but it was time to try something else. I pushed my magic into the bubble until it grew bigger and bigger, then I threw it right at the hydra's feet. It squealed and flopped around, almost like it *enjoyed* it. The hydra jumped up and down on all four feet like an excited puppy while spitting fire into the sky. It leapt off the ground straight up, and wings popped out of its back. It spun around in circles in the air squealing and flapping the new body parts that most definitely hadn't just been there.

Something bounced off its back— *Emersyn!* I pushed my wind right at her to catch her, but the hydra reached down and plucked her out of the sky. She screamed and tried to wiggle free while throwing fire balls at its face. I thrashed against the vines, but they only spread higher over my chest, squeezing my wound. I hissed as the pain made the world spin. *Lie still, dammit.*

"EMERSYN!" Tegan screamed. "I'm coming!"

She squatted down then pushed off her feet and shot into the night sky like a rocket. I smiled. *Come on, Kitten. You got this.*

She *flew* like Superman, with aim and direction. The hydra was completely engulfed in flames by the time Tegan got up there. I watched with my heart in my throat as she disappeared into the fire. The only thing I could see was the hydra's tail. Wind surged up and wrapped around them. They flipped and plummeted into the ground. *NO!* Dirt and fire exploded from their impact. Emersyn bounced into the air, hit the ground, and rolled to a stop beside me.

Where's Tegan? Where is she?

Em jumped to her feet with flames still dancing from her fingertips and hair. The dirt trembled, and vines shot out at her feet. She snarled and flicked little balls of fire then stomped them with her feet. The vines melted away. She smiled in victory then raced over to me. She dropped to her knees and gripped the vines holding me down. Within seconds, they vanished.

"Go get the others free," I said.

The hydra roared so loud the ground shook hard enough to knock the twins down.

"NO!" Tegan screamed.

Tegan. I sighed with relief. I hadn't seen her emerge from the fall. When I finally pulled myself up to my knees, I found Tegan standing between us and the monster.

It crouched low and whipped its tail back and forth

314

like a lion about to pounce. Four heads with smoldering red eyes were focused on my soulmate. Its wings flapped in the breeze.

"*No*," Tegan repeated like they were having a conversation.

She threw her arms wide, her long black hair whipping through the air. Her stance was wide and her fingers curled. She threw her arms forward, and water gushed from her hands like a geyser. The hydra's four heads snapped up in alert. She pushed the water into one giant wave, then slammed it right into the monster. I held my breath and watched. *Is she trying to drown it?*

The hydra squealed as the water covered its entire body. It dipped each head under one at a time...then *repeated* it. My jaw dropped. My mind went utterly blank. Tegan swirled her arms, and the hydra lifted into the air with the water still around it. If I hadn't known any better, I would've thought the creature was smiling. It looked down at Tegan and blinked a few times, its eyes a light aqua color. *What the hell?* The red was gone.

Tegan dropped her arms and sighed. "You're free now. Go home."

It shrieked again and did a few rolls then shot straight up into the sky until it was completely out of sight. I exhaled the breath I'd been holding and dropped to my knees.

"What..." Cooper coughed from suddenly right behind me. His big, warm palm landed on my shoulder, and he squeezed lightly. "What the hell just happened?"

Tegan spun around. She had a small smile on her face and a sparkle in her eyes. She opened her mouth to speak when the mountainside rumbled again. I braced myself for another hydra. When it stopped, a narrow cobblestone staircase emerged from within the rocks.

I sighed and stared at the staircase. "I think that's our way back home."

CHAPTER THIRTY-THREE

TENNESSEE

Tegan ran over to the base and looked up. She shook her head. "It's not going to be an easy one. I can't see the top."

Of course not. I nodded and peeked over my injured shoulder. "Is everyone all right?"

Willow and Chutney were pale and visibly shaking, but they nodded. I felt bad for them. They were young and had never experienced anything like this quest. Chutney rarely fought, and when she did, it was because she happened to be in the wrong place at the wrong time. Willow had had her battles with demons, but always on our home territory where we knew how to win.

Emersyn stood up and faced us with a bleak expression. Behind her, Deacon was crouched next to a dark object. *Royce.* My stomach turned.

"Royce is unconscious, but breathing." Deacon stood and scratched the back of his head. "I guess I'll carry him because we need to get out of here."

"I'll help you," Cooper said and ran over.

I pushed myself up to my feet, hissing through the scream of my shoulder. Fortunately it wasn't my leg, or otherwise we would've really been in trouble. I clenched my teeth and joined Tegan at the base of the stairs. When I looked up, my heart sank. The staircase ascended into darkness, and there wasn't an end in sight. *Talk about a stairway to Heaven.*

"Are you okay?" Tegan whispered. She reached up and squeezed my left hand.

Despite being numb from the sling, I still felt the warmth of her skin and the pressure in her hold. I smiled, though I worried it was mostly a grimace. "You're alive, so yes."

She blushed and looked at the ground. "There was so much blood when we landed... I thought...I thought..."

I tipped her chin up to bring her gaze to mine. "I'm okay, though. I'll heal."

"You better," she whispered.

"Okay, let's get this over with," Deacon grumbled, suddenly right behind me.

I jumped back and prayed it looked natural. *Saved*

by the bell. I'd been about to kiss her right in front of everyone. I cleared my throat and focused on Royce's big, unconscious body draped over Deacon and Cooper's shoulders. His feet dragged the floor behind them. They started for the stairs when a thought occurred to me.

"Hey, wait. Let Tegan take the lead."

Cooper frowned and peeked over his shoulder, and Royce's arm, at me. "You want Tegan to take the lead and not you?"

"I want the back. I want to make sure no one falls behind." I stepped aside and waved the girls forward. "Tegan can handle anything that comes at us."

Tegan nodded and pulled one dagger from her thigh holster. She gave me one hard look, then charged up the steps. Deacon and Cooper followed after her. With Royce hanging between them, they just barely fit on the staircase. Emersyn sprinted up the stairs after them. She held her hands out like she expected them to drop Royce at any moment. I waited for Willow and Chutney to go up before I started. I paused on the first step and held my right hand out. My sword flew into my palm. I shoved it into the holster around my hips then began my ascent.

I wasn't counting the steps as we went...but Chutney *was.* Maybe she didn't realize she was doing it. Maybe she needed the distraction. All I knew was that at step sixty-four, Tegan shouted about fog. At step seventy-one, I walked through the thin cloud of fog and emerged in full sunshine on step seventy-two. I squinted and looked down to shield my eyes. It seemed like we hadn't seen the sun in days.

Heat barreled down on us. With every step, my breathing grew heavier and heavier. My entire body was covered in a thin layer of sweat. It rolled in beads down my spine. My shirt was completely soaked and clinging to my skin. Every time I wiped my forehead, it seemed like I came away with a puddle on my forearm. My hair was drenched and dripping water like I'd just gotten out of the shower. I wanted desperately to pull it up on top of my head, but I only had one hand to work with, and I didn't want to make us all stop just so I could put my hair up. Not when Deacon and Cooper were carrying another person.

Chutney still counted steps, but she was way into the triple digits and I refused to hear it. I didn't want to know. I looked up and blinked through the sweat dripping in my eyes. Willow and Chutney had their hair tied up in a ponytail, and Emersyn had braided hers like Lara Croft. I didn't even need to look to know Tegan's wild hair was up in a messy bun. But I hadn't expected her to leave on the leather jacket. Tegan, however, didn't seem to be moving any slower than the rest of us.

I sighed and wiped the sweat off my brow with my arm. There was something off about these stairs. When we'd first started, Tegan and I had both tried to fly up them, but we only managed to hover a few inches off the ground for a second or two. Now, here I was dripping in water, and I couldn't even control it. I wasn't used to it. Water was my element, so it made no sense that I couldn't make it go away.

Tegan shouted and flew backward. She slammed into Deacon and knocked him and Cooper into the mountain wall. They stumbled and tried to catch Royce, but he dropped to his knees. Emersyn leapt forward and caught him around the shoulders, but his forehead still smacked against the stone step. Willow and Chutney slipped and stumbled into me. I somehow caught them with one arm and trapped them against the wall. I looked up to see what had attacked Tegan when a gust of wind hit me in the gut. My shoulder screamed in agony. I clenched my teeth and hissed through the pain. My magic rushed to the surface, pushing the wind up and off of us.

"Sorry, sorry!" Tegan cursed. She was back on her feet in seconds with her hands raised. Her magic billowed out of her palms in a faint rainbow swirl. The wind hit her palms then flew over our heads. "Was *not* expecting a hurricane! Hang on!"

"Where are we?" Royce groaned.

I gasped and turned toward his voice. "Royce!"

Deacon pulled his cousin up and re-draped him over his shoulder. "We're trying to get home now, cousin."

I expected him to smile and give us one of his classic one-liners, but he just frowned. His skin was pasty white and covered in a sheen that I assumed was sweat. His sapphire blue eyes were dark and hooded. His black eyebrows hung low. I hated seeing him like that. It broke a little piece of something inside me. I wanted to reassure him finding the Book of Shadows would help us get Henley back. Tegan kept insisting it would. I just... wasn't sure. False hope was a bitter pill to swallow.

"Tennessee!" Tegan shouted, her voice strained. "I can't hold it myself."

These damn stairs.

"Go ahead. Go help her in the front. I'll take the back." Cooper joined me on my step and pointed up ahead. "Deacon can handle Royce now."

I looked to Deacon, and he gave me a thumbs-up. Royce glared at the ground. I nodded and pushed through my friends until I stood beside Tegan. The wind slammed into me like I was standing outside during a major hurricane. I pushed against the force with my magic and let it tangle with Tegan's. Together, we weakened it enough to let us continue our path. By the time the wind subsided a little, I was struggling to breathe normal. My heart thundered in my chest. My arm throbbed. My legs burned. My shoulder felt like whatever had impaled me was still in there.

And then the mountain rumbled and dropped heaps of snow right on top of us.

I sighed. "Are you *kidding* me?"

CHAPTER THIRTY-FOUR

TEGAN

By the time the staircase from hell flattened out, I was practically crawling on all fours. My fingertips were a light shade of blue. My hair was rock hard, frozen in a knot on my head. My leather jacket kept my upper half warm and comfortable, but the rest of me trembled. My bones rattled against each other. Air burned my throat as I tried to breathe. I paused with my hands on the top step, trying to summon the energy to pull myself up.

"Here." Tennessee's voice was the only thing warm nearby.

I looked up and found his hand out. I slid my fingers against his and let him drag me up to the flat surface. My feet were heavy and weighed down. Several inches of snow were caked on top of my boots above my toes. I growled and the snow melted away. I grinned. My magic was back to regular.

Tennessee stomped his boots and shook his hair like a dog. When he stopped, he was dry. He looked himself over then glanced at me with a wide smile.

"Finally, right?"

"Finally," he half whispered, half sighed. He reached up and ran his good hand over my hair. The frozen, weighted pressure vanished instantly under his touch. "Let's help the others."

I turned and looked down at the staircase we'd just climbed. On the flat surface, the weather was clear and calm, a perfect spring day full of greenery. But one step down, a blizzard still beat up my Coven-mates. Snow piled on top of the stairs. The air was thick and gray, almost impossible to see through.

Deacon and Royce popped into view first. Snow completely covered their hair and dusted their eyebrows. They looked like identical twins. We pulled them up.

Royce coughed. "Deacon, put me down now."

"No, it's okay. I've got you," Deacon said, but his voice was barely more than a whisper.

"Deacon, please."

His cousin hesitated for a second before he hobbled them over to the wall of the mountain and propped

Royce up. The second Royce was on his own feet, Deacon slid down the green vine-covered wall to his butt. He squeezed his purple eyes shut and leaned his head back.

I waved my hand, and all the snow and water on them melted away. When I turned, I found Tennessee had helped the others climb onto the flat surface with us. Everyone sighed and looked around in relief.

"Well, well, well," a deep voice said.

I knew it instantly.

I spun around and found him standing there with his arms crossed over his chest. *Gabriel.* He looked exactly the same as he had when we entered the Garden of Eden. I had no idea how long it had been. It felt like years since we'd started the stairs. For all I knew, it could've been ten minutes. I pulled out my cell phone, and sure enough, it still read 6:02 *Sunday, August 26.*

"Hello, Gabriel," Tennessee said with that silky voice of his.

The glyph that covered Gabriel's entire body, the one that matched mine and Tennessee's, shimmered a metallic golden color. His white feathered wings reminded me of the snowstorm we'd just gone through.

He cocked his head to the side and watched me with his white and gold eyes. "High Priestess, you surprised me. That doesn't happen often."

My eyes widened. I opened my mouth then shut it again. I swallowed the nausea rolling up my throat. *Is that a bad thing?*

"A bad thing?" Gabriel repeated the question I hadn't asked. He pursed his lips and narrowed his eyes on me. After a second, he shook his head. "No, just not expected. You set the creature free. Why?"

Ah, crap. But then the hydra's expression when the water hit him flashed through my mind, and my confidence soared. I'd done the right thing.

I cleared my throat. "The animal didn't want to fight us. It waited a long time to engage, and only once we initiated."

"What do you call those vines?" Willow snapped.

Gabriel arched one eyebrow.

"Everything has to eat. I don't know what it was, where it came from, or why it was there..." I shrugged. I hadn't been sure if I should voice what I felt in that moment with the hydra, but looking up at Gabriel, I knew I had to. "It was barely fighting back until Tennessee chopped one of its heads off. Then, when he hit it with fresh water, it...like...*cried* with joy. I just saw it in its face. Then it grew wings and tried to fly away, even though it knew we were all alive down there. I only brought it back down to save Emersyn, then I gave the animal a little pool of water, and you should've seen how happy it was. The idea of hurting it just broke my heart."

"Its eyes changed from red to aqua," Tennessee added. "It splashed in the water."

"Exactly!"

Gabriel chuckled and shook his head. He looked at me with his white and gold eyes that sparkled in the sunlight. "The prophecy of Salem will be resolved by Samhain, one way or another."

I nodded.

He walked up and stopped in front of me. "Give me your hands, High Priestess."

I threw my hands out, palms up. My heart pounded in my chest.

He pressed his palms to mine, and a white light illuminated between us. "There may be hope for your world, after all."

My fingers tingled. Energy pulsed through my hands and up my arms. Gabriel pulled his hands back and I gasped. A massive, leather-bound book sat in my palms.

My pulse skipped with delight. Adrenaline rushed through my veins. I grinned down at the pentagram burned into the front cover. "The Book of Shadows."

"Yes, however..." Gabriel waited until I met his eyes. "Remember we are watching. If you don't deserve it—"

"I *will* deserve it. I promise." I'd just interrupted an angel, but I didn't care.

"You will find many answers in here. Take care of how you use them." Gabriel placed his hand on the cover of the book and tapped his finger.

"I will. I promise."

There hasn't been an Aether Witch in a few millennia, High Priestess, Gabriel said into my mind the same way I did to my friends. *Setting the hydra free proves that our selection wasn't a mistake. Remember what makes you who you are, for dark times lie in wait.*

Thank you, I thought back to him.

Gabriel stepped away and flapped his wings. He glanced at Tennessee then back to me. *Hope is not lost. Until then...* And then he was gone.

We were alone. We appeared to be on some kind of mountain ledge overlooking the Old Lands. Green grass swayed in the breeze under our feet. The trees were vibrantly full of color and life. The sky was a crystal-clear blue without a cloud in sight.

But my mind was a mess. Gabriel's words repeated like a broken record.

"So, you actually made it out."

I looked up and found Lonan leaning against the mountain wall with his hands in his black jean pockets. He was shirtless again and rippled with lean muscles, but it made sense for a guy who turned into a black dragon. Lonan looked like a tanner version of Royce, but with that wildness I loved so much in Tennessee—and that Emersyn feared.

"Lonan!" Chutney squealed and bounced over. She gave him a hug, which he returned hesitantly.

He chuckled. "You guys look like hell froze over."

I looked around at my friends. He was right. We were in rough shape. Our clothes were torn and grimy. Snow and sweat still lingered anywhere it could. We were covered in cuts and bruises. Blood was splattered everywhere, some of us worse than others. I knew from the strain in Tennessee's eyes that his wound hurt, even though he was acting tough. Royce looked like a zombie.

"Yeah, it's been a rough one," Tennessee said with a sigh.

"Listen, I know you all have a big prophecy on your hands right now..." Lonan's eyes flashed bright crimson. "I'll fly you back to Eden, but when everything settles, I think it would be good for our species to get to know each other more. Deal?"

I smiled. "Deal. Definitely deal." When a dragon shifter wanted to make friends, only an idiot would say no. Plus, Lonan had helped us out. I wanted to be friends with him. I wanted to learn about his species. I wanted to know why he was called the Banished One.

"Yes, for sure," Tennessee agreed.

"Let's get you home, then. You remember how to do this, right?" Lonan cocked a sideways grin. A dark shadow wrapped around him, and then a massive, twenty-five-foot dragon form stood in his place. He sank down to his belly and lowered his tail for us to climb up.

CHAPTER THIRTY-FIVE

TEGAN

I f possible, the flight back to Eden was faster than our first ride in the Old Lands. I knew my Coven-mates were excited to go home, but my mind was already working a mile per minute. I should've been happy, especially with my face pressed against Tennessee's back and my arm wrapped around his non-injured side. Warmth radiated off his body. For the first time since our last flight on Lonan, I felt comfort. Part of me wanted to close my eyes and sleep for days.

But I couldn't even if I wanted to. The prophecy of Salem had to be resolved by Samhain, or Halloween as Sapiens called it, but that was two months away. In the meantime, I had to find a way to lure the demon living inside my friend Henley back to our dimension...and then I had to trap it there until I could figure out how to separate the two. Without killing Henley.

I was told my answers were inside the Book of Shadows, and I finally had it in my possession. My fingers burned and ached from how hard I clung to the ancient leather-bound bible. There was no chance I was letting it get away from me. Gabriel had said I had to deserve it, and I was going to.

Before we left, I'd had visions of Henley being tortured by the demons in whichever hellish realm she resided in. Every time I thought about it, my stomach turned and threatened to empty. I just kept telling myself that Henley was tough, that she could handle it. But I believed it a little less every time.

"Landing!" Chutney yelled back to us. Our resident animal communicator was back to her smiling self, and I couldn't blame her.

Not everyone was cut out for what we just went through. I pressed my hand against Tennessee's chest, right over the glyph crystal that marked him as mine. His hand covered mine and squeezed. It wasn't much, but it was enough to let me know he was there and okay. I kissed the back of his neck and closed my eyes.

Hang on, Henley, I'm coming for you.

Tennessee tapped my hand then slid it down to his waist.

I frowned and sat up straight. But then I realized why he did it. We were about to land, and there were probably going to be a few pairs of eyes watching since we were flying a dragon in. The world passed by in a blur, and my stomach turned. I squeezed my eyes shut and breathed through my nose.

When is the last time we ate?

There was a loud whooshing noise, then a rumble vibrated through Lonan's back.

Whoa. I opened my eyes...and my jaw dropped. Lonan had flown us right into the center of Eden, in the courtyard in the middle of campus. The entire student body of Edenburg must've seen a black dragon flying overhead because there had to be *hundreds* of teenagers surrounding us. I glanced left and right only to find the same wide-eyed, jaw-dropped expression. No one spoke. No one pointed. No one screamed or ran away. They watched us slide off Lonan's back without reacting. It wasn't until Tennessee landed on the ground that everyone gasped. Except this time, they scurried *away* from him.

I frowned and looked over my shoulder at him to tell him to stop glaring at the civilians...but my words dried on my tongue. His eyebrows were set low over his eyes, blocking the beautiful colors from view. His lips were set in a firm line. His hair was wild and disheveled, sticking out in every direction. But it was the blood caked on his face and dripping down his body that set the tone. His left arm bandage and left hand were completely soiled a dark red from dried blood. If possibly, it made him look more dangerous.

I got the feeling no one had ever seen an injured Tennessee. And it seemed like it terrified them.

Finally, one kid whispered, "If something hurt the Emperor, we're screwed."

I smiled with pride.

Tennessee strolled up to stand in front of Lonan. "Thank you, Lonan. If we want to find you again, do we go to the place?"

Lonan snorted and looked to Chutney.

"Okay!" Chutney grinned up at our dragon friend with a rosy blush. "I'll tell him."

"Perfect. Take care of yourself." Tennessee smiled.

I waved. "Thanks, Lonan!"

Lonan nodded then pushed into the sky like a rocket. He flapped his wings then shot out of sight. There was a rush of whispers in the crowd on the far side of the circle of students. A second later, a tall, slender man with tortoiseshell glasses and a three-piece suit emerged from the crowd. I had no idea who he was, but I got the impression he was important somehow.

"*Tennessee?!*" the man all but squealed.

"Hello, Daniel." Tennessee smiled and led the rest

of us over to him. "Sorry about the dragon. He's a friend of ours."

Daniel flushed and pushed his glasses up. He swallowed and looked up at the sky. "A friend, you say? With a dragon?"

"Well, at least *that* dragon." Tennessee frowned and looked around the crowd. His gaze was sharp. He turned back to Daniel. "Where are Constance, Kenneth, and Timothy?"

Daniel blanched. "They went to Tampa to help. The demon attacks have intensified."

"Help? Attacks?" Tennessee shook his head. "What are you talking about?"

"Emperor...you've been missing for five weeks."

THE COVEN HAS no idea what's coming for them in Book Four of the Elemental Magic series, THE BROKEN WITCH. Want to know if Tegan and Tennessee can keep their love hidden long enough to save Henley? CLICK HERE to sign up for my newsletter and you'll receive an email alert when it's available early summer 2018!

TURN the page to see the cover and get a sneak peek at
THE BROKEN WITCH!

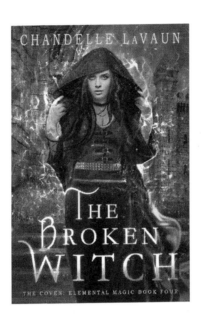

DESPERATE TIMES, desperate magic.

I finally have the Book of Shadows. The pages call to
me, begging me to devour their hidden power. There are

more than just spells inside, and there are things only the High Priestess can see.

And now I know everything I wasn't supposed to.

My Coven likes to keep secrets...well they're about to get a taste of their own medicine. Rescuing Henley from the demon's possession won't mean a thing if we can't close the Gap in Salem. Samhain is our deadline, and it's right around the corner.

The question is...can I dig into the world's ancient secrets without losing myself? I don't know, but i'm about to find out.

THE BROKEN WITCH releases early summer 2018! CLICK HERE to sign up for my newsletter to get an email alert when it comes out!

ABOUT THE AUTHOR

Chandelle was born and raised in South Florida. She is the ultimate fangirl. Her love of Twilight, Harry Potter, and The Mortal Instruments inspired her to write her own books. When she's not writing she's on the beach soaking up the sun with a book in her hand. Her favorite things in life are dogs, pizza, slurpees, and anything that sparkles. She suffers from wanderlust and hopes to travel to every country in the world one day.

78513876R00212

Made in the USA
San Bernardino, CA
05 June 2018